JAY McLEAN

To the dads in my life who prove time and time again that blood is not always thicker than water, and that your family is what you make it.

My non-husband Warwick McLean – who loves me, flaws and all.
My father-in-law Richard "Pa" McLean – who has always encouraged me to take a chance. (Fire truck cancer)
And last but not least, to a man I've loved since I was five, my (step) Dad Steve "Gam Gam" – whose only advice has and will always be: to do what makes me happy.
Dad, because of you, I am happy.
But most of all, I am.

PROLOGUE

With my eyes closed, I could feel every stone, every bump, every crack of the pavement. The wheels spun—gripping tightly to form that perfect relationship with the ground.

The board, the ground and me—we were one—nothing to hide, nothing to lose.

I heard the dribble of the basketball and silence for a second, then the ball bouncing off the metal hoop. Hunter's feet scraped across the asphalt, kicking loose gravel around on the half-court we'd been coming to since we were kids. I opened my eyes and set my foot on the tail of the deck, slowing down, and then finally coming to a stop. I didn't join him in our usual game of Skateball, a game we'd made up when we were kids. Instead, I sat on the bench; shoulders slumped from the proverbial weight that'd just been dumped on them.

"What's wrong?" he asked, sitting down next to me.

Blake Hunter had been my best friend since I could remember, so of course he could tell. Or maybe I was shit at hiding it. I looked down at the board beneath my feet as I moved it from side to side, itching just to jump back on, coast away, and chase that high of being alone.

Alone with just me, the deck, and spinning of the wheels.

"Natalie says she pregnant."

Hunter's foot landed on the nose of my skateboard, stopping it from moving. "Josh?"

I heard the weariness in his voice, but I didn't look up. I didn't want to see what his eyes would convey. Probably pity.

"What are you going to do?" he asked.

I shrugged. "She just dropped the news on me and told me to leave—that she didn't want my input on *her* decision."

"That's bullshit."

I shrugged again. "I didn't know what else to do so I gave her what she wanted."

"What do you want to do?"

"Not think about it."

"You can't ignore it."

I lifted my gaze, but still avoided his. "I don't want to think about it because I don't want to have my mind or my heart set on something and she chooses the opposite."

"I'm sorry," he said, and I laughed. Because really? What the hell else could I do? He added, "I didn't even know you were having sex."

"Twice," I told him. "Condom broke the second time."

"Fuck."

I sat back and crossed my arms. "Yeah. That pretty much covers it."

He sighed loudly, but I still couldn't look at him. "So we wait until she decides and we go from there."

"We?"

"Always *we*, Josh. Whatever you need."

I stood up. "I'll see ya, Hunter." And then I pushed off the ground with one foot, the other on the board, and headed home—wondering the entire time what Hunter's face would've looked like when the word "pregnant" left my mouth. I laughed. It was dumb to laugh, but like I said, what the hell else could I do?

For two weeks Natalie talked and I listened. She went back and forth a thousand times over, repeating the same questions. Then one day, she sat down next to me in the school cafeteria and placed my hand on her stomach. My eyes snapped to hers. Her bright blue eyes seemed to sparkle when she flicked her blonde hair over her shoulder and pushed out her stomach. And then she smiled. "Promise me we'll do it together?" she asked.

And I found myself smiling with her. "Of course," I said. And I meant it.

We were sixteen and pregnant. And at the time—we were *happy*.

We told her parents first. She said it would be easier if she did it alone, but I refused. Natalie and the baby were my soon-to-be family, and I sure as hell would take responsibility for them. Her parents were disappointed. Her dad looked like he was going to punch me. Truthfully, I'd geared myself up for it. Natalie was an only child, like me, and she was their baby. But they weren't around much. Her dad was a hotshot industrial realtor who traveled a lot. Her mom was his trophy, and she'd follow him wherever. We were lucky though—they understood that the decision to keep the baby was ours, and they said they'd support us to a certain degree. But they were done being parents, and not ready to be grandparents, so not to expect too much support.

My parents? That was a whole other story. My dad actually did what I thought Natalie's dad would do. Yeah. He punched me. My mom cried. Natalie cried. My parents yelled some more. My mom kept mumbling about how she should've forced me to go to church with her every Sunday. My dad called me useless and told me to pack my bags and leave. Mom cried some more. I caught her gaze once, pleading with her to try to talk some sense into Dad. She knew what I was silently asking, because she said, "No, Joshua. This is your mistake. You deal with the consequences." I did what they wanted. I packed my shit and left. No one would ever call my child a mistake. No one.

Natalie drove home.

I skated to Hunter's.

He saw the bag in my hand and the fresh bruise under my eye and opened the door wider.

I slept in his guest bedroom for a while, walking on eggshells around his asshole dad. Then one day Hunter said, "You wanna look for an apartment or something? We could get jobs and split the rent." And I knew what that meant without him actually coming out and saying it. His dad wanted me out. He added, "I'd offer you the guesthouse, but Mom's moved in there."

"What?"

"Yeah. I think it's easier to hide her drinking."

I called Natalie. She picked me up and took me back to her house. Her parents said I could stay in the bedroom down in their basement until I found something more suitable just as long as no one knew about it. They didn't want to seem like the type of parents who encouraged sex and teen pregnancies. With them being gone so much on business, Natalie and I made a home for us in my temporary bedroom and played house during the day. We never argued, never had a bad thing to say to each other. It was nice. Actually, it was kind of perfect.

My parents never called.

We combined all our savings and the money that her mom had secretly given her to buy clothes and diapers and everything else the Internet told us we'd need. We went to all the doctor's appointments together, and when she started truly showing, she stopped hiding it from the kids at school and everyone else. I was proud of her. I was proud of us. And on the day that Thomas Joshua Christian was born, I was the proudest damn man in the entire world.

She said she didn't want to give him my last name. She wanted to wait until we were married and then she'd change it... something about not wanting to be looked down on when she gave people their different last names. I thought she was being stupid, but she had gotten ridiculously moody toward the end of the pregnancy so I chose my battles, and I let her win every single one.

I really wish I knew what happened between the months leading up to the birth, until the few weeks after. All I could think of is that we actually had the baby. Natalie—she complained a lot about everything: breastfeeding, exhaustion, having to do it all on her own, me not helping. I didn't know how much more I could do. I changed every diaper, every outfit. Even when she was awake for feedings, I'd wake up with her so she didn't have to feel alone. She was exhausted, and I understood that, which is why I helped out as much as I could.

So, gone were the days of playing house, of never arguing, of everything being perfect.

All of it gone.

And then, on Tommy's one-month birthday, so was she.

I woke up to him crying in the middle of the night. I searched the house for her but I couldn't find her anywhere. I even knocked on her parent's bedroom door and asked them where she was. They said they had no idea and went back to sleep. All the while my baby cried, hungry, in my arms.

I tried to call her.

She didn't answer.

I looked for her car.

It wasn't there.

Then I saw it: the note on the nightstand next to the framed picture of *my* family.

I'm sorry, Josh. I just couldn't do it.

It'd only been two weeks since Natalie took off when her parents asked to talk to me. I was still living in their basement, eating their food, using their water and electricity. I'd never asked for more of them. In fact, they barely even looked at their grandchild. "I know this is hard, Josh," Gloria, Natalie's mom, started. "But we didn't agree to this living arrangement."

I stared down at my son, not even two months old, sleeping peacefully in my arms. He had it tough for a few days after Natalie left. I had to buy special formula to wean him off the breast milk. He didn't take too well to it. I had gone through three different brands before I found one that he could actually keep down. I'd stopped going to school. Hunter—he came around to bring my homework, even though he knew I wouldn't do it. Honestly, I think he came just to see Tommy. He was kind of obsessed with the kid.

"Josh?" Gloria said, pulling me from my thoughts. "I hope you understand."

I didn't.

I couldn't.

I couldn't understand how anyone could turn their backs on their family... and yet here I was—facing nothing but backs.

I nodded and pushed back the tears threatening to fall. Never looking up from my son, I asked, "Have you heard from her?"

William, Natalie's dad, cleared his throat. "Yes," he said. "She asked for money."

Silence descended on the table, my mind reeling, my rage building. Then I finally spoke. "Did she ask about us?"

Gloria answered, "No, Joshua. She didn't."

William stood up, bringing my attention to him. He pulled out his wallet and dumped two hundred-dollar bills in front of me.

"Thank you," I said, standing up and grabbing the cash.

I called Hunter once I was in my room packing everything I thought we'd need.

"Where to?" he asked after I'd installed Tommy's car seat in his car and sat in the back with him.

"Home, I guess."

My dad slammed the door in my face. My mom cried.

When I got back in the car, Hunter looked pissed. "I'll be back," he said, and marched up to my parent's front door. He pushed it open and walked past my dad, slamming the door behind him.

I don't know what they spoke about, but it was loud. Mom cried harder. Dad yelled louder, but Hunter—he yelled the loudest.

We went to a hotel. Hunter paid for a week in advance on his mom's credit card. "She's too tanked to even know it's missing," he told me.

I didn't argue.

After we unloaded his car and he helped us settle into the room, he sat on the edge of the bed, his shoulders slumped and head bent.

I asked, "What's wrong?"

He looked up at me and I could see the sympathy behind his glazed eyes. "I hate that this is happening to you."

I sighed. "Tell you what…" I removed Tommy from his car seat and handed him to Hunter. Hunter looked down at him, smiling as soon as my son was in his arms. "Look at him, Hunter. Look at him from my eyes and tell me any of this isn't worth it."

Hunter let me borrow his car, opting to skate anywhere he needed.

Thank God for Hunter.

I spent the week looking for jobs. Turns out no one wanted to hire a seventeen-year-old high school dropout who brought their baby to interviews.

Even though two hundred dollars seems like a lot—it's not, especially when you have a baby.

"Your card's been declined," the clerk behind the register said.

My heart stopped. "What?"

She shrugged. "Sorry."

I took out my wallet and fished around for cash. I had a twenty but that wouldn't cover what I needed. I looked at the formula, wipes, and diapers sitting on the register, trying to decide which one I needed less. "Take out the wipes."

She shook her head. "Still not enough."

I ignored the grumbles from people in the line behind me. My heart was thumping now, finally cracking under the pressure. "I need the formula and diapers," I pleaded with her, knowing it was useless.

She shrugged again. "Sorry."

She wasn't sorry. She didn't give a fuck.

"Fine. Just the formula."

· · ·

I walked to my car in a complete daze, wondering what the hell else I could possibly do. I searched the diaper bag in the trunk of Hunter's car, hoping Natalie may have hidden an emergency stash. Nothing. I searched my plastic bag of clothes and found an old T-shirt. I looked from the shirt, to Tommy, and back again. And then I had no choice but to use it as a diaper. I had no idea how to wrap it, or what to do, and this wouldn't last long before he needed to be changed again.

I needed money.

And I needed it fast.

Then I saw it—hiding beneath Tommy's port-a-crib. My IXO longboard. I'd saved up almost a year just to drop $1500 on it. I'd used it to compete in street comps. It was my pride and joy pre-Tommy.

I pulled it out without a thought and finished dressing him, then walked to Deck and Check, the skate shop two doors down from the grocery store.

"I'll give you fifty for it," Aiden said from behind the glass counter.

"Bullshit, Aiden, you know what this is worth."

Aiden leaned forward to examine the board again. "I get it, Josh. But the punks around here—they don't care for this kind of shit. Only you do."

Tommy started crying.

I tried to soothe him.

Aiden added, "You're the only one around here that knows what this is worth. I don't want it for myself, and I can't sell it. I'll give you a hundred."

I felt my heart tighten. Another crack. Tommy cried harder.

"Aiden, please!" I begged. "A hundred won't cover his diapers. I need diapers. I need gas. I need a place to fucking sleep tonight. You gotta help me out, bro. Please."

Aiden stood taller. "I feel for you, Josh, but this is my business. One fifty. That's it."

Tommy was wailing now.

I dropped my gaze. "One fifty will barely get me a hotel room."

"I'm sorry." He wasn't.

"Fine."

I took his cash and in return, I said goodbye to my old life.

I bumped into someone waiting behind me, apologized, and walked out the doors to my uncertain future.

I took three steps around the corner and into an alley. And then I finally let the cracks from the pressure break me.

I placed Tommy, in his car seat, on the ground and I cursed.

I kicked the brick wall.

And I broke some more.

Tommy cried louder.

I slid down the wall until I was next to him and pulled him out of the seat and into my arms. Rocking him. Soothing him.

And I cried—tasting my tears mixed with his sweat on his forehead as I kissed him. "I'm sorry, baby. I'm sorry. Daddy's gonna make it okay. Daddy isn't going anywhere, okay? I'll never leave you. Never. I promise."

I wiped my eyes and nose with the sleeve of my hoodie and tried to calm down. But we were both crying, and his cries made me cry harder, because as much as I promised to make it right—I had no idea how to.

Then the strangest thing happened.

The tiniest ray of sunlight shone between the two buildings. The strength of it causing Tommy to flinch, then open his eyes, long enough to possibly see the outline of my face.

He stopped crying.

I stopped crying.

Then something dropped next to my feet. My longboard.

"What the…"

I looked up.

An old lady was smiling down at me. She had dark skin, like

she came from an exotic island somewhere. "You need gas money? I need a young man to help me shop for groceries and give me a ride home." She had an accent.

I sniffed and stood up, Tommy still in my arms. Then I looked down at my board. "What? How did—"

"Let's go."

"Wait…"

"What are your names?" she asked.

"Joshua." I lifted Tommy slightly. "This is my son Tommy."

She raised her arms, her eyes soft and pleading. There was a hint of pride in her expression—the way my mom used to look at me before everything went to shit. For that reason, I felt safe enough to hand over the only thing that mattered to me. She smiled warmly and looked down at my son. "He's beautiful." She motioned her head toward the car seat and my board. "Don't forget your things. Let's go."

"Wait," I said again, picking up the items off the ground. "W-what's your name?"

"Chazarae."

I followed her around the store while she did her grocery shopping. She kept her hold on Tommy and asked me to collect things for her cart. She said, "I have my niece staying with me next week. She has a newborn, like Tommy. So get what you think I'll need for the baby."

I grabbed a box of diapers and wipes. She said to get a tin of formula just in case. The entire time I was in a trance, still worried about where the hell I'd be sleeping that night. She paid for the groceries and we headed back out to Hunter's car.

He called the second we were all settled. "I was wondering if I could borrow the car tomorrow. Dad's set up a meeting with a recruiter."

I laughed once. "It's your car man, I'll uh…" I glanced over at Chazarae sitting next to me. "I'll call you later. We can work it out."

I didn't want Chazarae hearing that I'd planned on sleeping in it that night. I had enough shame to deal with.

She directed me to her house about ten minutes away. "Just up there," she said, pointing to a garage apartment. The main house was to the right of the driveway. It was two-story—nice enough—with a perfectly kept garden. She took Tommy, still in the car seat, up the stairs to her apartment while I carried her groceries. I left the first batch of bags at the front door and went back twice more before lugging them all inside. She set Tommy on the counter of the tiny kitchen and started to turn on some lights in the small space. I helped her unload, noticing when she powered up the fridge from the outlet behind it. *Weird.*

Once the groceries were put away, she turned to me. "How about a ride back to my car now?"

My eyes widened. "But you said—"

She stepped forward, cutting me off, and held my hands in hers. "Joshua. I saw you at the grocery store. I saw your heart shatter when you could not care for your son the way you wanted. I saw that same heart disintegrate when you let go of something you cared about in that skateboard shop."

"There is no niece, is there?" I choked out.

She ignored me and looked around. "I know it's not much of a house, but you and Tommy—you can make it your home."

I get asked a lot how I do it: raise a kid on my own and not be bitter about the life that'd been handed to me. Here's the answer: I wake up every morning.

That's it.

There are no hidden secrets, no words of wisdom or encouragement.

I wake up.

Breathe new air.

And fall even deeper in love with a kid I created.

Tommy squatted in front of the cereal aisle, his face contorting with that look I'd come to recognize over the past year of his existence. Then he started to grunt.

I grimaced. "I bet it's a big poop, huh?"

His face turned a shade darker. He grunted louder and I couldn't help but laugh. He watched me watching him through his clear blue eyes. I'd read somewhere that a lot of babies are born with blue eyes but they can change over time. A part of me had hoped that his would change, become brown like mine. Because every time I looked in his eyes, I saw Natalie. It didn't make me angry or pissed off like it would most. It just kind of bugged me. Like, I wish he had more of me in him than her. You know… considering she wasn't even around to see the epic poop-face that I was currently witnessing.

A diaper change and two aisles later, I heard, "Josh, is that you?" and I turned to see my Uncle Robby and his wife walking toward me, huge grins on both their faces. Uncle Robby was my dad's stepbrother. He was only ten years older than me so he was more like a cousin than anything. We didn't see each other often, once a year maybe, twice if we were lucky, but not once since Tommy was born.

I stopped pushing the cart and waited for them to join me. Robby's wife, Kim, smiled even wider when she saw Tommy.

"Who's this little guy?" Robby asked, and my heart dropped and realization set in: Dad was so ashamed he didn't even tell his family about us.

I cleared my throat and raised my chin, my pride overpowering the need to sulk. "This is my son Tommy."

Robby's eyes went wide. "Your son?"

I nodded.

He looked from me to Tommy and back again. "Your dad never mentioned it."

"Yeah, well my dad's kind of an asshole," I murmured.

"How old is he?"

"Nearly one," I told him.

"Huh," he said, then added, "You guys want to grab some lunch?"

"Can't. Gotta get this stuff home and unpacked and Tommy needs to nap." I turned the cart to face the exit. "What are you guys doing here anyway? I thought you moved to Charlotte?"

Kim answered, "We moved back a month ago. How about we take you boys out for dinner tomorrow night?"

Something felt off. When people found out I had a kid there were normally two reactions. (1) They ran the other direction and (2) They looked at me with so much pity in their eyes I wanted to punch them.

The last person who welcomed me was Chazarae and, honestly, I believe that was a higher person's doing. I wasn't religious, didn't believe in a God, not unless she came in the form of a quiet but sometimes-kooky old Hawaiian lady who talked to her plants.

Kim smiled warmly and it finally hit me—which of the two reactions she was having. *Pity.* People can't hide pity—it lives in their eyes, not in their fake smiles. "We're good," I said, starting to turn away. "We don't need your charity."

"Whoa!" Robby grabbed my arm. "Josh, I don't know what your problem is but my wife just invited you to dinner. Nothing else. If you don't want to go you can just say no. You don't have to throw her kindness in her face."

I stepped back; my shoulders slumped in defeat. "I'm sorry," I said, and I meant it. So maybe I was being oversensitive. I guess hearing the fact that your own father had completely cut all ties with you could do that to a person. I rubbed my eyes.

"Are you okay, Josh?" Robby asked.

"Yeah. Listen, I'm sorry. How about you guys get some

takeout and bring it to my place? I'm starved, but I gotta get Tommy home."

Kim smiled again—the pity in her eyes completely wiped.

I gave them my address and told them to give me an hour or so to get Tommy settled.

By the time I got home, Tommy was asleep in the backseat. I put him in his crib, unloaded the groceries and a moment later, they showed up. We ate and made small talk in-between the long awkward silences. They asked if I was seeing anybody and I told them I wasn't really interested in girls at the moment.

"What, you're gay?" Robby shouted.

I threw a plastic fork at his head. "Shut up. You'll wake Tommy. And no, I'm not gay!" I shook my head at him. "I just mean that Tommy takes precedence and I haven't really been with anyone since Natalie."

"Tommy's mom?" Kim asked.

I nodded. Honestly, it felt good to have someone to actually talk to that spoke back. Hunter was gone on an impromptu road trip so it didn't leave me much as far as adult conversation went.

"How's the skateboarding going?" Robby asked.

"It's not."

"What to do you mean? You loved skating."

"Yeah," I shrugged, "But I love Tommy more, and I couldn't have both."

"So you just gave it up?" Robby said, eyeing Kim sideways.

"That's a big deal, Josh. It's a huge sacrifice," Kim said.

I laughed awkwardly. It was my go-to reaction when people started pushing the wrong buttons. "Nothing I do for Tommy is a sacrifice."

Robby cleared his throat, then asked, "You still hang out with that basketball kid?"

"Hunter? Yeah. Well, kind of. I mean I hope so. Things have changed."

"Changed?"

"He got engaged," I said with a shrug.

"Oh yeah?" Kim asked. "That's a little young."

I stayed silent—opting to leave out the parts about their road trip and Chloe's cancer diagnosis.

"Josh?" Kim said, and this time—I didn't have to look in her eyes to *feel* her pity. "Are you okay?"

"I'm fine," I said. But the truth? I'd been alone since Hunter had left. And not just alone or isolated or disregarded, but I was *lonely.* Though I'd never admit that to anyone.

The next day, I half-assed it through closing at the bowling alley where I work and sped home. Robby had called earlier and said that he and Kim wanted to drop by to talk about something. Honestly, when they mentioned they'd keep in touch, I didn't believe them.

They came in and sat on the only couch I had and I pulled up a chair from the kitchen table.

I watched them.

They watched me.

Occasionally, they'd watch each other.

"So, good talk. Thanks for dropping by," I said.

Robby laughed a little.

Kim cleared her throat and sat up straighter while Robby took her hand in his.

My eyes narrowed, my gaze moving from her to Robby. He smiled but it was tight. Then he kissed his wife on the cheek and focused his attention on me. "I know you said you didn't want charity and we're not here for that."

I crossed my arms. "So what do you want?"

He glanced over at his wife again. "Kim—she loves kids. We both do… and that's kind of why we're here," Robby said.

Confusion set in, only for a moment before I realized what the hell he was saying. "What the fire truck?" I got to my feet and started pointing fingers. "You can't have my kid!"

His eyes widened. "No, dickhead. We're not asking for your kid."

I sat back in my chair and uncrossed my arms. "So why are you here?"

"I wanted to offer you a job—one that I'm sure pays better than that bowling alley."

"What kind of job?"

"I started my own construction company here. It has the potential to be pretty big thanks to the old man's money. That's why we moved back. I need laborers, Josh. There's room to move higher in the company—if that's something you'd be interested in. There'll be deadlines to get a job complete, but you could make your own hours… work it around Tommy." He sucked in a breath, then added, "I know you said you're driving around in your friend's car, which is fine, but if you were interested in the job you'd need to use the company truck. It's a crew cab, so you'll have room for Tommy in the back. It'll be hard work, I'm not going to lie, but I'll make sure the pay's worth it." He nudged Kim.

"Oh, me?" she asked, surprised.

He nodded.

She looked nervous.

It made *me* nervous.

She said, "I was wondering—I mean, if you decide to take the job… if maybe I could watch Tommy while you were working? I don't work at the moment and it would be my pleasure." She pulled out her phone from her pocket. "I can give you the numbers of personal references if you don't feel like you can trust me right away. We can start a couple hours a week. Whatever you want, Josh. It would save you money on daycare—"

"Why?" I cut in, raising my chin and squaring my shoulders. "Why offer me a job, let me work my own hours, pay me well? Why give me a car and offer to watch my kid? *Why?*"

Robby answered, "Because you're family, Josh, and regardless of how the world has shown you otherwise, decent people —they don't turn their backs on their family."

I took the offered job. I'd be stupid not to. Maybe it would help give me and Tommy a head start instead of living paycheck to paycheck and counting dimes.

When I went to hand in my two weeks' notice, the manager at the bowling alley told me to leave on the spot and not to bother coming back. It was kind of a blessing because it meant I could start work with Robby right away.

The work was hard, especially considering I'd been used to merely handing out shoes and taking people's money. The pay, however, was good—a little too good. I tried to talk to Robby about it. I specifically told him he was paying me way too much. He called me a dickhead and told me to get back to work.

The first day, I pulled Tommy out of daycare and let Kim watch him. She came by the job site twice. I didn't know if it was for her benefit or mine but I was grateful she did because truthfully, I was worried about how they'd get along. The fact that Tommy didn't want to leave her house when I'd gone to pick him up sealed the deal.

And so for the next two years, I didn't feel so alone, at least not in the grand scheme of things. I had help, emotional and financial, and I no longer felt like I was cracking under the strain of my life.

Until *she* came along.

CHAPTER 1

BECCA

---

fear

> **noun**
>
> **an unpleasant emotion caused by the threat of danger, pain, or harm.**

It's also a completely strange and difficult and sometimes unjustifiable emotion.

I've lived with fear for all of the reasons listed above. But now I'm experiencing it for an entirely different one.

Uncertainty.

I look out the window while my grandmother speaks to me from the driver's seat. "I want you to feel comfortable. My home is your home now. Your father…" she says, and I tune her out, choosing instead to focus on the trees that line the streets and the rays of sunlight filtering through the leaves. I wind down my window and inhale deeply, feeling the heat against my cheeks. Then I close my eyes and rest my head against the seat. It feels good just to be able to breathe. Just *breathe*. Because the simple act of breathing is a constant struggle when you live your life in fear.

Her car sways as she drives over a bump, pulling me from my daze. "There they are," she says, and I look out the windshield at some guy opening the driveway gate. *There who are?* I think to myself. The guy smiles, or more like grins like an idiot and yells out to some kid running toward the car. He picks up the kid quickly and moves out of the way so Chazarae (or *Grams*, as she wants me to call her) can park in front of the house.

Once Chazarae's out of the car, I grab the bag by my feet and hold it to my chest, looking up at the two-story house that's apparently now my *home*.

"Rebecca," she calls out and my eyes drift shut.

I step out of the car and meet her at the trunk. "Becca," I tell her, my voice cracking from lack of use.

"What's that?" she asks, the pity and confusion clear in her voice.

"My name's Becca. Rebecca is my mother." *Was my mother*, I should have said.

Her eyebrows furrow and the aged wrinkles around her eyes tighten when she quietly says, "I'm sorry."

"It's fine," I murmur, feeling guilty for her reaction. Slowly, I reach up, wanting to touch her, to show her that *I'm* the one who should be sorry. But the fear of uncertainty prevents the contact and I drop my hand to my side, the other still clutching my bag.

"This is the boy I was telling you about," she says, just as the guy, still holding the kid, steps beside her. "Joshua, this is Becca. Becca, this is Joshua."

She must have mentioned him in the car after I'd tuned her out because all I can think is *what boy?*

Joshua places the little boy carefully on the ground and removes his hat, revealing his shaggy dark hair and dark brown eyes—eyes that squint as they look directly at mine. He blinks hard and blows out a breath and I wonder if he's spotted one of the many scars I try so hard to hide. Then I remember they're not visible—at least not to anyone else.

"Hi," he finally says, raising his hand between us. I look down at the hand, and then at my grandmother, panicked, pleading with her to understand me.

The confusion on her face passes quickly. She grabs Joshua's arm and spins him to face her. "I'm glad you're here. We need your muscles."

Joshua's still looking at me even though he's facing her and I don't know why. So I avert my gaze and look down at the little boy who's looking up at me, his grin wide and unassuming. And I decide then and there that he may possibly be my favorite person in the entire world. He won't ever care enough to ask questions I don't want to answer—questions I've heard way too many times before.

I raise my hand in a small wave and he smiles wider. And I realize then that his smile is identical to Joshua's. I quickly look between them both. Joshua must realize what I'm thinking, or at least guessing, because he says, "That's my son. Say hi, Tommy."

"Hi Tommy!" the kid shouts, and I almost smile.

Almost.

"Becca's my granddaughter," my grandmother tells Joshua. "She's going to be staying with us for a while."

Us?

After a moment's silence, I hear Josh say, "Cool." Right before he sets my suitcase by my feet. I pull up the handle and that's all I do because I don't know where I am and who I'm with and what the hell I'm doing.

"Josh lives in the garage apartment," my grandmother informs and I nod in response.

"Did you need a hand carrying your bags up the stairs?" Josh asks.

I look back up at him but he's already watching me—his eyes focused on mine like they were before.

"No," I tell him, but it comes out a whisper. I swallow nervously, my mouth dry and my heart racing—no doubt caused by his impenetrable gaze. "But thank you." This time I actually do smile. It's fake as shit but it's still there, and if I'm lucky enough, he won't notice.

I don't think he hears me though because he doesn't seem to respond, he just continues to stare.

So I take a step back, away from all of them, rolling my suitcase with me as I look down at the kid; my new best friend. I raise my hand in another wave and somehow his smile gets even wider. He grabs onto his dad's leg before shouting, "Bye Tommy!"

CHAPTER 2

JOSHUA

Her eyes are the color of emeralds.

And that's pretty much all I remember about her. Even now, after hours have passed, all I can think about are those eyes.

I get through the obstacle course of toys on the floor and answer the knock on the door. Chazarae stands on the other side greeting me with the genuine smile I've learned not to confuse with pity.

"Everything okay?" I ask.

"Everything's fine. I just wanted to apologize to you about the Rebecca—I mean *Becca*—situation. It was very last minute and very—"

"You don't need to apologize for anything. It's your house."

"No, Josh. It's *our* house, and if I'd had more time I would've run it by you at least. I don't want anyone—"

"It's fine, ma'am. Really. I don't mind at all."

"Good," she says, clearing her throat.

"So she's staying for a while? Is everything okay? I didn't even know you had a granddaughter."

"I do." She sighs. "She's just graduated high school in

Mississippi and she'll be here—well, it's a long, complicated story. One that I wish to stay between Becca and me. Okay?"

"Sure," I tell her, though I don't really know what I'm agreeing to. "She's not, like, in trouble or anything is she?"

"Define trouble?" she mumbles, but it's more to her than me so I leave it alone.

She turns to leave but before she does, I ask, "Is there anything I can do to make her feel more welcome or something? Anything?"

She sighs again, long and slow. "I think it's best if you just leave her alone."

CHAPTER 3

BECCA

---

intrigue
   verb
   arouse the curiosity or interest of; fascinate.

I watch from my bedroom window as Joshua shakes hands with the guys who just delivered a mountain of soil and more plants than I can count. He and my grandmother stand side by side, Tommy is between them, as the guys get back in the truck and drive away. As soon as the truck's gone, Joshua throws his arm around my grandmother's shoulders and shakes his head.

Whatever he says makes her laugh, or at least I think it does. I don't actually hear the sound, just see the tilting of her head and her eyes brighten when she turns to him. She reaches up and cups his cheek with one hand, her smile as genuine as the ones she's been giving me the past two weeks since I've moved in.

Josh nods and starts walking toward the garage, his smile

matching hers as he looks up. Up. UP. And when his eyes land on mine, his smile drops.

So does my stomach.

Shit!

I close the curtains and turn around, my thumb already between my teeth when I bite down on it.

My heart races and my eyes squeeze shut from the pain of it all.

My gaze, unfocused, settles on my thumb when I pull it out. The imprints of my teeth fade away as the blood slowly recirculates.

A moment later there's a knock on my door. I get up and answer it. "Is everything okay?" my grandmother asks.

I nod. "Why?" I whisper.

I whisper a lot.

"Josh said he saw you looking outside. We're working on my garden today. Do you want to join us? Maybe get some fresh air? Some sun?"

With a shake of my head, I close the door in her face.

Of course I feel bad for doing it, but I don't control my actions—*fear* does.

I wait a few seconds before going back to the window and parting the curtains, just slightly, and look back down to the driveway. Grams comes out of the house and straight to Josh who seems to be waiting for her. They speak and whatever she says has him looking up. Up. UP. *Again.* To *me.*

I repeat the exact same process as last time. I shut the curtains, sit on my bed, bite down on my thumb until the pain numbs me and then I stare at the wallpaper.

I stare at the wallpaper a lot.

I've come to love the wallpaper.

Now though, I can't seem to keep still. Maybe it's because my heart's racing, or my legs are shaking, or my fingers are itching to push aside the curtains again.

I groan from deep in my throat and my eyes snap shut at the sound of it. I sound like a monster that hides under beds, watching, waiting. Or like *my* monsters who don't bother to hide at all.

Finally, I give in to the urge—to the *intrigue*—and I look out the window again. Josh and Tommy are both pushing wheelbarrows. One real one. One toy one. That's all I see before I run back to my bed, afraid he'll spot me again.

I sit still for a shorter time than the last before I jump up and part my curtains again. Tommy has a bucket now. Josh and my grandmother are speaking to each other while looking at the garden bed between the fence and the driveway. My grandmother points at a few things while Josh stands with his hands on his hips and nods.

That's enough, I tell myself, and go back to sitting on my bed... to staring at the wallpaper.

Then I repeat the process.

Over and over again I go from my window to the bed until an hour has passed and I'm spending more time looking out the window than I am at my wallpaper.

The wallpaper is stupid.

Tommy's on a scooter now as Josh wipes his face with the bottom of his shirt—his back to me while Grams inspects what I'm sure, at one stage, was a bright yellow flower.

I decide right away that it's my favorite of all the flowers.

I sit back on my bed, chew my thumb, just for a few seconds before looking back out. Grams is in her car now, reversing out of the driveway. Tommy's got the bucket from earlier on his head, and Josh's in the garden bed, one foot in the soil and the other on a shovel... right underneath my just-declared favorite flower.

His foot presses down and for some reason there's a sharp ache in my chest. My gaze switches from his foot to the flower, over and over. Time slows and his foot moves and so does the flower as the shovel tilts, separating the plant from its roots and before I know it I'm yelling, "Stop!" Only nothing comes out and I curse myself for not speaking enough. I grab my bag —the one I held on to for dear life on the bus ride here—the one I've held on to every day since I got here—the one that holds the only thing left that matters to me—and I run down the stairs, open the front door, and go straight to the flower.

Josh jolts a little—I guess from the shock of my presence. "What are you doing?" I whisper loudly—not intentionally— but because I'm out of breath from racing down here.

He eyes me sideways. "Your grandmother wants all new plants put in. I'm getting rid of the old ones. Why?"

"Can you wait a minute?" I ask, my voice louder, but no more clearer.

With a shrug, he answers, "Sure," and backs away as if he thinks I'm crazy.

He's right.

I take a moment and inspect the flower just like I'd seen Grams doing, then I open the bag and feel the cold metal against my fingertips. My hand curls around the leather grip and when I'm sure I have a solid hold, I pull it out—my camera —and bring it straight to my eye, removing the lens cap at the same time. I take one shot, and then another, and another; of a single yellow flower whose life has almost ended.

"Why are you taking a picture of a dead flower when there's close to a million fresh ones around us?"

"Because." I replace the lens cap and focus on putting the camera back in its place as I clear my throat. "Some things will always be beautiful, even in the face of death."

CHAPTER 4

JOSHUA

Who'd have thought that windows could be so distracting?

Okay, so maybe it wasn't the window itself but the person behind it. An entire day has passed and I'm still thinking about her. Yesterday, when she'd snuck up beside me, scaring the shit out of me, I turned to her quickly and got trapped again—trapped in her eyes.

Her eyes were the first thing I noticed about her. One of the only things I could remember, really.

Then she spoke.

And I remembered why it'd taken me so long to shake the thought of her the first time. It was her voice. It wasn't horrible, but it was deep and raspy. Husky almost. The first time I heard it I remember thinking it was odd—that it didn't seem like the type of voice that would belong to someone like her. Most pretty girls had annoyingly high-pitched voices. After she'd spoken yesterday, I'd decided that it was no longer odd. In fact, it was kind of hot.

So was she.

She was also completely fascinating.

Not that it matters.

I look at her window again—catching her watching me for the fifth time this morning. With a sigh, I go back to digging a hole in the dirt while Tommy plays with his cars in the driveway. Chazarae had left for church half an hour ago and had given me strict instructions on where to dig. She left out the part about what to put where. So, here I am spending a perfectly sunny Sunday digging holes.

An hour passes and the temperature rises. I take a break and sit down on the driveway, staring at the dirt lining the fence. In my head, I count how many holes I've dug compared to how many more I need to and just as I go to lean back on my arms and curse the North Carolina sun for being so damn hot, something cold taps against my arm. I face it quickly; it's a glass of iced water. Becca stands above me, blocking the sun. I look back down at the glass again and take it from her hands. "Thank you," I say, but I'm talking to her back because she's already walking away.

I down the entire thing in one go, set the glass down next to me, and a moment later the cold sensation's on my arm again.

A new glass.

Same Becca.

She doesn't speak. She doesn't even non-verbally respond as I take it from her. She picks up the used glass and walks over to Tommy with a plastic cup, hands it to him, and walks away.

So I do what anyone with a curious mind would do; I stare at the fence, down the water, and set the glass next to me. And then I wait.

This time, I see her shadow before I see her. Apart from that, she doesn't make her presence known. She simply replaces the empty glass with a full one and does the same with Tommy's.

I repeat the process.

So does she.

Tommy laughs.

He thinks it's a game.

To me—it kind of is.

I drink my third glass of water in two minutes and wait.

After a while, I hear the screen door slam. I turn around to see her sitting on the porch steps, a tray of glasses and two jugs of iced water set down beside her. I face the fence again, trying to hide my smile.

"More!" Tommy shouts.

I turn and see her start to stand. "It's cool," I tell her, standing up faster than she can. "I got it."

She sits back down as I gather our empty cups and walk them over to the tray. I fill them up slowly just so I can prolong her presence. "Fanks," Tommy says when I hand him back his cup. She watches him and from the corner of my eye, I watch her. When Tommy's done, he hands her back the cup. She places it on the tray and stands up. I think she's going to go back inside but she doesn't. Instead, she walks over to the flower pots at the top of the driveway and for some unknown reason, I follow her.

Squatting down, she inspects each of the plants; the flowers, the leaves, even the stems. Then she looks up at her window, her eyebrows pinched in concentration. She picks up a pot and places it about a third of the way down the driveway, then looks over at me. She holds up her hand as if asking me to wait and I nod in response because her *eyes* tell me to.

A moment later her bedroom curtains open, and I mean *open*. Not just the tiny gap that I normally see her between. She disappears a second before returning, pointing to the phone in her hand, the same time my pocket vibrates with a text.

> **Unknown:** Can you move the pot back a couple feet?
> **Joshua:** How did you get my number?
> **Unknown:** Grams.

Joshua: Oh.
Unknown: So?

I look from my phone and back up to her and give her a cheesy-as-hell thumbs up before picking up the pot with one hand, the other sending a reply.

Joshua: I'll walk backward. Just raise your hand
when you want me to stop.

After reading my text, she returns my cheesy thumbs up with one of her own and I start taking small steps back until she tells me to stop.

When she comes back out, she silently goes through all the pots and lines up what must be the ones she wants to see from her bedroom window against the fence line. This only takes a few minutes and when she's done, she turns to me. "I think maybe we should wait for my grandmother to come back. I don't want them there if she doesn't. I don't want to upset her," she says, her voice knocking all sense out of me.

Again, I agree, because her *eyes* tell me to.

Becca spends the rest of the time watching me dig holes from her bedroom window, only now she doesn't even try to hide it.

When Chazarae comes home and asks about the plants against the fence, I just point to Becca's room.

Chazarae smiles.

I smile.

And then I plant those flowers with more attention and care than I've ever planted anything before. When I'm done I look up at her window. She's already watching me, not a single emotion on her face. I wave for her to come down and she gives me another cheesy thumbs up. She shows up with her camera in her hand and without a single word spoken, spends the next hour taking pictures while I watch her and continue to dig holes, not just for the plants, but for myself, because I'm pretty sure I've never been more compelled by anything or anyone in my entire life.

CHAPTER 5

BECCA

---

envy

verb

desire to have a quality, possession, or other desirable thing belonging to (someone else).

My grandmother doesn't work which means she's home a lot. And when she's home she likes to ask a lot of questions. I don't like to answer them. So instead of feeling bad when I walk away or pretend like I don't hear her, I just sit in my room and stare at the wallpaper.

Josh works and most of the time he takes Tommy with him. But not on Wednesdays. On Wednesdays he stays here. And Wednesdays are my favorite of all the days. Tommy calls me Becs. I like it. And I like him. I told him that. I also told him he was my best friend. He agreed that I was his. So now we're best friends. Friends who can communicate without talking. When I whisper, he thinks it's a game and whispers back. When I actually do speak, he doesn't look at me like I'm a freak.

I am a freak.

But I like that he doesn't know that.

Josh pulls into the driveway and the second the car's stopped, he looks directly up at my window. I know this because I'm watching him. I quickly move behind the curtain to hide my smile. I've stopped biting my thumb when he catches me now because it doesn't feel wrong to be watching him anymore, so I no longer feel the need to punish myself with pain for doing something *bad.*

"Your dad's home," I tell Tommy, who's sitting on the floor of my bedroom drawing. I like being alone with him so we spend a lot of time in my room. I don't like the looks my grandmother gives me when she sees us together. I can tell by the way her brow bunches and her lips pull down to a frown that, in her head, she's coming up with more questions that'll inevitably be left unanswered.

I kneel down in front of Tommy and start packing the crayons.

He whispers, "Can I show Daddy my drawings?" and I nod and gather all fifty pieces of paper, the majority of which have a single jagged line through the middle.

Voices from downstairs filter up to my room and then footsteps thud up the stairs. I know it's Josh because the steps are loud and heavy. My grandmother creeps around like I'm an injured animal and I'll attack if spooked.

A panic sets in at the sound of his steps and then escalates when he knocks on the door. I look at Tommy—but all he's doing is smiling—a smile identical to his father's. Tommy answers because I'm too busy trying to look preoccupied with putting the crayons back in their box.

"Hey, bud," Josh says to Tommy. "Did you have a good day with Becca?" He uses a voice suitable for talking to kids.

My teachers were the only ones who used that voice with me.

"We drawded," Tommy whispers.

"Why are we whispering?" Josh whispers back.

"It's a secwet," Tommy tells him, and I turn my back on them to hide my smile again.

"Okay," Josh says, his voice still low. Then louder, he asks, "I brought some burgers and fries home. You want to ask Becca if she'd like to join us?"

"Come on, best fwend!" Tommy shouts.

I stand up and set the crayons on my bed and pick up the drawings. Without looking at either of them, I hand Josh the papers and pass him on the way down to the kitchen. I hear Josh ask Tommy if he drew them, and then the fake surprise in his voice when he says, "Wow! These are amazing!" And as hard as I try not to be envious of Tommy in that moment, I am.

I wait in the kitchen for them to join me and my grandmother—who's already going through the bags of food at the counter.

Josh and Tommy enter the room holding hands and Josh shouts, "No!" making me jump in my spot. "You know the rules, ma'am. Sit down at the table. You, too, Becca," he says, but he's not angry, he's smiling.

He smiles a lot.

And again I find myself envious of Tommy for having a happy parent—or at least one who's decent enough to fake it around him.

Grams takes a seat at the table and motions for me to join her. I sit down next to her while Josh and Tommy busy themselves in the kitchen. Josh hands Tommy a bag and Tommy comes to the table, kneels on a chair and goes through it. The bag's filled with paper plates, napkins and plastic knives and forks. Tommy gets to work, walking around and setting the table for us; a plate each with a knife placed on one side and a fork on the other with a napkin beneath it. He does this silently, his lips pursed and his eyes focused. Once he's done, he walks back to the kitchen counter and asks his dad where the cups are.

"Take this," my grandmother whispers from next to me. I look down at her hand between our plates holding a single dollar bill.

"Why?"

"You'll see."

Tommy returns a moment later with plastic cups and places them next to his and Josh's plate, then comes around to our side and does the same with ours. "Now?" he asks loudly, speaking to his dad.

Josh looks up from emptying the bags and rolls up the sleeves of his shirt at the same time. His forearms are tanned and muscular. And kind of hot. I've never noticed forearms before. Ever. I wonder what his hands are like.

"Looks good, bud," Josh says, and I blink once and tear my gaze away from his arms. "Great job!"

"Excellent work, young man," My grandmother states, handing him a dollar.

"Fank you, ma'am." He walks over to me and grins from ear to ear. "Did I do good, Becs?"

"No one's ever set the table for me before," I tell him, trying on the kid-voice used earlier. Josh and my grandmother laugh, and for a second I don't know why. Probably because they think I'm kidding.

I'm not.

I hand Tommy the dollar just as Josh places a tray in the middle of the table; burgers (cut in quarters), fries, and two other things coated in batter.

"Dig in!" Josh shouts, rolling up his sleeves even higher.

When did arms become attractive?

I wait while everyone loads their plate (Josh loads Tommy's) and when they're done I grab one of everything. I keep my eyes on Tommy, using him as a guide on what the proper protocol is.

He picks up a flat, round, batter-covered thing and throws it in his mouth. Then he chews and chews until he swallows.

I look down at my plate and pick up the same looking thing. Then, without wanting to look out of place, I shove it in my mouth and chew.

I choke.

The taste overpowers all my senses, even my nose. "What is this?" I mumble, bringing the napkin to my mouth.

Josh and Tommy laugh as I spit it out onto the napkin then use it to wipe the taste off my tongue. Tommy's still laughing, but Josh has contained his reaction to a smirk—a smirk almost as hot as his arms. "You're not a fan of fried pickles?"

I shake my head.

"Your eyes are watering! They're not that bad," he says, shoving one in his mouth to prove his point.

My nose scrunches in disgust.

Then fingers brush the side of my face, moving my hair, and I gasp and flinch away from my grandmother's touch. My heart pounds while I look down—watching my chest rise and fall. I bite down on my thumb, my eyes drifting shut when the pain consumes me. I try to calm my breathing but I can't.

I can't run.

I can't hide.

When the pain becomes too much to handle, I release my thumb and open my eyes. I focus on the imprints of my teeth and wait for them to fade and the color to return. When I'm satisfied and can breathe without pain, I muster the courage to look up, already aware that everyone'll be watching me. "I'm sorry," my grandmother says. "I guess I forgot."

"It's okay," I whisper, and look over at Tommy. He hasn't noticed a thing. But then I look at Josh, and that's all I do.

41

Because he's watching me, his eyes dark and sad and worried and confused, all at once. He tries to smile, but it's fake. I know, because I've watched him enough to know the difference. And I've seen enough of this particular smile to know what it means.

Fear.

CHAPTER 6

JOSHUA

"So Tommy upset Kim yesterday," Robby says, sitting down beside me on my makeshift bench during our lunch break.

"Shit. What did he do now?"

He laughs once. "Nothing like that. He told her he had a new best friend. Her name's Becs and she's prettier than Kim."

"Is she upset because he has a new friend or because Becca's prettier?"

"Is Becca real? I thought she was his imaginary friend..."

"Yes, she's real," I say through a chuckle. "It's my landlord's granddaughter. Have I not told you?"

"You mentioned something about her staying for a while, I didn't know she was still there or that Tommy was hanging out with her. I know how you get with him spending time with strangers."

"Yeah well..." I trail off.

"Anyway. Honestly, I think Kim's more upset about the pretty part."

"Yeah, she should be."

"So it's true then?"

"What is?" I ask, playing dumb, even though I can feel the heat creeping to my cheeks.

"That she's prettier?"

"I mean…" I drop my gaze and focus on the dry wall dust covering my shoes. "Don't get me wrong, Kim's hot for her age and I still don't know how you struck gold with her, but Becca —she's something else completely."

His eyes burn a hole in the side of my head, but I don't look at him. After a long ass moment, he whistles, low and slow. "Holy shit, Joshy! Have you got a crush?" He pokes my side.

I punch his arm. "Fuck off!"

He returns my punch by stomping on my foot. "You do!"

"Fuck off!" I repeat, but I'm laughing this time. Because really? What else can I do? Even if I denied it he wouldn't give a shit.

"Hey, boys!" he shouts to all the other workers. He stands up and cups both hands around his mouth. "Our little boy Joshua has finally hit puberty!"

"Fuck you," I mumble, shaking my head as he walks away.

After a few steps, he turns to me. "So are you going to do anything about it?"

"No. What am I going to say? Hey… wanna get some food with my kid? You can watch him lick the boogers off his ice cream like I have to. It'll be fun!" I say, the sarcasm in my tone unmistakable.

He stands with both his hands on his hips, his head cocked to the side and his eyes narrowed. "Or we could watch Tommy and you could take her out on a proper date. Or… are you afraid?"

"Fire truck yeah, I'm afraid. You've seen me in social situations, right? I mean, you were there at Michael's bachelor party when I told the stripper her tits were perfect for breastfeeding."

"Thanks for getting us kicked out of that club, by the way,"

44

Michael says, patting my shoulders as he walks behind me. "Fucking creeper."

"See?" I tell Robby.

He shakes his head and sighs heavily. "At some point you're going to want to move on and find someone."

"And I will," I assure him. "Once Tommy's in college."

He laughs. "Anyway, Kim asked if we can have Tommy overnight?"

"Sure."

"You're done here, by the way. There should still be enough light left in the day for you to get some skating in, right?"

I get in my truck without a second's hesitation and rush home to shower and change. People get excited and anxious for a lot of reasons: money, power, food, sex (it's been so long, I don't think my memory of the sensation of sex can even qualify as a legitimate memory anymore). For me—it's skating.

The last few days had been quiet on the site so I got to leave early, which meant skate time with Tommy in the driveway. He's good for an almost three-year-old but he loses interest and gets distracted real quick.

I'd seen Becca watching a few times from her window hoping she'd make an appearance like that day when she brought us drinks.

She never did.

So you can imagine my surprise when I pull into the driveway and see her standing there, one foot on Tommy's skateboard, the other on the ground, and her hands out by her sides.

CHAPTER 7

BECCA

---

safe

adjective

protected from or not exposed to danger or risk; not likely to be harmed or lost.

"Shit!"

I drop my arms and jump off the board, my gaze anywhere but on him. His car door opens and my panic sets in so I do the only thing I can think to do.

I run.

"Wait!" he shouts, and I freeze on the porch steps, my shoulders heaving with each breath.

His door shuts and then his footsteps near and I swear the air's thicker and harsher than it was a few seconds ago.

"You don't have to—"

"I'm sorry," I cut in. "I shouldn't be using your stuff without—"

"Becca."

I inhale deeply, my fists balled so tight my nails dig into my palms.

"Did you want me to teach you to skate?" he asks, and I can hear the plea in his voice.

I turn to him, completely surprised by his words. "What?"

"I can teach you," he rushes out. "If you want to learn, I mean. I uh…" He pauses a beat. "I can try to do it without touching you… if that'll help."

My chest tightens at his words—at the fact that he'd even think of it. "I don't think I'd be very good."

He smiles. *Holy shit*, does he smile.

He motions for me to come back down and I do because he's still smiling and I'm still panicking, though not as much as I was before.

I follow behind him, watching his broad shoulders move with each step. "Where's Tommy? You're home early," I mumble.

He faces me, the smile still in place. "He's staying at my uncle's, and were you skating because you thought no one would see?"

I shrug even though we both know he'd caught me. I'd seen him and Tommy out here so much and it looked like fun and, yeah, I was curious. But, clearly, it's not as easy as it looks because I suck. I tell Josh all that and his head throws back with his laugh before he eyes the skateboard, still in the middle of the driveway. "Well, yeah, it would be hard. You're using the wrong board. That's Tommy's. It's made for toddlers."

"Oh."

"Hey," he soothes, "it's no problem." He reaches into his pocket and pulls out his keys, then opens the huge metal toolbox in the bed of his truck. He grabs an armful of skate-boards and drops them to the ground. There has to be at least seven of them. He picks a black one and pushes it toward my feet. "You can use that one."

I put my left foot on the board, and the other on the ground, and then I look at him, waiting for his reaction. He bites down on his full bottom lip as he takes me in. "You gotta —" he breaks off on a sigh, picks up one of the boards and sets it next to mine. "You gotta move your left foot up a bit and straighten it a little. It's better for balance." He gets on his own board and shows me how to place my feet.

I follow his instructions and his smile gets wider. "That's it. Now all you have to do is kick and then push."

I kick back and push off the ground, but I don't get far because my balance is off and like I said, I suck. "This is dumb," I tell him, getting off the board. "And I'm sure you have better things to do—"

"I was just gonna skate," he cuts in. "So this is kind of perfect."

"Yeah but—"

"See the problem is…" he starts, jumping off his board and walking over to me, "…you're just doing a whole lot of kicking and no actual pushing."

"Okay?"

He rubs the back of his neck, his bottom lip between his teeth again. His gaze moves from my feet, up my entire body until his eyes lock on mine and all I want to do is yell *Fire!* Because that's what I feel like—like my entire body is on fire— my cheeks especially.

"Um… shit," he mumbles, looking away. Then he does the worst possible thing my flaming body can handle; he steps up on *my* board and stands behind me. "Maybe you just need to get a feel for it—let the wheels take you," he says, his voice low and completely intimidating. "Maybe… I mean, I know you don't like being touched but what if you touch me? Is that the same?"

I stare straight ahead, my breaths coming out in tiny, shaky spurts as my stomach fills with knots.

"If I put my arms out like this," he asks, lifting his arms straight out on either side of me. "You can hold on to me and I'll push us along. If you want."

"Okay," I whisper, my fingers trembling as they settle on his wrists.

"Are you good?"

"Yes," I whisper again.

And then the most amazing thing happens. Warm air hits my face and blows through my hair and my hands grip tighter and I *breathe*. I hear the wheels spinning—feel them beneath me —and I close my eyes, blocking the tears from forming because in this single moment—with my heart racing and the world whooshing by around me—there's a sense of freedom I'd never felt before.

And freedom, I've come to learn, is a feeling that often gets taken for granted.

He comes to a stop and when I open my eyes I'm face to face with the garage door. "Again?" he asks, his breath warm against my ear.

"Yes," I whisper, and then clear my throat so I can actually speak. "Please."

He doesn't drop his arms as he pushes us backwards and does his best to turn us around while I'm still on the board. "Ready?"

"Yes."

He repeats this a few times, going back and forth up and down the driveway, and I know this isn't what he had in mind when he said he planned on skating but I don't want to ask him to stop. I want to keep feeling this—this *free*—for as long as he'll let me.

"You want to keep going?"

I nod.

"All right. I just need to rest my arms for a second."

"Sorry." I release my death grip on his arms and look down

at my feet.

After a moment, his arms are back in place and I settle my hands on them, but they're not on his wrist anymore, they're closer to his elbows and before I can work out why, I feel his front pressed against my back and his breath against my cheek, causing me to hold in my own. "Becca?" he asks.

"Yes?"

"I *really* like it when you talk to me." Before I can respond we're moving again. "Ready?" he asks, and I have no idea what he means, not until my hands are no longer touching him.

My eyes snap open. "What the—" Something catches on the wheels and then next thing I know, I'm landing on all fours, my hands and knees scraping on the concrete.

"Holy shit!" Josh yells, and I look up just in time to see him squatting in front of me. "I'm so sorry. I shouldn't have let you go. Are you okay?"

"I'm fine."

He gently brushes off my knees, his brows bunched while he inspects them. "You didn't break skin. That's good." He looks up, the concern in his eyes evident. "Palms?" he asks, his hands out waiting.

I show him my palms and he pouts. "You got a little booboo," he says, but I'm too busy staring at him to know what he's talking about. "I'm sorry." His eyes flick to mine quickly before returning to my palms. Slowly, he lifts my hand—just as slowly as his mouth lowers.

I suck in a breath.

Hold it.

And then I wait.

When his lips press softly against my skin, kissing it lightly, I try to release the breath.

Try.

"All better, right?"

51

I open my eyes to see him watching me, a half smile pulling at his lips. "Kisses make all booboos better."

Shit, he's cute.

My grandmother's car pulls up to the curb and she steps out and walks up to the house, eyeing Josh's car suspiciously. But not as suspiciously as when she sees us sitting in the middle of the driveway.

After claiming my hand back, I finally exhale. "Thank you," I tell him, standing up. "Bye." I practically run into the house and go to my room so I can settle the beating of my heart, because I sure as hell can't do that with Josh around. I throw myself on the bed and look down at my hands just as my grandmother enters my room.

"You let him touch you?" she asks.

"Yes."

"How was it?"

"His hands are rough."

"Well, he uses them every day and he works hard."

I sit on the edge of my bed and look up at her. "But they're gentle."

She smiles warmly.

"And safe. His touch is *safe*."

CHAPTER 8

JOSHUA

You know when you're in middle school and you have a crush on a girl and you make up reasons to try to get her to notice you? You walk past her for absolutely no legit reason or say something funny when she's in earshot hoping she'll hear you and think you're hilarious? Or, like, you find ways to sniff her hair?

Not that I did that.

I'm just saying.

Anyway, that's pretty much me right now. Normally when I didn't have Tommy, I'd street skate for hours and when it got dark and I knew the place would be empty, I'd hit up the skate park. Instead, I'm doing lame ass tricks on the driveway, hoping she'll notice me and come back out. I almost knocked on her door, but what would I say? *Hi. Can Becca come out and play?*

I see her, though, standing at her window watching me. I don't let her know I see her—that means she'll know I'm watching her just as much as she's watching me. Plus, I don't want to give her a reason to stop.

I laugh at myself and drop my foot on the ground,

wondering why the hell a twenty-year-old guy is spending his rare free time skating in the driveway trying to impress some girl. Shaking my head, I look at her window for the hundredth time in the past four hours. She's still there and I still have no idea what she's waiting for.

She let me touch her. That has to mean something. Right?

I pick up my board and go back to my apartment where I spend the rest of the night alone and lonely because, in my case, they're two different things. And sometimes that loneliness makes me do or think stupid things. Like how I never knew that Chazarae even had a granddaughter, or any kids at all. And then I wonder if I'm a bad person for never caring or asking about her life before. Then I think about my parents—and wonder if they've ever met someone who's surprised when they find out that they have a son *and* a grandson. And then I do something that puts stupid on an entirely new level. I think about Natalie—something I rarely let myself do. And I wonder if she's happy—if turning her back on us made her *happy*. Almost three years gone and she's never once asked about her son. I wonder if she's just as selfish as she was back then. Or *selfless* maybe. Because in her case, she could be both. I just don't know which one. And I think that's what bothers me the most—not knowing *why* she left.

∼

I call Robby as soon as I wake up and shower the next morning because I'm sick of the silence and I don't know what to do with myself.

"Are you sure?" he asks, "We don't mind having him until after lunch."

"Yeah. I forgot I had plans with him," I lie.

. . .

I grab my board and go back to skating in the driveway, waiting for them to show up. A half hour later they pull in and as soon as Tommy's free from his seat he jumps out of their car and right into my arms. And all my other thoughts, feelings and questions become completely insignificant. "I missed you, buddy," I tell him.

"Me, too, Daddy," he says quietly, squeezing my neck.

Robby walks over with Tommy's backpack and hands it to me. "You good?"

I pretend to focus on brushing Tommy's hair aside so I don't have to look at Robby and, hopefully, he won't be able to read me. "Uh huh. Thanks a lot for bringing him back."

"He hasn't had his morning snack," Robby calls out as I climb the stairs up to my apartment.

"I'll take care of it. Thanks again."

After putting the bowl of fruit on the counter in front of Tommy, I ask, "Did you want to spend the money you earned? We could hit up the toy store and see what they got for you?"

His eyes light up with his smile. "Camera!"

My eyes narrow, but inside, I'm smiling. "I think you're going to have to work a lot harder if you want a camera."

His smiles drops, and so do his shoulders. "Okay."

"What about a sandpit or something? You like the one at daycare right?"

He shrugs as he chomps on a piece of apple, his eyes lowered, and if a kid could get an award for being the saddest most pathetic looking apple eater in the entire world, he'd definitely win.

"Why do you want a camera, anyway?"

"Because Becca."

"Because Becca has one, you want one?"

"She said it makes her happy."

"Oh yeah? She said that?"

He nods, looking up at me now.

I tilt my head as I eye him curiously. "Does she talk to you a lot?"

He nods again.

"What do you guys talk about?"

With a shrug, he says, "You."

"Me?" I clear my throat, my pulse spiking and my ears thirsty for more information. "What about me?"

"Can Becca come?"

"No. Tommy. Listen. This is really important. What does she say about me?"

"She can't come?"

"Tommy!"

He finishes his fruit and gets off the stool, then walks the bowl to the sink. "Moneys?" he says, his hand out waiting.

"What does she say?" I ask, frustrated and fully aware of how tacky it is that I'm using my kid for intel on a girl I might possibly be crushing on. What can I say? I'm that kid in middle school and Tommy's my best friend. He's also hers. So right now, in my mind, it makes complete sense.

"I get da sandpit," he says, shoving his hand right under my nose.

I bend down so I'm eye to eye with him, and then I do something really pathetic. "I'll give you moneys if you tell me something she's said about me."

He smiles. "Five."

I rear back. "What?"

"Five moneys."

"How the hell old are you?"

"Naughty word, Daddy."

With a roll of my eyes, I reach into my pocket, pull out my wallet, fetch a five-dollar bill and slap it in his tiny little hand.

His smile widens. "She wikes my smile," he says, and starts walking to his room.

I follow him. "That's not about me! What does she say about *me*?"

"Me handsome like you, daddy."

I tell him he can invite Becca.

I also tell him not to hold his breath. Which apparently is a dumb thing to say to a kid. *Why would I hold my breath?* That's a question he asks over and over while I change my clothes, over and over, and search the bathroom for the cologne I hadn't worn since the bachelor party with the breastfeeding boob stripper.

"But why would I hold my breff?" he asks again, taking my hand as we descend down the stairs. It's worse than the time I told him to *hop* out of the bath.

"It's just a figure of speech, buddy."

"Finger of peach?"

I can't help but laugh. "Yeah. Finger of peach."

He runs up their porch steps and knocks wildly on the door, cackling the entire time. Chazarae answers and before she can speak, he runs into the house yelling, "Becca! Becca!"

Chazarae smiles as her eyes move from him to me.

"He wanted to invite Becca to hang out with us if that's okay?"

"I hope he doesn't get too disappointed. Becca hasn't left the house since she's been here."

"Yeah, I figured," I tell her. "It's just he asked and I couldn't—"

"You smell nice," she cuts in, coming closer and sniffing me once. "New cologne?"

I shrug. "It's old."

"Hmm." She eyes me sideways. Then reaches up and runs

the back of her fingers across my cheek. "You're blushing, Joshua."

The human body is stupid.

Even though it knows that embarrassment is something you want to hide—it makes sure that you can't hide it. I lower my head. "No, I'm not."

Tommy squeezes between me and Chazarae and runs to my truck. "She said yes!"

You know what's worse than your landlady calling you out on wearing cologne purely because you want to impress her granddaughter? I'll tell you what. Being in the confined space of a truck while your son tells said granddaughter about how you paid him five moneys for him to tell you about what she said about you. *Yeah.* That's happening. And if I thought the human body was stupid before, I'm pretty sure I hate it right now.

From the corner of my eye I can see her smiling, even though her head's lowered—probably trying to hide her own embarrassment. I don't know why *she'd* be embarrassed. She's not the one getting called out for being pathetic.

I focus on the road. Nothing but the road. Not her legs. Or her short blue dress. Or her cowboy boots. Or her hands settled on her lap, her thumbs circling each other.

She clears her throat and I refocus on the road I thought I was focused on. "Where are we going?" she asks.

My fingers grip the steering wheel tighter while I try to piece myself back together. "Toy store. He gets to spend the money he's earned. You know when we were there for dinner and you and Chazarae gave him the dollar for setting the table? That's kind of like his allowance and once a month I take him toy shopping for whatever he wants."

She nods slowly.

I add, "I know it might seem weird. You know, considering his age, but I just want to start him off early—to know that hard work pays off and nothing comes for free. I just think it's important. I don't really know why. I don't really know what I'm doing when it comes to being his dad. I guess I just do my best. I try to teach him manners and respect and hopefully it's something that'll stick with him. It's hard, you know… being a single dad and making all the decisions and trying to work out…" I trail off, my eyes wide when I realize all I've just said. "I've just given you way more information than you asked for." I glance at her quickly but she's looking down at her hands. "I'm sorry. I ramble a lot." I pull into a spot in the parking lot at the mall, and then switch off the engine—my eyes still wide and my awkwardness at an all-new high.

She shifts in her seat but I'm too afraid to look at her. I see her hand moving across the bench seat, coming closer and closer to mine. I swallow nervously. Time slows. And when her little finger brushes across my wrist, every single muscle in my body tenses. Her palm covers the back of my hand, her fingers sliding between mine. "Josh?" she whispers, and I finally look at her. "You're doing an amazing job. Tommy—he gives me the courage to push on. You know… after I kick."

"Like skating?"

She nods, her gaze lifting and locking with mine.

Then Tommy huffs in the back seat, breaking our stare. "My boogers taste like finger of peach."

CHAPTER 9

JOSHUA

Tommy and Becca pretty much ignore me as they walk hand in hand through the store. They seem to have their own silent language—one that I'm completely unaware of. They smile. A lot. Not just at each other, but in general.

They pick out one of those plastic shell sandpits. She waves a hand in the air, indicating to all the different colors. He points to her, then her eyes, and then he chooses *green*.

After checking out, they lead the way, hand in hand, to my truck, where I dump the sandpit and all the accessories (buckets, shovels, you name it) in the back. It costs a lot more than the money he'd earned over the last month but who am I to say no? Especially when getting the extra stuff meant spending more time with Becca. And him, of course.

When everything's strapped in, I turn around and see them having another one of their silent conversations. Tommy rubs his belly, and then points to her. She purses her lips and looks up to the skies, then rubs her own belly. He gives her a thumbs up and she returns it. Then they both look at me, a question in their eyes. And I stand there silent and unmoving because, seriously? What the hell just happened? Tommy crosses his arms. Becca quirks an eyebrow.

I nod.

They celebrate.

I sigh. "Okay, I'm going to be honest. I have no idea what you guys just said, or asked, or whatever."

Tommy sighs louder than I just did and throws in an eye roll. Sometimes I truly question how old the kid is.

Becca bends at her waist so she's eye level with him, then holds up three fingers.

He nods and looks up at me. "Me and Becca are hungry. Can we eat?"

"*That's* what that was?"

Becca snorts with laughter. Legit, snorts. And no lie—it's kind of hot.

I take them to Tommy's favorite place—Chuck E Cheese, where we scoff down our meals and I double-dog-dare Becca to have another fried pickle, which she refuses. We spend the rest of the afternoon playing games and going from one ride to the next. Normally, I'd find an excuse to cut out after an hour or so but honestly, it's not so bad with Becca around. It's actually kind of fun. The two of them still live and play in their own worlds, but occasionally, they'll try to get me involved in it. It's a whole lot of pointing and nodding and head shaking and holding up one or two fingers—whatever that means.

After three hours, Tommy's finally had enough and he asks to go build his sandpit. We get in the car and five minutes later I can see him in the rear view mirror—his eyes heavy as he starts to nod off.

"Don't fall asleep, buddy!" I say loudly, trying to keep him awake.

He doesn't respond.

"We'll be home soon and we'll set up the sandpit and you can play there for the rest of the day." I reach back and shake his leg while I keep my focus on the road. "Don't sleep."

He lifts his head slowly, his eyes hooded. "I won't," he says through a yawn.

I glance at Becca quickly. Her brow's bunched in confusion as she looks from me to Tommy. "Can you try to keep him awake?" I ask her. "Shake his hand or something. Anything. I can't transfer him from the car to his bed anymore and he turns into a little turd if he gets woken."

She nods and shakes Tommy's arm.

"Stay awake, buddy!" I yell, knowing full well how ridiculous this might seem to her.

After a minute, she turns back around and faces the windshield. "I'm sorry," she says. "He's out."

"It's okay. He should be worn out. It was a big day for him."

"So what do we do?"

"I normally just drive around or park somewhere until he wakes up on his own but I can drop you home first."

"Or not," she says quietly. "I don't mind driving around. Or parking."

I drive to the half-court and park in the middle. Normally I'd crack a window and skate close enough to the car that I'd still be able to see or hear Tommy. But for obvious reasons I choose to stay in the truck this time.

After switching off the engine, I turn to her. "Thanks for coming out today. He was really excited to ask you and I know you haven't really been out much since…" I trail off.

She shrugs and takes out her camera from the bag sitting on the seat between us. Then switches on the screen at the back and starts flipping through pictures.

63

"Is it because you don't know the area well or something? Because I can show you around if you want."

She shakes her head, her eyes still focused on the camera.

I thought, or at least hoped, that after what happened yesterday and the time we'd spent together today, that she'd at least talk to me—maybe give up a little more of herself. Maybe I was wrong. Maybe I'd hoped a little too hard. I rest back in my seat and let the disappointment wash through me. I hear the unbuckling of her seatbelt and face her just in time to see her move to the middle of the seat. She smiles as she leans into me, her arm touching mine as she lifts the camera and shows me the picture on the screen.

It's of Tommy—his face covered in dirt mixed with sweat and his smile from ear to ear. Probably the same as mine is right now. "When did you take this?"

"Wednesday," she says quietly, then clears her throat. "There's a whole bunch of them." She leans even closer into me, so close her chest is against my arm and I panic. I move my arm and settle it on top of the seat behind her. She starts flipping through the pictures quickly and I take in every one. Then she gets to a bunch of close ups of her and Tommy. "Wait." I cover her hand. "Go back."

"Here." She hands me the camera and somehow moves closer again. Now her forearm is on my leg and I can feel her warm breaths against my chest. I do my best to hide the shakiness of my hand and slowly flip through the pictures of her and Tommy. They've been taken outside. I can tell because her eyes are brighter—and, yeah, it doesn't escape me that I pay way too much attention to her eyes.

I pause on one of them sitting on the porch steps. I can see her arm extended, taking the shot as she looks right at the lens… but Tommy's looking at her, his eyes shut tight and his nose against her cheek. The next one has him kissing her cheek, her nose scrunched a little but her smile wide. I swallow loudly, my heart thumping against my chest. My thumb traces over the picture while I take in every single detail of it— mentally burning the image in my mind. There's an ache in my chest, not from the beating of my heart, but from the breaking. Still, for some reason, I want more of whatever is causing the pain. "Can I get a copy of these?"

She doesn't respond but I can feel her shifting next to me. The warmth caused by her breaths leaves my chest and returns a moment later, only now it's against my neck and my eyes close when I feel her exhale softly against my skin, then hear her inhale through her nose, sniffing me. I'm about to back away from her but her hand moves to my nape, keeping me with her. She runs her fingers through my hair and I keep my eyes closed; goose bumps pricking my entire body. I wonder if she can feel it. If the hairs on the back of my neck tickle her fingers as her hand moves down and her face moves up and she kisses right under my ear and I swear to God everything stops. *Everything.*

My breath.

Her hands.

My heart.

Her lips.

My *world.*

Everything.

Stops.

Then she exhales.

And my eyes snap open.

She whispers, "You smell so good."

And everything starts again.

Everything.

Only this time, it's amplified.

My breaths.

Her touch.

My pulse.

Her kiss.

Because she's *kissing* me.

From my neck to my jaw, and I meet her half way—but the second my mouth is on hers and the softness and the warmth of her lips invade all my senses, I freeze. I sit there, my mouth on the hottest girl I've ever and possibly will ever see and I choke.

Literally *choke*.

I cough into her mouth and she pulls back, her nose scrunched, only for a moment before her eyes widen and she grabs a bottle of water from her bag and I'm thumping my chest, my eyes watering and seriously, fuck my life.

She uncaps the water and hands it to me; the surprise on her face replaced with concern as she slowly rubs my back.

I close my eyes, too embarrassed to face her as I drink and drink and drink like the water is more important than air because in this moment it is.

"Are you okay?" she asks as soon as I'm done.

I burp.

Right in her face.

Fuck, I'm a class act.

"Run, Becca."

"What?" she says through a chuckle.

"Seriously, run. I'm a mess."

"No you're not," she whispers, her eyes soft and her smile wide. She laughs a little and I can't help but laugh with her.

I chuck the empty bottle on the floor of the car. "It's just… it's been a while since I've done anything like this and I'm a wreck and you—you're so intimidating."

"*I'm* intimidating?" she asks incredulously.

"Well, yeah," I tell her, still not facing her. "Have you seen you, Becca? Your beauty alone is intimidating and just the thought of kissing you…"

"Josh," she whispers, her hand on my shoulder turning me to her. "No one's ever said I was beautiful before."

"Clearly, you're surrounding yourself with either the blind, the stupid, or the pathetic. I'm the pathetic."

"Stop it. It's no big deal. It was just a kiss, right?"

I shake my head, avoiding eye contact. "That's the thing, though. I want to kiss you, Becca. You have no idea how much and how often I've thought about it and I never ever dreamed that you'd—"

"Throw myself at you?" she cuts in.

"No. I was going to say *give me the chance to.*"

"So what happened just now?" she asks, and a part of me wonders why it seems so out of character for her to be confident in the situation when I'm a mess, but I push it aside because she's actually *talking* to me.

She's talking and she's letting me touch her and I'm pretty sure nothing else matters. "I freaked out. *Obviously.* It's just I know how fast things can escalate and kissing isn't just kissing. Kissing leads to touching and touching leads to sex and sex is frightening as fuck for me."

"Why?"

"You've met my son, right?"

She smiles. "Okay. I get it."

"That's what frightening sex leads to. At least in my mind. It's years of diaper changes and months of potty training and finding peas in underwear and dirt in pillow cases and freaking out over every cough and every sneeze and—"

She clamps her lips between her teeth, fighting to contain her laugh.

"You think it's funny?" I ask, finally facing her. I look at her now, right into her eyes, and raise my eyebrows.

After placing her hands on my chest, she whispers, "I just really wanted you to kiss me."

"And that's the other thing—why is it always up to the guy—"

She fists my shirt and pulls me closer, cutting me off. And then she leans up and kisses me. *Holy shit*, does she kiss me. Properly. Not the shit version of a kiss I attempted. Her mouth covers mine, her wet lips moving across my lips. Just once. And then her tongue repeats the process and, *fire truck,* I give in to her and her kiss and her hands and her everything. I take everything she gives, returning it as best I can. Time slows, but my pulse doesn't and when she pulls back slightly—gasping for breath—I take the opportunity to hold her closer and kiss across her jaw, down her neck and to her shoulder. Her hands move to the back of my head, her fingers lacing in my hair and I've never *ever* felt anything sexier in my entire life. "Maybe…" she says through a shaky breath. I jerk back so I can look at her but all I can see is her chest heaving up and down, up and down, and my gaze locks on her cleavage because *BOOBS!* "Maybe you're right… about kissing leading to other things. I think maybe we should stop and get out of here."

I open my door and get out. She follows. I pull out two boards from the toolbox and drop them by her feet. "You want to practice some more?"

She nods and steps on the board. I stand behind her, my arms out straight by her sides, like we did the day before. Only this time, she grabs my wrists and places my hands on her hips. She smiles when she tilts her head up and looks at me. I kiss her quickly.

I can't not.

"Now I'm ready," she says.

So I kick.

And I push.

CHAPTER 10

JOSHUA

"How the hell did we forget the sand?" I say through a laugh, staring at the empty sandpit and all the toys that go with it.

"But I wanted to play in my sandpit," Tommy whines.

I check the time. "Everything's closed now, bud. It's almost bed time for you and you haven't even had dinner."

"But I wanted to play in my sandpit," he says again.

"I don't know what you want me to do, Tommy. All the sand shops are closed."

"But I wanted—"

"I *know*, buddy. We can get it tomorrow."

"But you said I could play today!"

"I *know* I said that but—"

He starts to cry.

I thump my hand on my forehead.

Becca pouts.

"Don't look at me like that," I tell her.

She looks down at Tommy and back up to me and pouts again.

"What can I do?"

She steps closer, not touching me, but close enough so I can hear her whisper over his cry. "He's so sad."

"Well—"

"You did tell him."

"You're not helping me right now."

She pouts again and goes to Tommy, squatting down so she can hold him. "But Daddy said," he cries, and I roll my eyes.

Becca rubs his back and whispers in his ear. I don't hear what she says but it doesn't seem to calm him and now they're both looking at me with their sad, pleading eyes and stupidly adorable pouts.

"Fine!" I shout, and point to the sandpit. "Get the buckets and shovels and get back in the truck!"

I start walking to my apartment.

"Where you, Daddy?" Tommy shouts.

"Getting trash bags!"

When I get back in the truck, Tommy's already buckled in and Becca's sitting in the middle of the front seat. "Where are we going?" she asks, trying to hide her smile.

"The stupid beach."

We get McDonalds drive-thru on the way. I never let Tommy have this much crappy food in one day but I have no choice. We eat in the car in the parking lot at the beach. "I like today," Tommy says.

I adjust the rear view mirror so I can look at him. He's shoving fries down his shirt. Eying Becca sideways, I say, "I like today, too, buddy. It's a shame Becca was here. She smells."

Becca gasps and throws a fry at my head.

Tommy giggles.

I throw one over my shoulder at him.

He laughs harder.

Then Becca throws a handful at me.

I pick them up and eat them.

"You fun today, Daddy!" Tommy says.

I turn to face him. "What do you mean *today*? I'm fun every day."

He shakes his head. "No you not." Then he points to Becca. "Becca makes us fun!"

It takes me and Becca a half hour to fill one trash bag with sand using the toy shovels and buckets and I curse myself for not bringing one of the fifteen actual shovels Chazarae has stored in the garage. Tommy's too busy rolling around in the sand to help us. "That's one," I tell Becca. "Another what? Five or six to go?"

Becca just smiles.

I pick up the bag to take it to my truck. It splits at the bottom and the last half hour becomes a waste.

I groan, but Becca—she cackles with laughter.

"How is this funny? We just wasted all that time!"

She shrugs and points around us. Tommy's ankle deep in the sand, the ocean is still, and the sun is setting, turning the atmosphere an eerie orange. "Look around us and tell me again you'd rather be somewhere else," she says.

I watch her closely as she puts one bag inside another and starts to fill it with sand. After glancing at Tommy quickly and seeing that he's distracted, I squat down next to her. "Tommy's right, you know? About you making us fun."

Her gaze lifts, first to Tommy, then to me. She kisses me quickly and then looks away. "I *love* today."

"Can you watch Tommy for a second? I'm just gonna grab my phone from my truck."

She nods.

I go to my truck, get my phone, and dial Robby's number.

"What's up?" he says in greeting.

"Hey... is that mini loader at your house?"

"Yeah, it's still on the trailer." He pauses a beat. "Why?"

"What are you doing right now?"

I tell Becca not to worry about the sand anymore but don't tell her why. So when the flood lights and the roar of Robby's truck appear out of nowhere, Tommy instantly stops what he's doing (using his shoes to shovel sand down in his pants) and squeals, "Uncle Robby!"

Both Robby and Kim jump out of the truck, their smiles matching Tommy's. Tommy flies into Robby's arms. "I hear your dad's a goofball and forgot to get you sand for your *sand*pit," he says, tickling Tommy's side.

"Daddy a poofdoll!" Tommy laughs.

Becca comes up beside me, her arms full with all the stuff we'd brought to collect the sand. "Who's this?" Kim says, walking toward us with a face-splitting grin and it already makes me afraid of the shit that'll come out of her mouth. She stands in front of us, her hand out waiting. "I'm Kim."

Becca smiles and motions to her full arms. She nudges my side and I face her. Her eyes are wide, pleading. And for a moment I'm confused. Then it hits me. "This is Becca," I tell them, forgetting she can't—or doesn't like to speak. Or touch. I guess that's why she's carrying all that shit. She nudges my side again and jerks her head toward my truck, then lifts her arms slightly.

I nod. "I'll give you a hand," I tell her, pulling my keys out of my pocket.

"I guess we better start getting this sand for you, huh?" Robby says, but my back's already turned and I'm walking toward my truck. He adds, "You ever operated a front hoe loader before?"

"Yes," says Tommy, and Robby laughs.

Kim says, "Only your dad would go to this extreme to make you happy, Tommy. You're one lucky little dude."

CHAPTER 11

BECCA

---

shame

   noun

   a painful feeling of humiliation or distress caused by the consciousness of wrong or foolish behavior.

That's exactly what I feel. Not for me, but for Josh.

"I'm sorry," I whisper, looking down at my now empty hands while we sit in Josh's car.

"You have nothing to be sorry about, Becca."

"I embarrassed you."

"You did not."

"I'm a freak."

"What? Why?"

"You know why… the not talking or touching…"

"Hey…" He comes closer but I pull away. He sighs, his hands hovering in inch above my leg. His voice lowers to a whisper. "What's going on?"

With my gaze still lowered and my voice strained, I tell him,

"Maybe this was a bad idea. You and me… doing what we're doing…"

He clears his throat and moves further away from me. His reaction doesn't surprise me. Not even a little. I'd give up on me, too. "I don't really know what to say," he says, his words drawn out. "Today's been…" He laughs once. "Today's been one of the best days I've had since I can't even remember… and that has everything to do with *you*. If you're not comfortable with us, you know, getting closer or whatever, then that's cool. I mean, I'll be upset, for sure, but I don't want to stop hanging out with you. I like you, Becca."

I gather my courage and look up at him, but he's already watching me, his eyes fixed on mine. I swallow my nerves. "I like you, too."

He's quick to close in on me, and even quicker to smile. "So what's the problem?" he says, his hand resting on my leg now.

And I let him this time. I bite my lip and point out the windshield to the loader dumping sand into the back of a truck while Tommy squeals with excitement. "That. The real and outside world."

He shrugs. "Fuck the real world then. We'll just live in our own."

"That's not possible, Josh."

"You think?" He arches an eyebrow and *dammit* he's cute. "Watch me make it possible." He comes closer again, his eyes drifting shut right before his mouth meets mine. He kisses me once, soft but quick. Then he pulls away, his hand rubbing his heart. He huffs out a breath, his cheeks puffing with the force of it.

"What's wrong?"

"I think you broke my heart a little bit just now."

"Shut up!" I laugh out, leaning into him. He puts his arm around my shoulders while I place my hand on his stomach, feeling his hard muscles beneath it. And because I'm curious, I run a single finger down from his chest.

Dip.

Dip.

Dip.

His hand covers mine, stopping me from going any lower. "What are you doing?" he murmurs, his voice rough.

I look up at him. "Playing."

He shakes his head, his eyes on my mouth.

I lick my lips.

He does the same.

A tapping on the window interrupts us. Josh winds down the window. "We're done. I'll meet you at your house?" Robby asks.

"Yep!" Josh says, louder than normal.

Robby's eyes drop to Josh's hand on my leg. "I'd take Tommy but his seat's not in my truck."

Josh's fingers press down on my leg when I try to move away from him. "It's cool. Can you just um... put him in his seat? I can't really get out right now."

What? I think. But Robby says it out loud. Then after a beat, he laughs. "Oh!"

Oh what?

"Sure," Robby says.

What's funny?

As soon as Robby's gone, Josh squirms in his seat, his hand on his lap covering himself.

Oh! "Oh!"

Josh shakes his head.

I stare out the windshield.

Kim puts Tommy in his seat. "See you guys there," she says, smiling and waving just outside Josh's window.

He gives her a two finger wave.

I blink.

77

He drives home.

I don't speak.

Neither does he.

Not until we get home and he switches off the engine. I turn to Tommy. And then I laugh.

"What?" Josh follows my gaze. "He fell asleep!"

My grandmother takes Tommy into the house and tells us he can stay with her overnight so we can unload the sand and prepare everything for him for the next day.

Josh talks with Robby and Kim while they work. I try not to listen. At some point, Robby leaves for a short time. When he returns, he's carrying a case of beers. Josh gathers some lawn chairs and sets them up around the sandpit. I place the last of the dump trucks in the middle of the sandpit and stand up, brushing the sand off my hands. I tap Josh on the shoulder just as he sets down the third and last chair. He turns to me and sits down on it.

I wave good night.

His brow bunches and he reaches for my hand. "Where are you going?"

I point to my house.

"Why?"

I don't really know why he's asking me questions when he knows I won't answer him. So I just stare him down, waiting for his next move.

His next move is to smirk, which just confuses me more. Then he grips my hand tighter, the other on my waist, and pulls me down and onto his lap.

My eyes widen but he just keeps the smirk in place. He raises his hand not on my hip and the next second he catches a beer. He uncaps it and passes it to me, then repeats the process.

"Wait," Robby says, "You're legal right, Becca?"

Josh scoffs. *"I'm* not even legal." Then he runs his nose across my shoulder until his mouth is next to my ear. "Just relax, Becca. I got you."

I relax. I could blame it on the beer, but I don't think that's all it is. It's Josh, too.

They talk a lot of shit. A lot of funny as hell shit. Mainly about Josh as a kid. I can tell they're trying to embarrass him and it works. They don't talk directly to me, but they also don't make me feel like an outsider. I smile a lot. And I laugh. They're silent laughs, but still, they're there. They talk about Tommy and his cute and crazy antics. Kim mentions something about being replaced and how she's jealous that I'm his new best friend. She doesn't say it with malice though, and for some reason that makes me trust her. Just a little.

"Did you get any skating in yesterday?" Robby asks.

Josh shrugs. "A little."

"Street or park?"

He points his thumb to where the trucks are parked. "Driveway."

"Really?" Robby says. "I let you take half the day off and you fuck around in the driveway?"

Josh smirks and taps my leg. "I got distracted."

Without even knowing I've done it, I raise my hand. All eyes snap to me. I clear my throat. "He tried to teach me but I suck."

I'm met with silence and confused stares and I instantly wonder if they're just as freaked out about my voice as I am. My gaze drops and Josh's hand moves from my leg to my stomach, pulling me closer to him.

Robby's the first to speak. "Becca, you know I'm the one who bought him his first skateboard when he was seven?"

I shake my head, looking up at him through my lashes.

"I'm just saying," Robby adds, "if anyone should be teaching you to skate, it should be me."

His wife smacks him on the back of the head. To me she says, "Have you seen Josh skate, Becca? Like, *actually* skate?"

I open my mouth but the words catch in my throat and I hesitate. Josh—he must sense that because he kisses me, right under my ear. Then he pulls away and with a single finger under my chin, he makes me face him. He's smiling, his dark eyes twinkling under the moonlight, and there's something about the way he looks at me that completely confuses me—like he's proud and accepting of me, just as I am, and I want to give him a reason to see me in that way.

It's as if he's kicked off the ground, and now it's up to me to push.

I tear my gaze away from him and look at Kim. "Just around in the driveway," I whisper.

Kim raises her eyebrows at Josh.

I turn to him. "Am I missing something?"

"Nope," Josh says quickly.

"Is there more?" I ask.

"Nope," Josh repeats.

"But it—"

"Shh!"

"I just—"

He presses his lips to mine, cutting me off. I smell the beer on his breath, and when he opens his mouth and runs his tongue across my lips, I taste it. His hand tightens on my waist, the other going to the back of my neck holding me to him. And I forget everything else and get lost in his kiss. In him. He moans into my mouth, his hips lifting slightly and now my hands are in his hair and I'm dizzy. *So dizzy.*

"We're gonna go," Robby says and my eyes snap open and then shut tight when reality hits. For a moment, I'd forgotten we had an audience. I hide my face in Josh's neck while he mumbles something incoherent. It sounds like he and Robby high five right before Robby chuckles and says, "It's cool. Don't stand up."

Josh squirms beneath me.

And then I understand why.

We hold our positions, not a single word spoken, until we hear Robby's truck roar away. Josh chuckles lightly, his breaths shifting the hair on top of my head. "You want to come up and watch a movie or something?" he drawls.

He doesn't wait for me to answer, just helps me to stand, takes my hand and leads me up to his apartment. And I let him. The entire time my heart hammers furiously in my chest, but not at all from the reasons I've been accustomed to.

There is no fear.

No anxiety.

No shame.

Just excitement.

We sit on the couch with the TV on mute. He looks at me. I look at him. A slow smile builds on his beautiful face and I find myself doing the same. "So," he says.

"So," I whisper.

And his smile gets wider.

"Is Robby your brother?"

Turning his entire body to face me, he shakes his head, his arm going on to the back of the couch, his free hand resting on my leg. "He's my uncle. My dad's stepbrother."

I nod slowly, my eyes on him and his smile falters, just for a second. "Can I ask you something?"

He sighs. "You can ask anything as long as I'm not expected to answer."

"That's fair."

He raises his eyebrows.

"You guys talked a lot about you and Tommy... but you never spoke about your parents. If they're your family…"

He clears his throat and looks over my shoulder. "It's because my parents aren't really part of my life. They kind of disowned me when Natalie got pregnant."

I hate everyone named Natalie. I've never known one before but I hate them already.

"They both know it's a no-go zone for me so they don't talk about them. Ever."

"Okay," I say with another slow nod. "And they mentioned skating, like it was something—"

"Something I don't want to talk about," he cuts in.

"Okay."

"That's it? Just *okay?* You're not going to push it?"

"I'll never force you to talk about something you don't want to."

He smiles. Right before leaning in and kissing me soft and slow. When he pulls back, he lets out a quiet groan, then presses his lips together.

"What?" I ask, running my fingers through his hair.

"I think... just the beers and today and being alone with you and your eyes... and *fuck* you're ridiculously beautiful. I'm trying to stop my mind from going places it shouldn't go…" He bites his lip, his eyes trailing down my body. And I've never felt more wanted or appreciated in my life. His hand automatically goes to my waist when I sit up a little.

"What are you doing," he mumbles, his gaze lifting from my chest to my eyes while I straddle his lap.

"We're both adults, Josh." I drop my mouth to his neck as his hands move from my waist to my ass, pulling me closer to him. "We just have to stop before things go too far."

He rolls his head back, giving me access to his neck. "*You* have to be in charge of stopping it," he mumbles, his hand on the back of my head.

Then our lips crash together, our hands everywhere, all at once. His hips push up, and I push down, grinding against the hardness trapped in his pants. The room fills with the sounds of our breaths, our moans, our lips, our tongues. But in my head, all I can hear is the thumping of my heart. His hands are on my back now, holding me to him. His hips keep moving, matching mine. My breath catches when a familiar ache builds in the pit of my stomach, and my eyes squeeze shut. "Stop?" he asks, his breathing heavy.

I nod, still refusing to look up.

He cups my face and makes me look up at him. Then smirks as he runs the back of his fingers across my cheek. "What happened?" he asks, but he knows what happened. He thrusts up, just once, and my eyes roll involuntarily. "Are you okay?"

I try to get off him but he holds me in place. "What? You've gone back to not talking to me?"

I slap his chest and try again, in vain, to move way.

He kisses me once and finally releases me, but I don't move.

His smile slowly fades as his eyes search mine. "Can I ask you something?"

"Same rules as you?"

He nods.

"Okay."

"Why don't you talk?"

I drop my gaze and focus on my fingers tracing the outlines of his abs through his shirt. "I haven't always spoken like this. With this voice, I mean. I hate the way I sound and the way people look at me when I speak. You saw how your aunt and uncle responded when they heard me—"

"Yeah..." he interrupts, "that's because I told them you were mute and a germaphobe."

"What?"

83

"I just didn't want to make you uncomfortable so I lied. I'll tell them later that I was kidding. They won't even question it. I say stupid shit all the time." He taps my leg twice. "So what happened to your voice?"

"It was a car accident. I wasn't able to wear a seatbelt. When the car collided with the tree, I flew forward and the dash flew back and landed right against my throat. I was stuck that way until they were able to pull me out. But it was kind of too late. The damage had already been done to my vocal cords."

"Holy shit. Are you okay? I mean, how badly did you get hurt?"

I shrug. "It wasn't so bad. I'm alive, right? Anyway, the doctors told me not to talk too much because it can make it worse, so can whispering. But it's hard to get used to not using it at all, especially when *physically* I can. But because of how I sound, I whisper more than I talk. It's not that I don't have anything to say. Trust me, I hold back a lot. But I don't know, after the accident, there were just a lot of people asking a lot of questions and I used the whole no talking thing to get out of answering them. Plus, like I said, I sound like a freak so it's no big deal."

His brow bunches and I can see the thousand questions flickering in his eyes. He raises his hand, his fingers gently stroking my neck, and out of all the questions he can possibly ask, he asks the one I can never answer. "What do you mean you weren't *able* to wear a seatbelt?"

"Did I say that?"

"Yeah."

"That's not what I meant."

He nods even though I'm sure he can tell I'm avoiding. Then he asks, "Do you talk to your grandmother?"

"Not really," I whisper, glad he's not pushing me.

"But you talk to me?"

"Because you understand. You get that I don't *want* to talk

84

all the time. She's one of those who ask *a lot* of questions *all* the time."

"So *tell* her that, Becca."

My eyes snap to his and whatever he sees in them has his face falling. "I'm not scolding you. I'm sorry if that's how it sounds. I just know your grandmother. I know her heart—and I know it would be killing her to think that she's not helping you or that she's doing something wrong. And I can see it in the way she looks at you. She loves you, Becca, just like she loves me and Tommy. She was the only one there when we really needed someone to save us. And she did. She saved both of us, no questions, no demands. She's the only one who hasn't turned her back on us and up until my aunt and uncle came along, she was the only family we had. She'll understand, Becca, whatever it is you're wanting to keep to yourself, she'll let you do it. I just think you should give her something. *Anything.* Because having you give even the tiniest piece of you is a million times better than having nothing at all. Trust me."

His eyes fix on mine and I nod because he's right. And because I'm pretty sure he and my grandmother are the closest thing to family I'll ever have. "Okay," I whisper.

"Good." He smiles. "So movie?"

I return his smile. "Okay."

CHAPTER 12

JOSHUA

We're lying on the couch, the movie's on mute and she's fallen asleep. There's a strand of hair stuck to her lips, but it moves every time she breathes. I know all this because I can't stop watching her. Then suddenly, her breathing stops and she jerks in my arms. I sit up slightly, waiting to see if she's okay. She whimpers and exhales slowly and I smile, watching her body relax and her breathing return to normal. But it only lasts a few seconds before she whimpers again, her body shaking now. "Stop," she whispers, her hands forming fists.

"Becca!" I whisper loudly, trying not to spook her.

"No," she cries.

I shake her shoulder but her eyes won't open. "Becca!"

"Please," she cries, louder this time.

"Becca!" I sit up now, my legs under hers, my heart pounding, struggling for breath while I watch a single tear trickle from her closed eyes. Her head moves from side to side, her hands gripping my shirt. I scoop her up and onto my lap. "Becca." I run my hand through her hair, rocking her, trying to get her to wake up. But she won't. She's crying now—silent cries and broken breaths.

She gasps loudly, her eyes squeezing shut and I lift her head and bring it to my chest. I keep rocking, keep soothing, all while she cries in my arms. "Becca you need to wake up. Please!"

But she doesn't. Her cries grow louder. Her grip gets tighter, pulling my shirt down and away from my body.

"Stop!" she shouts, the fear in her voice causing a fear in my heart.

"Becca." I kiss her forehead.

Rocking.

Soothing.

I don't know what else to do.

Suddenly, she tenses in my arms. "You did this," she whispers, and I don't know if she's talking to me or—"I didn't mean to," she cries. She repeats this. Over and over. And each time she does the fear in my heart escalates.

"Wake up," I whisper in her ear. "Please, *baby.*"

Slowly, I feel her body relax. Mine doesn't. I watch, and I wait, hoping she's come to. Her cheeks are wet with tears, soaking through my shirt—the shirt she slowly releases. Her eyes stay closed while her hand glides up my chest and to my neck. She whispers my name, and I finally release the breath I'd been holding. But then she starts to cry again, quiet and contained, and it hurts more than when she was dreaming— because she's aware now, and whatever she feared in her sleep is the same fear she has when she's awake.

I kiss her temple.

I rock.

And I soothe.

"It's okay," I tell her. "I'm here."

She cries harder.

I stay silent, not wanting to make it worse.

I hold her.

She lets me.

And after minutes that feel like hours, she pulls away, her eyes lowered. Without a word, she stands up and heads for my door. I go after her. "Becca, you don't have to go."

She stands still, hands at her sides, refusing to meet my gaze. She opens the door.

I follow.

"Becca."

Finally, she looks up, and my heart hurts.

My emerald eyes should never look so broken.

"I have to," she whispers.

I reach for hand but she flinches and pulls away.

She's not letting me touch her.

"Becca."

She turns away.

And then she walks away.

CHAPTER 13

BECCA

I try not to blink.

Even that millisecond of darkness brings back the fear.

And I *hate* the fear.

As much as I hate the darkness.

My grandmother sits up higher on the couch when I enter the house. I check the time. It's close to midnight. I open my mouth.

Her eyes widen.

I want to tell her she shouldn't have waited. I decide not to tell her anything.

She sighs and closes the book in her hands, then sets it on the coffee table. She gets up, closes in on me and every single part of me turns to stone. "I'm sorry," she says, standing a few feet away. Her eyes look tired. And worried. "I know you're an adult but I'm not used to having someone living with me. I can't help but wait and worry about you, Becca." She pauses a beat. "And I guess maybe you're not used to having someone waiting and worrying about you, either." She smiles, one that deepens the wrinkles around her eyes. "We might have to work on this."

She starts to leave but I grasp her hand—remembering Josh's words.

Her breath catches and her gaze moves from my hand up to my eyes. Her eyes are dark, matching her skin. She's beautiful. I've wanted to tell her that before, but I hadn't known how. I look at the contrast of our skin colors. I'm a shade lighter—a mix of races. Then I lift my gaze, and through the fear of the darkness and the aching of my heart, I *smile*. "Good night, *Grams.*"

CHAPTER 14

JOSHUA

I wait anxiously, my hands on Tommy's shoulders, while Chazarae runs up the stairs to get her. The first thing he asked when he woke up was to play in the damn sandpit, of course, followed closely by whether Becca could play, too.

Footsteps approach and the louder they become, the louder my heart beats. I'm not sure if I'm excited or nervous or afraid or if possible all three at once. She comes into view, wearing pajamas, her hair a mess and her eyes tired. "Did we wake you?"

Without looking at me, she shakes her head and bends down to Tommy's level.

"Come play in my sandpit?" he asks.

She smiles the saddest smile I've ever seen and slowly shakes her head. She holds her palms together and puts both hands on the side of her face, indicating that she's tired.

Beneath my hands, Tommy's shoulders slump. "Little bit?" he asks.

She stands to full height, her head still lowered.

"Becca's tired, bud. Why don't you go ahead?" I release him and motion to the back yard. "I'll be there in a minute."

"Okay," he mumbles, before leaving us alone.

I wait until he's out of earshot before speaking. "Are you okay?"

"Tired," she whispers.

"You didn't sleep well?"

She sighs and finally looks up. She starts to speak but my phone rings—cutting her off. She raises her hand in a wave and slowly closes the door in my face.

"Fuck," I whisper, reaching into my pocket. Chloe's name flashes on my screen and for a moment I panic. I hit answer. "Everything okay?"

"Jesus Christ, Shitstain, I'm in remission, not on my deathbed. You don't need to panic every time I call."

I chuckle under my breath. "You're bright and chipper this morning. I'd call you names, but it's not nice to tease girls. Besides, your life sucks enough. You're married to Hunter."

She cries out in pain.

"What? What happened? Chloe!"

She cackles with laughter. "Sorry, I was just reacting to your epically shitty burn."

I shake my head and make my way over to Tommy. "What do you want?"

"Well… I'm here visiting my parents."

"Oh yeah? Hunter's playing away this week, right?"

"Yep."

"So what's up?"

"Tommy."

I laugh. "What about him?"

"Can I come and play?"

A half hour later she shows up with gifts from her and Hunter—mainly Duke merchandise and a little Duke jersey with Hunter's name on the back. We've been to his games a few times and Hunter always manages to get us all access tickets, locker rooms and all. I don't think Tommy fully understands how much of a big deal his *Uncle Hunt* really is. "You didn't have to get him all that," I tell her, walking her from her car to the back yard. I glance up at Becca's window for the tenth time this morning. She's not there. She never is.

"So what's been going on?" Chloe asks, catching me distracted by my phone.

"Same old, C-Lo. You know me."

"No," she says, standing up and walking over to me while wiping sand off on her jeans. "Something's going on. I can tell."

I figure *fuck it*. I have no one else to talk to about Becca, at least no one who's not going to give me shit about it like Rob and Kim. So, I spend the next fifteen minutes talking while she listens and Tommy plays. I don't tell her everything. I keep out the parts I know are too private or personal. She smirks at first and I know deep down she wants to tease, but she doesn't. She just nods and tells me to go on. I tell her about last night, about Becca's nightmare and how she hasn't spoken to me since. And as each event, each word, leaves my mouth, I can see Chloe's frown deepen.

"So that's it," I say. "And I don't know what to do now."

Chloe clears her throat, her eyes on Tommy. "You know, I get it. I mean, you were there from the very beginning with Blake and me. You saw me push him away, afraid I'd hurt him with the whole cancer thing. You remember what you said to me?"

I shrug. "Honestly, no. Did I call you a bitch?"

She punches my arm and laughs so loud it frightens Tommy.

95

I add, "Because I'm pretty sure that's what I was thinking at the time."

"Shut up!" she whines. "I've had cancer. Don't be mean."

"You can't pull out the cancer card whenever you feel like it. It doesn't work like that."

"Bullshit, I can't. I can do whatever I want."

I laugh. "So what did I say?"

"You said that if he wanted to spend time with me—that it was his choice. But I had to let him make it."

"I don't see how that's at all relevant."

"Make your choice, Josh. You want to see her"—she points to the main house—"go see her. But be ready to get turned down—because if she's anything like me—she'll keep pushing. Don't give her the chance."

"So what you're saying is I should do what Hunter did and propose to your crazy ass."

She laughs again and throws her arm around my shoulder… then gets me in a headlock and starts ruffling my hair. I wriggle out of her hold and stand in front of her. All joking aside, I say, "Thank you, Chloe."

"You're welcome."

I tug a strand of her short hair. "And I'm kidding—about the bitch thing, kind of. You're just lucky you're beautiful."

She pouts. "I have a feeling you'll be fine, Warden."

I nod and shove my hands in my pockets.

"What are you doing?" she asks.

"What?"

"Don't just stand there! Go get your girl."

"Now?"

"I got Tommy. You got time. What you don't have is excuses. Go!"

CHAPTER 15

BECCA

---

secret
  adjective
  not known or seen or not meant to be known or
seen by others.

Josh's voice filters from downstairs up to my room and I sit up slightly—afraid he's going to be at my door at any moment. But it's not him that comes. It's Grams. She's holding a box, smiling like the Cheshire cat. "Joshua just dropped this off for you," she says, setting the box on my bed by my feet. She slowly backs out of the room, her eyes shifting from me to the box and I can't help but smile. I raise my hand and wave for her to sit down on the bed. Her smile widens as she picks up the box and hands it to me. "What could it be?" she says, rubbing her hands together.

I wonder if this is what it's supposed to feel like—to have someone in your life who shares your excitement and your fears and your *secrets*.

I look down at the box, but there's no writing or labels that indicate what it might it be.

"Open it," Grams encourages, tapping the envelope that's taped to the box. I do as she asks and pull out the note.

> You know what comes after you kick and push?
> You coast.
> Coast with me, Emerald Eyes?

I cover my smile with my hand and drop my chin to my chest, hiding my blush.

"Are you going to open it?" Grams asks.

I nod, lifting the lid on the box.

It's a bright green skateboard.

My very own skateboard.

I look up at Grams, unable to contain my grin. Then I realize I'm shaking and I have no idea why. "It's a beautiful day out," she says.

And before I know it I'm out of bed, changing my clothes, grabbing *my* skateboard and running down the stairs. I stop half way and run back up to Grams. She's waiting at the top with my camera bag in her hand. I thank her—actually say the words *thank you*—but that's not why I came back. I hug her with one arm, my body buzzing with excitement. She hugs me back. "Praise Jesus, what a blessed day," she murmurs.

I practically run out of the house and toward his apartment, skateboard under my arm. Before I get to his stairs, I hear Tommy yell my name from the yard and my gaze snaps to him and Josh and… my heart drops to my stomach.

Josh walks toward me, his smile wide but I can't move.

I can't think.

I can't pull my mind off the beautiful girl standing next to Tommy.

Josh's smile fades as he approaches. "Becca?" he says, but I still can't move. I can't breathe. His hands are on my shoulders now, and his face is in my vision, and for some reason I want to punch him. And puke. And if I could do both at the same time I probably would.

"Come meet Chloe," he says. "My best friend's *wife*."

"So do you really like it?" he asks, one hand on the steering wheel and the other on my leg.

I look down, feeling the warmth of his touch spread across my skin. "I love it, Josh. Really."

"Good. That's good. I mean, it's lame, because I'm giving you something that's kind of *my* thing, but I don't know. I wanted to share something with you, you know? And maybe next weekend we can do something with your photography?"

I face him. "You want to learn about it?"

"I want to learn everything about you, Becca."

My breath catches.

He adds, "Well, as much as you want to share…"

Ten minutes later we're pulling into a skate park. Once he's parked, he turns to me and rolls his shoulders. "Ready to skate?"

"Ready to try not to suck at skating? Yeah."

The second I'm out of the truck, he takes my hand and leads me to the path alongside the concrete playground. "Drop your board," he says, and I carefully place it on the ground. For some reason, this makes him laugh. "Boards are durable, Becs. You don't need to be so gentle."

I look up, one eye squinting against the sun behind him. "But it's so pretty and perfect."

He smiles at that, his hand curling around my neck and his lips lowering to mine. He stops an inch away from my mouth. "You know what else is pretty and perfect?" he says, his voice husky. "You." And then he kisses me. Just once. But it's more than enough. He pulls back and taps my foot with his. "Get on."

So I do, trying to remember how to place my feet from the last time he showed me. Once I'm settled, he grasps my waist and walks beside me, rolling me along. I ignore how his touch makes me feel and concentrate on trying to keep myself steady on the board. "Relax, Becca, I got you."

Relax, he says, like it's that easy. If only he knew that *he*'s the reason I can't relax. That it's *his* presence causing my feet to wobble. *His* touch causing me to tense. *His* breaths on my cheek preventing my own breaths from forming. We get about ten feet before I hear, "Well, well, if it isn't Joshua Warden!" I look to the guy standing right behind Josh.

Josh moans and rolls his eyes at the same time. Without turning around, he says, "I'm a little busy here, dude."

"Sorry," the guy says, kicking his board and holding the end of it like I'd seen Josh do a few times. "I just wanted to see if it was you."

Josh straightens and turns to him. "Do I know you?"

The guy shakes his head. "No man, but I know you. I used to watch you skate this park when I was a kid. It's good to see you back around. You doing any comps?"

Josh shrugs. "Nah. I gave that up a few years back."

"Sucks. I mean it's a shame." The guy's gaze shifts to me. "Have you seen him skate?"

I shake my head.

"I have these videos I took of him when I was, like, thirteen." He looks back at Josh. "You were fifteen I think, doing shit that the pros do and you did it so effortlessly. I still have them if you want me to email them to you."

"I'm good," Josh answers quickly.

"Right," the guy says, nodding. "Well, my buddies and I are on the half-pipe. I was telling them about your mad skills, but they didn't believe me. I kind of made a wager…"

"A wager?" Josh quirks an eyebrow. "What do you win?"

"A Benjamin."

"And what do I have to do?"

The guy laughs. "Just show off, I guess."

"What do I get?"

"Dude." The guy takes a step back. "You can keep the hundred. Hell, *I'd* pay a hundred to watch you in action."

Josh looks over at me. "What do you think, Becca?"

I just shrug, my eyes wide.

Laughing, he helps me off the board and holds me to him. To the random guy, he says, "I'll get my gear."

He gets his gear.

I get my camera.

We climb the ladder to the top of what I've been told is a half-pipe. Josh helps me to sit on the landing, my legs dangling off the edge. For the first half hour of watching him I ignore the camera in my hand. What he's doing—what I've been *witnessing* —deserves to be seen with my own eyes and not through the lens of a camera. It isn't until the random guy from earlier, who introduced himself as Chris, sits down next to me and asks if I've been getting any good shots that I finally start snapping away.

"He's amazing, right?" Chris says.

I nod.

"Do you know what happened to him?"

I set the camera on my lap and face Chris, my eyebrows raised.

"Josh—he was like a God amongst men out here. Rumor had it he had sponsors knocking on his door and then one day he just disappeared. People thought he'd died." Chris laughs. "For a year or so people had sworn they'd seen him out here in the dead of night. He was his own urban legend."

I look away from him and back to Josh as he skates to the top of the half pipe, stands upside down on one hand—his feet in the air—as he holds the board. I gasp loudly. Chris nudges my side. "This is child's play for Joshua's skill level. Don't worry, he's all good."

Somehow, Josh lands perfectly back on the pipe, eliciting cheers from the people watching.

"So?" Chris asks, pulling my attention away from Josh. "Do you know what happened?"

I shrug and press my lips tight.

Josh skates toward us, doing one more trick and then swiftly turning at the top of the pipe and sitting down on the other side of me, grabbing his board as he does. "We gotta get going."

"Thanks man," Chris says, offering Josh the hundred he promised.

Standing up, Josh raises his hands. "All good, man. Keep it."

Once we were back in his truck and driving away, I ask Josh, "You didn't want the money?"

He shakes his head.

"Does that happen often? People paying you to skate?"

He shrugs. "In another life. One I don't really want to talk about."

He takes us to a hole in the wall restaurant; literally a door into a basement that I would've never known was there. We eat in silence because I can tell his mind is elsewhere and I don't want to ask the wrong questions even though my thoughts are racing with them. He settles his hand on the table between us—his palm up. I place my hand in his the same time he says, "Sorry. I've kind of killed the mood haven't I?"

I shake my head and smile at him.

"That guy—Chris—I remember him from way back. I remember he used to follow me around with his camcorder telling everyone he was recording history in the making. But like I said, it was another life for me and not one that I like to look back on or think about."

"Because you gave it up for Tommy?"

His gaze moves to somewhere behind me, somewhere far, far away. "It's just skating, right? It's no big deal."

"It is if it's something you love," I say quietly.

With a sigh, he looks back at me. "There are some sacrifices greater than love. And some loves greater than any sacrifice. Tommy's greater than both."

My gaze drops and I try to ignore the ache in my chest—the one caused by *envy.*

He picks up my hand and kisses my palm. "Let's get out of here."

Josh drives a few minutes to the same basketball court from yesterday.

"This is my playground," he tells me. "My safe place."

I stay silent as he leads me to the middle of the court and sits down, tugging on my arm for me to do the same. I sit opposite him, my legs crossed. He scoots closer and settles his hands on my thighs. Then he just stares at me, his eyes on mine, and I haven't felt so open and so vulnerable since when my mother used to look at me that way. I wait for him to look away—to be the first to break. And just like my mother, he doesn't. Instead, he asks a question worthy of a thousand answers. "Do you have a safe place, Becca?"

I release a shaky breath, but I can't seem to look away. "Yes," I whisper. And I hesitate, just for a moment, from telling him the truth. *"You."*

He doesn't respond, not with words, but he brings me closer and holds me to him. Seconds, minutes, hours pass—I have no idea. When he finally releases me, he takes out his phone, taps it a few times, waits for a song to start and then puts it on the ground between us. Then, with his hand holding one of mine, he lies down flat on the ground and I do the same.

So here we are, lying side by side, hand in hand, listening to music on the middle of a basketball court with nothing but darkness surrounding us and I swear it, my world has never looked so bright.

"Becca?"

"Yeah?"

"I'm going to ask you something, and if you don't want to answer, just tell me okay?"

"Okay," I say, my heart aching from the beat it just skipped. I pray and I beg; please, *please,* don't ask me about *her.*

"Do you not like being touched because you've been hurt? Because *someone* has hurt you before?"

Tears form in my eyes just as fast as the lump rises to my throat. I hold my breath, hoping he can't hear the sob forcing its way out of me. Silence fills the air as one song ends and another starts and I still can't find it in me to answer. I feel him shift next to me and suddenly his face is in my vision, looking down at me. I can see the concern in his eyes, matching the tears in mine and I start to shake, because everything inside me is fighting, clawing its way out, trying to get free and I can't—

I can't let it happen.

I release my breath, my sob, and my tears all at once.

"Baby," he whispers, wiping the tears off the side of my face.

And then he's gone, back to lying next to me, his hand still holding mine, but now his touch is different.

It's tighter—as if he's scared to let go.

"You never have to be afraid of me, Becca, I'll never hurt you. And as long as I'm around, no one else will either."

CHAPTER 16

JOSHUA

Two weeks.

That's how long it's been since I'd asked Becca to coast with me.

And we have been.

Kind of.

We spend a lot of time together but mainly when Tommy's around. We sneak in the occasional touch, steal the occasional glance, but as soon as Tommy's bedtime comes around she chooses to leave, giving me a quick, chaste kiss and the next day we repeat the process.

It's like she's reluctant to take the next step. Of course I've wondered if it's because of what happened when I took her to the half-court... or if she's afraid of getting too close and doing what Chloe had said—pushing me away. I've tried plenty of times to think of a way to bring it up but every time I build the courage to actually do something it's like she can sense it somehow and she focuses all her attention on Tommy.

So for two weeks I've been stuck in this weird limbo of kind of dating a girl sometimes maybe.

Fuck, that doesn't even make sense.

Yesterday, Chazarae managed to pull me aside while Tommy and Becca were playing in the sandpit. "It's Becca's birthday tomorrow," she said, and my mind went into frenzy—because ask any guy, even those like me who've never *technically* been in a serious relationship: Girls and birthdays are the worst.

Especially if you have no idea where you actually stand with said girl.

And, even more so if you only have a day to work it out.

So I do what anyone in my situation would do—I call the closest thing I have to a friend who's a girl: Chloe. She doesn't answer. Which means I only have one other choice. Reluctantly, I call Kim. She gives me ideas. They aren't great but they'll have to do.

Becca's eyes light up; matching the candles burning atop the camera cake Tommy and I had made her. Kim had sent me the link with instructions. I sent her a picture of the cake when it was close to completion. She wrote back: *pinterestfail.com*

My aunt's a smartass.

"You made me a camera cake?" Becca whispers, her gaze darting between Tommy and me.

"Tommy made the cake. I was just the funds behind the grand operation. Right, bud?"

His little eyes move from me to the cake, his smile huge as he watches the candles flicker.

Becca gets out of her chair and hands her grams the camera. Then she picks up Tommy and sits down next to me with him on her lap—one hand on his stomach, holding him in place, the other on my leg. She leans down to Tommy's ear. "Ready, buddy?"

He doesn't reply—just sucks in a whopping breath and blows until all air leaves his lungs. And then he does it again. And after that, I don't really know what happens because Becca's watching me and I'm watching her and the world has stopped and the room's hot and her eyes drift shut and somehow I find myself leaning in and just as my lips are about to touch hers, the snap of the camera brings me back down to earth and to the vision of Tommy sitting on Becca's lap—his face buried in the cake.

Becca snorts with laughter and scoots back in her seat to get him away from the cake while Chaz giggles and fusses in the kitchen—I assume to get something to clean him up. She comes back with a wet dishcloth and starts wiping at his face. "I want a copy of that picture," she says, looking between me and Becca.

Chazarae's attempt to clean up Tommy with a dishcloth is a fail the moment he decides his hands and feet want the same fate as his face. The cake's a goner, but no one seems to mind.

"Grams has him in the bath," Becca says, stepping out of the house and sitting down next to me on porch steps. She lifts her gaze and smiles as she looks up at the stars. "This was a great birthday, Josh. Thanks for spending it with me."

"I wouldn't want to be anywhere else."

She turns to me, bringing her smile with her—only now it's wider and aimed at me.

"I got you something," I tell her, reaching into my pocket and pulling out the little green bag. "It's not anything special but I didn't really have much notice."

Her eyebrows pinch and her eyes move from the bag to me. "But you made me the cake."

I hand her the bag and shrug at the same time. "Yeah, but this is something you can keep."

Her smile's gone now; her features bunched in a way that makes her look confused for some reason. She widens the opening of the bag and empties its content onto the palm of her hand. After setting the bag on her knee, she picks up the ring. It's a quarter-inch thick, silver and has the words *I shoot like a girl* engraved with a picture of a camera. It's also extremely lame. And going by the look on her face, she thinks so, too.

"It's stupid," I rush out, smacking it out of her hands.

She catches it quickly and turns her back to me, inspecting it further. After a few moments, she faces me, a single tear streaming down her cheek.

My eyes widen, and then roll stupidly high. "Great, I've made you cry with the ugliest present known to mankind."

"Shut up, Josh," she whispers.

I try to reach for the ring but she pushes me away.

"It's so beautiful and thoughtful and perfect and you're ruining my moment with it." She slips the ring on her pointer finger and smiles. "It was made for my shooting finger," she says, shoving her hand under my nose.

"It's stupid."

"Stop it."

I look over at her now—her smile back in place and her emerald eyes gleaming under the porch lights.

"It's lame," I say, because apparently I like beating dead horses. Or maybe I just need her to assure me that it doesn't suck.

She purses her lips and narrows her eyes at me. "You're lame!" Then she scoots closer and hugs my waist, and swear it —I think I actually sigh. She clears her throat before saying, "I've been thinking about something lately, but I don't really know how to bring it up…" she trails off and I know that whatever it is—it's not good.

"So just say it," I tell her.

"The other day, when your friend Chloe was here, I thought it was Natalie."

"Yeah. I figured."

"I don't know, Josh. I kind of just felt weird about it."

"Is that why you've been a little…I don't know, standoffish?" She shrugs. "Is she nice?"

"Who? Chloe?"

She shakes her head.

"Natalie?"

She nods.

"I don't really know. She hasn't been around since Tommy was born."

Her eyes widen. "Oh. I thought maybe—"

"No," I cut in.

"Have you thought about what you would do if she came back in your lives?"

"Every day."

She doesn't respond, not with words, but she backs away and lowers her gaze.

With shaky fingers, I take her hand, bring it to my lips and kiss it softly. "Becca, I need you to say what you're thinking."

With her eyes fixed on our joined hands, she whispers, "Would you want her back?"

"No," I say quickly. "That ship's way past sailed."

"So…"

My shoulders drop with my forced exhale, causing her to look at me. "She's Tommy's mom, Becca. I'm not going to lie, if she came back and wanted to be part of Tommy's life, I can't, and I won't, stop that from happening. I've spent nights thinking about it. At first, I told myself that she would have nothing to do with him. That I'd shut her out and protect him. But then I realized I wasn't protecting him. I was protecting my heart… and he deserved to have both parents. *If* the time ever comes…"

"Do you still love her?" she asks.

I hesitate.

And that slight hesitation is answer enough.

"I can't lie, Becca."

"I understand."

"Do you, though?"

She glances toward her house, where the sound of Tommy and Chazarae's laughter echo through our surroundings. "Nothing can replace a mother's love," she says, but there's something off about the way she says it, almost like she's mad that such a statement exists.

Chazarae opens the door and pokes her head out. "Tommy's all tucked into my bed. He asked if he could stay the night?"

I nod. "Sure."

Becca releases my hand and stands up. Then she gives me a quick kiss on the cheek. "Goodnight, Josh, and thanks again."

Hours go by and I spend those hours in bed, tossing and turning. And then tossing and turning some more. I check my phone for what feels like the millionth time.

It's just past two in the morning.

Finally succumbing to the voices in my head, I pick up my phone and dial a number.

Not hers.

Hunter answers, whispering a "Hey."

"Sorry to call so late."

"No such thing, Shitstain. Everything good with you?"

I nod even though he can't see it. "I met a girl."

"So Chloe's told me. I've been waiting for this call," he says, and I picture him smiling lazily. "Tell me everything." A door clicks shut at his end and footsteps sound, as if he's walking away from the bed he shares with his wife. "What's she like?"

"Insanely hot."

He laughs. "What are we talking here? An eight? Nine?"

"Eleventy-three."

"Niiiice."

I bite my lip, preventing the grin from forming. "We're such pigs."

"True. But I know you, Josh. She's not just hot. That's not why you're calling me at two in the morning. So?"

I cover my eyes with my forearm and sigh heavily. "She asked about Natalie."

"What about Natalie?"

"She asked if I still loved her."

"You told her the truth, didn't you?"

I clear my throat. "I didn't have to."

"You know, I was thinking about you the other day."

"Yeah? Was I naked?"

"Shut up, asshole."

"Continue."

"Natalie—she's kind of like your version of cancer."

With a chuckle, I say, "Wow. We've called her a lot of things before but never a terminal disease."

"No. Hear me out. It made sense when I was thinking about it... maybe not so much now." I wait a moment, knowing he's gathering his thoughts into words. "So, before I met Chloe, she'd been afraid to get close to people because of the cancer. It was always in the back of her mind, you know? Forming a relationship and then having to end it... I mean, I get it, but I wouldn't accept it. She pushed and pushed me away until she finally realized I wasn't going anywhere." He blows out a breath and continues, "Natalie—she's kind of your cancer. She's the thought that plagues your mind—that haunts you—so much so it makes it hard for you to move forward, to build

113

relationships, to fall in love. And one day your cancer might appear, just like it did with Chloe. But it shouldn't stop you from building the life you want. There are some things you have no control over, and some things you can take control of. How you deal with the Natalie issue is your choice."

I let his words sink in, and I think about Chloe and how little my problems seem compared to hers. "I'm sorry. About Chloe and the cancer."

"I'm sorry, too," he says. "About Natalie. You shouldn't be sorry about Chloe, though."

"Were you scared when you found out?"

"Yeah. Just like one day, whoever you're with will be scared that Natalie *might* one day show up in your life. But if the girl loves you half as much as I love Chloe, she'll stick around. And she'll regret it if she doesn't. You and Tommy—you're worth sticking around for."

I laugh to hide my true emotions. "You're such a little bitch, Hunter."

But Hunter will know I'm faking it because he knows me better than anyone. Still, he laughs. "And you, dear Joshua, need to get laid."

"Why the hell do you think I'm calling you at two in the morning?"

"Because you woke up from a dream about me naked? That's cool."

"Good chat."

"Nice talk."

"Later, Hunter."

"Josh?"

"Yeah?"

"All bullshit aside, I meant what I said. Don't sell yourself short. Don't settle. The world owes you and Tommy. You'll get it one day. You'll have it all."

I swallow the lump in my throat. "Tell C-Lo I love her."

"Will do."

"Go back to your wife."

"Go back to your rub and tug."

I hang up and stare at my phone. Then I shoot out of bed, forgetting the time and everything else that's important. I draw open the curtains and look at Becca's window. Then I dial her number.

"Hello?" she squeaks.

"Can you look out your window?"

"What time is it?" she whispers.

"It's late. And I'm sorry. I just really want to see you."

The instant her curtains separate and I can see her clearly, I can't help but smile.

She has one eye barely open and her face is scrunched. But damn, she's beautiful. "What's up?" she says, her voice scratchy and her eyes unfocused.

I tap on my window and her eyes dart to mine right before they widen in surprise.

"Hey…"

"I get scared," I tell her truthfully, trying to collect my scattered thoughts.

Her eyebrows pinch and she looks so damn cute that I have to turn away because if I keep looking at her I'll lose the courage to tell her everything. "I'm sorry that I hesitated when you asked about Natalie. It's not easy for me to talk about my feelings about her. I hate her but I can't. I feel like I *shouldn't* love her, but I look at Tommy and I see her in him and she gave me that, you know? So I can't love her. I can't hate her. She just is. But when it comes to you and me and whatever we *might* be —she doesn't matter. Or at least she shouldn't." I scratch my head in irritation because I'm rambling, but I can't stop. "And I'm sorry because I feel like I'm saying all the wrong things at the worst possible times. I mean, yeah, I've always kind of imagined having that conversation we had with someone far,

far into my future. I didn't expect to find someone who I had to explain that to so early on and I'm not even sure I'm prepared for it *at all*. So just kick my ass if I do something wrong. Because I'll change, or I'll try. I guess what I'm asking you—begging you—is to please, *please* be patient with me. Because I really don't want to let go of this. And *you*—I don't want to let go of you." My voice drops to a whisper. "Of us."

Moments pass and I wait for her response. It never comes. I inhale a sharp breath and muster all the courage I need to finally face her, but her curtains are closed and she's gone. I check my phone—she's still connected. "Becca?"

Then there's a knock on my door that echoes through my phone and I practically run out of my room and down the hallway—tripping over my own feet to get to her. I end my magnificent display or overly-excited clumsiness by crashing my shoulder into the wall. I recover quickly and brush down my clothes, attempting for a look of "casual-calm" when I open the door. But it doesn't matter how I look because when she rises to her toes and plants her lips on mine—phone still to her ear—whatever calmness I'd faked is replaced with everything good and right in the entire fire trucking world.

She pulls back, a half-smile playing on her lips and holds her hand to my chest. "Sweet dreams, Skater Boy."

I watch her jog back into her house and I can't contain my grin as I close the door. And when I drop my gaze, my eyes catch on a piece of paper on the floor by my feet. I quickly pick it up and turn it over. It's the picture her grams had taken earlier that night. Tommy's sitting on her lap focused on blowing out the candles… and behind him Becca sits, her eyes open and her smile full force, but she isn't looking at the cake, she's looking at me, just like I'm looking at her and even through the picture I can tell how badly the boy's falling for the girl, just like the girl's falling for the boy. I sigh/laugh—the kind of reaction you have when something unexpectedly phenomenal happens. That's a Hunter term, FYI, and I've never understood it until now. I carry the picture, along with the healed heart, to my room, and set the paper against my lamp on the nightstand. And I fall asleep with a smile on my face and my heart in her hands.

CHAPTER 17

BECCA

---

joy

noun

a feeling of great pleasure and happiness.

"Happy toomuffvenessee," Tommy yells, flowers in his hands and big goofy grin on his face.

I open the door wider and look from him to Josh who's wearing the same goofy grin.

"What's this?" I ask, taking the flowers from him.

Josh leans over Tommy and kisses my cheek. "What he was trying to say is Happy two month anniversary."

My jaw drops and so does my stomach. "I didn't get you anything," I whisper.

Josh rolls his eyes. "You mean you forgot?"

"I didn't—"

"I'm kidding," he cuts in. "I was just being lame."

"No!" I mouth, then pout while I sniff the flowers. Grams

comes up behind me, sees the flowers, sees Josh standing in front of me, and does what I didn't know I wanted—she takes Tommy and shoves me out the door, right into Josh's arms. Josh waits for her to shut the door behind us before taking a few steps back and leaning against the porch railing, his hands on my waist, pulling me between his legs. Then he grabs the flowers and throws them over his shoulder.

My jaw drops, again, and my eyes widen in shock.

He shakes his head. "I don't even know if it's our anniversary, and I picked those flowers from the neighbor's yard. I just wanted an excuse to ask you to go out with me—like, on a proper date. Dinner, movie…"

Without meaning to, I scrunch my nose.

He tilts his head back and looks down at me. "Or a helicopter ride to my penthouse mansion, maybe?"

I scoff and laugh at the same time. Something he calls a scaff, and it's something I apparently do a lot.

"So that's a no to the date?"

My lips purse tight.

His smile widens as his hand rises—his thumb brushing against my lips. "I think I've gotten pretty good at reading your facial expressions but I don't know what this one means."

I place my hands flat against his hard chest and look up at him, and I just stare at him for a while because really, who wouldn't want to? I clear my throat, my mouth dry. "I like what we do," I tell him, and it's the truth. The last couple of months we've spent every spare second together, even after Tommy goes down. He tells me about his work and what jobs he's doing, and what Tommy's up to. Sometimes he'll apologize for talking too much but he really enjoys having someone to talk to, and the truth is, I really enjoy listening to him talk. I mean, one of us has to, right? I add, "I don't really think we need to go out and do anything fancy."

"But you don't want to… I don't know." He shrugs. "You can get all dressed up, I'll get dressed up, we'll go out…"

I lean closer and undo the top button of his work shirt, then press my lips to his chest. "I'd rather you dress down," I tell him.

He engulfs me in his arms, holding me to him. Then lowers his mouth to my shoulder. His breaths warm against my ear, he says, "I'm so lucky to have you." Slowly, he releases me but I don't go far. He adds, "I just don't want to fail on all my boyfriendly duties."

I try—unsuccessfully—to suppress my grin.

"What?" he asks, giving me a crooked smile I've come to love.

"Boyfriend," I whisper.

He nods slowly. "Well, yeah. Am I not that?"

Returning his nod, I smile full force.

"Your *only* boyfriend, right?"

I roll my eyes and plant my lips on his, kissing him longer than the last. His hand drifts under my shirt, rough but gentle. He moans into my mouth as I bite down on his lip. Then he curses and half-heartedly attempts to push me away. I don't budge. Not even a little bit. "So this date?" I ask.

He nods, his eyes on my chest pressed against his.

"Where would Tommy be?"

"I was going to ask Kim and Rob to watch him," he says to my breasts.

I tug on his hair to make him look at me. He just laughs—no shame. "So what if we do have a date… but instead of going out, we stay in?"

His smile fades. He blinks. Once. Twice. Then he swallows. "W-w-we can do that."

"Okay."

His eyes drop to my chest again.

"So when?"

"Huh?"

"Josh."

He finally looks up.

"Focus."

He smirks.

"When?"

"Next Friday?"

Josh slumps down next to me on his couch after putting Tommy to bed. "That took forever. He just kept wanting to tell me story after story."

"It's cute."

"The first two, yeah. The ten after that, not so much."

"What did he say?" I ask, turning to him.

He grabs my legs and puts them over his. "Anything. Everything."

I fake a smile and somehow he knows it's fake. He shifts me until I'm on his lap and his arms are around me. "Are you okay?"

I rest my head on his shoulder but don't look at him. "I'm just tired. I didn't sleep well."

With his finger on my chin, he makes me face him. There's a frown on his face—one I'm sure I caused. "Did you have another bad dream?"

My eyes shut when he holds me tighter and I hesitate to nod because I don't want him to know how fucked up I am.

"Do you want to talk about it?"

"Not—" My voice breaks, and my hand automatically comes to my throat. "Not really."

His eyes narrow, his frown deepening. "Is your throat sore?"

I nod again.

He replaces my hand with his. "You been straining it?"

"I think so," I whisper.

His thumb, gentle and soft, rubs across my neck. "I got this tea for you—it's supposed to be able to help with that."

He moves me off him, stands up, and goes to the kitchen. I follow. After pulling out a bag from the pantry, he leans back against the counter and starts reading the instructions on the back.

"How did you know what to get?" I ask.

He shrugs. "I looked it up online and went to this herbal store on one of my lunch breaks."

"Josh…" I press up against him, my hands on his stomach. "You did that for me?"

"Well, yeah," he says, like it's the dumbest question in the world. He touches my neck again. "I know it hurts you sometimes. I just thought it might help."

With a pout, I wrap my arms around his waist, my face on his chest while I fight back the tears. His hand finds the back of my head and slowly strokes my hair. "You sure you're okay?"

"Yeah…" I say, picking at his shirt. "I don't know. I just feel like I spend my days waiting for you to come home and as soon as you get here I'm kind of all over you. I just don't want you to get sick of me or anything and today—" I break off on a sigh. "I just really missed you today, is all."

He pushes me back a little and makes me face him again. He's biting down on his lip but I can still see his smile forming. "And that makes you what? Sad?"

"Scared," I admit.

"Why?"

I shrug.

He smiles wider. "Becca, I'm buying you herbal tea on my lunch breaks. I think about you *all* the time. I miss you like crazy when you're not around. If anything, I worry you're going to get sick of me asking you to hang out with me. I get it. It's scary. But it's mutual, right? So that kind of makes it okay."

He doesn't wait for a response, just leans down and kisses me softly. At first. But then his arms tighten around me and his mouth pauses on mine, before slowly lifting to a smile. His lips part and skim mine from side to side.

"Daddy?"

Josh groans, frustrated, and I can't help but laugh. "Yeah, buddy?"

"I think I'm going to wee in da bed."

"What?" Josh shouts, his arms tense. "You're *going to* or you *have?*"

Tommy shouts back, "I'm going to! No. Now I have!"

Ten minutes later, Tommy's in the shower cackling with laughter while Josh changes his sheets, cursing, and glaring at me while I try to suppress my laugh. "It's not funny!"

"I'm not laughing because it happened," I say. "It's the way he said it. So cute."

He shakes his head and finishes making Tommy's bed, then throws the old sheets out in the hallway. "I'm going to wash you and you're getting right back in bed and going straight to sleep," he tells Tommy when he walks into the bathroom.

Tommy laughs harder.

"Okay?" Josh says in his tough-dad tone.

"Okay, Daddy!"

I pick up the sheets and throw them in his washing machine and a few seconds later I hear Josh growl. "Tommy! I'm all wet now," he huffs. I walk out just in time to see Josh's shirt and jeans flying out of the bathroom. I take them, too, and bring them to the laundry room. I empty his pants pockets before throwing them in. After switching the washer on, I go through the scraps of paper and coins and that's when I see it.

A note.

A name.

A number.

I stand, frozen, still looking at it when Josh walks in minutes later. "You doing my laundry?" he asks, and I can hear the smile in his voice.

For the first time, I'm glad I don't speak often because it's given me the experience to formulate proper words instead of just blurting them out like most people do. Only now, I can't think of anything to say.

His hand settles on the small of my back as he looks over my shoulder. His breath catches—he knows he's been caught. "Becca?" he says through a sigh. "It's not what it looks like."

Slowly, I turn to him and try to ignore the fact that he's standing in front of me wearing nothing but boxers. I do my best to ignore the muscles on his shoulders, the ripples of his chest and the dips of his abs, and that perfect V of his that turns my insides to dust. I look back up at him and clear my throat. "Who's Angela?"

He doesn't skip a beat. "She's just this mom from Tommy's daycare. She invited Tommy over for a play date and gave me her number. That's all."

"So... what? You go to her house and drop Tommy off?"

"Well, no. I'd stay there while they played. I don't feel comfortable leaving Tommy alone with someone I don't know that well."

"So you'd be there... with her."

He nods. "And our *kids*."

"Is she pretty?" I ask, even though I really, really don't want to know.

He shrugs. And it's all I need to push him out of the way. He doesn't let me though. He stands in front of me, his shoulders squared. "What's wrong?"

I drop my gaze. "Don't be dumb. You know what's wrong."

"Say it."

I glare right at him.

"Say it," he says again, smirking this time.

"Say what?"

"You're jealous."

"You're mean."

He chuckles lightly and bends down so his mouth's to my ear. "You're crazy cute when you're jealous."

"Shut up," I try to say, but it's barely a squeak because his bare chest and arms are wrapped around me now, forcing all the air out of my lungs.

"So cute," he murmurs, his mouth on my neck. "I was kidding, by the way. She's like forty and goes to church with your grams."

I push against his chest but he doesn't move, just chuckles louder and a second later I'm being lifted onto the washer.

"Why would you make me feel like that?" I whisper.

He settles between my legs and pulls me closer to him. "Like what?"

"Josh…"

"I'm sorry," he says, but he's not. I can see it in the stupid smirk and the stupid amusement dancing in his eyes.

"No you're not."

"So I like it that you got jealous. Sue me." His hands drift down my back and settle on my ass while his eyes drop to my chest. And the amusement in his eyes is gone and replaced with something else completely. He licks his lips, his eyes moving to mine.

"What?" I whisper.

He squeezes my ass, pulling me fully against him. "You know what."

I curse my hands when they move, almost on their own, to his bare chest, the tips of my fingers warming from the heat of his skin as I lower them to his stomach—my gaze following my movements.

With one hand on my back, the other in my hair now, he

tugs lightly and tilts my head back. His lips lower; already parted when they cover mine and my eyes drift closed just as he kicks the door shut and reaches over to switch the light off. "Let's play in the dark," he says, and there's absolutely nothing sexier than feeling him between my legs, his breaths warm and heavy against my neck and his hands everywhere all at once. The sounds of my breaths mingle with his while his mouth trails from my mouth down to my neck, kissing every inch like he kisses me lips. I run my hands all over his torso, his shoulders, his arms. *Goddamn, his arms.* His muscles flex beneath my touch. His hands are on my thighs now, moving higher and taking the hem of my skirt with them. His kisses are soft against my throat, and my legs tense when I feel his fingers skim the fabric of my panties. "Fuck," he spits, pulling away and gasping for breath. I take the opportunity to return the favor and kiss down his neck to his shoulder. His fingers dig into my thighs as I lick down his chest until I find his nipple. My tongue flicks across it, eliciting a deep guttural moan from him. "Jesus, shit," he whispers, cupping my face. His thumb searches for my mouth in the darkness of the room and when I open my mouth and wrap my lips around his thumb, he loses it.

We both do.

Our lips crash together, our hands searching for something, anything. Between our frenzied kisses, we gasp for air. His hand covers one of my breasts, squeezing gently and my hips jerk at his touch but it just makes it worse because now I can feel him hard against my sex. He's pushing into me and I'm pushing back and he's kissing me harder until I'm forced against the wall behind me. My hands skim down to his stomach and—"Shit."

His thumb rubs against my panties, between my legs, slowly moving up and down.

My hips jerk forward. The backs of my fingers run through

the tuft of hair just above the band of his boxers—the band I'm slowly lowering…

He whispers another "fuck" as he pulls down on my top, revealing my bra. His lips, wet, skim the top of my breast just as my hands find their way to his—

"Daddy!"

"DAMMIT, TOMMY!"

CHAPTER 18

JOSHUA

I double check the measurements against the list Chazarae had given me as I stand in the middle of the driveway planning out my day. Soft hands cover my eyes and Becca's breasts press against my back. "Morning," she whispers and I can't help but smile.

I turn slowly, removing her hand at the same time. The morning sun beats down on her, making her skin glow and her eyes the brightest shade of green. "Morning." I kiss her quickly, not wanting my mind or my body to remember how her lips made me feel last night. You know… until Tommy ruined it all. "How'd you sleep?"

She shrugs and glances at Tommy scooting up and down the driveway. "I missed you."

I cup her neck and run my thumb across her throat, waiting for her to tilt her head back before leaning down and kissing it. "Me, too."

"Next Friday, right?" she says, her hands fisting my shirt.

"The next week is going to be so slow."

"It'll be worth it."

A delivery truck pulls into the driveway and I open the gate for it. Chazarae had asked me to build some garden beds in the back yard for her and Tommy so that's how I'm spending my weekend—which I guess will help keep my mind and my hands off Becca.

I wait for the truck to reverse into the driveway and introduce myself to the driver when he hops out. "Brad," he says, shaking my hand, but his eyes are on Becca and Tommy sitting on the porch steps blowing bubbles. His gaze moves from her face to her legs and back again.

I've never wanted to punch someone. Hunter and I have come close a couple times but that's just boys being boys. But this guy—I want to punch him. And if he keeps looking at Becca the way he is, I will.

Because I'm frustrated.

Emotionally.

Sexually.

All of it.

We unload the truck. Well, I do. He's too busy looking at her. "You want to do your job or should I just keep doing it for you?" I snap, taking another bag of soil from his truck.

He's silent as he finally looks away, his eyes narrowed, before he grabs the end of a piece of timber.

It doesn't last long though. A couple minutes later I catch him doing it again. And I've had enough. I drop the supplies and for a moment question whether or not I can actually take him. He's a few years older, but I'm bigger. Plus, I have a reason to fight. He doesn't. I take the steps to get to him and his eyes widen when my fists ball his collar and I shove him against his truck.

"What's your problem?" he says, like *I'm* the one with the fucking problem.

I glance at Becca quickly—she's rushing Tommy in the

house and calling out to her grandmother. My fists ball tighter. *"You're* my fucking problem."

"Josh," Becca calls out, her voice strained. She steps up beside me now, her hands on my chest pushing me away. "Stop, babe."

I release my hands but not my anger. "Quit fucking looking at her."

"It's a free world," he says, smirking as he looks her up and down.

Becca stands in front of me when I take a step forward. "Please," she says, her eyes pleading and filling with tears. "Just don't." She rises to her toes, her hands on my shoulders, and kisses me until my anger fades.

"Okay, I get it," Brad says, but still—we don't pull apart.

He sighs and starts to actually do his job, the entire time, my lips don't leave hers and I know it's just going to add to my frustration but her kisses, her touch—they're like my drug... and I can't quit.

Once the truck's unloaded and the asshole's left, Chazarae and Becca take Tommy with them to run errands and go shopping while I work alone in the yard. Alone with me, myself, and my thoughts—and sometimes, that can be a deadly combination.

I knew I'd lost it—which is something I rarely do. And it wasn't just because that dick was looking at her the way he was. It's because deep down, I knew he could've had her. And he would've been better for her than I was. Everyone would be better for her. At least they could actually do things without being weighed down by a kid. They could date, *properly*. They could get intimate without worrying about being interrupted. They could have the freedom to enjoy each other, fall in love even... without all the extra baggage. And these are the thoughts that make me question everything to do with Becca. That and the fact I still don't know anything about her. Not really. But like I said, I'm addicted to her. To every single thing about her. And even though I know it's bad, it feels so damn good.

These thoughts still plague my mind hours later when they all return. "Hey," Becca says, beaming up at me. Her smile falters when I don't return it. She walks toward me, her head tilted as if assessing me. "You okay?"

"Yeah," I lie, leaning against my truck and wiping the sweat off my face with the bottom of my shirt. "What did you guys get up to?"

Her smile returns. "Grams got me a new printer! I've only got this little portable one and she bought me this one that does all these things and I'm going to play with it all weekend!"

The excitement in her voice is reason enough for my mood to switch. With a chuckle, I link my fingers with hers and just stare at how fricken' perfect she is.

"What?" she asks, her smile wide.

"You're such a cutie when you get excited."

"I've never had anything like this before. Not for myself."

My smile widens with every word she speaks. "I don't think I've ever heard you this excited before. Ever."

She shrugs and looks down, her cheeks darkening. "It's a big deal for me."

"I know," I tell her. "I love it—seeing you like this."

"It's big," she says, spreading her arms out as wide as they can go. "And it's in the trunk. Can you get it and haul it up to my room? Please?"

"Sure."

The second I release her hand and take a step away she smacks my ass. "Thank you."

"How the fuck old is your computer?" I ask, looking down at it while I set up the printer on her desk.

"Not that old. It was like, three years old when it was given to me."

"How long ago?"

She shrugs. "Four years ago."

"And it still does what you need? I mean, you have to run some pretty heavy stuff on there for your photos, right?"

"It's not so bad. It's better than not having one at all."

"I'll be back."

"Where are you going?"

"Just wait here."

I return a minute later with my laptop—one I was conned into buying. Well, not so much *conned,* but the guy at the store talked it up so much that I was convinced I needed all the pixels and aspect ratios and graphics—whatever the hell they meant. One thing led to another and the next thing I knew I was handing him my credit card.

I've used it twice.

"Here." I dump the laptop and charger on her desk.

"What's this?"

"It's my computer. It's a year old and I don't use it. Like, *at all.* You can borrow it."

"Josh, this is MacBook Pro."

"See, at least you know what it is."

"I can't—"

"You will." I sit down on her desk chair and switch it on. "I'll just change my password and get rid of any and all incriminating evidence."

She laughs just as Chazarae calls out, "Becca!"

"Becca!" Tommy repeats.

"Oh no." I sigh. "Has he been playing echo with you guys all day?"

She shrugs. "I don't know. Has he been playing echo with you guys all day?"

"I'm sorry," I laugh out. "But it's your fault. You taught him about echo."

"You taught him about echo."

"That's so annoying."

She giggles. "That's so annoying." Then she tilts my head up from behind me and plants a kiss on my nose. "I'll be back," she says, before practically skipping out of her room. Her steps thud, fast and free, down the stairs and regardless of how I felt no more than fifteen minutes ago, I realize I'm happy. She makes me happy. Especially this side of her. Because with Becca—there *are* two sides. And I'm pretty sure I'm in love with both.

The front door slams shut and I hear Tommy's voice, but he's outside and a minute later, I hear Chaz's car start.

I hit the right keys, change the passwords and delete my porn just as Becca walks in with two cans of soda and, going by the look on her face, she *knows* exactly what I've been doing. "Porn?" she whispers.

"Pshh! I barely know how to use this thing let alone download porn on it."

She smirks, setting the cans on the desk before pushing me back in the chair and sitting down on my lap. She scoots back until her ass is pressed up against my stomach, then takes my hand and places it on her bare legs. I rest my chin on her shoulder and try to fight off the excitement stirring in my dick. "Where's your grams?" I ask, kissing her neck while her index finger moves the curser to a trash icon on the laptop screen. She clicks it twice, and the first thing that pops up is a folder titled *Porn*.

"You're supposed to empty the trash if you want to hide things from me."

I chuckle lightly and drop my forehead to her shoulder. "Shut up."

Her fingers comb through the back of my head as she shifts on my lap. I hold my breath, my hands moving higher on her legs, taking the hem of her dress with them. "The store forgot to give us the paper we bought so Grams has taken Tommy with her to get it. She said she might take him to a park after," she says.

I swallow loudly. "So... we're alone?"

She tilts her head to the side, inviting me. I kiss her—my hands drifting higher on her leg. "What were you doing anyway?" she asks.

"I'm just loading the drivers for the printer."

"Mmm. Keep talking nerdy to me."

I chuckle against her skin and jerk my hips up. "Yeah? You like that?"

"Mm-hmm." She starts grinding, her ass making slow circles against my cock.

"Megabytes. Hard drive. Gigawatts."

"Shut up," she says through a chuckle, turning her head to face me. She runs her tongue across my lips and I no longer have to question what she wants. I capture her mouth with mine, one hand on her breast and the other between her legs.

Breaking the kiss, she moans as she spreads her legs wider. I kiss her shoulder while I cup her sex. She pushes against my hand and whispers my name.

"Is this okay?"

"God, Josh... I want..."

I lick up her neck and bite gently on her ear. "Tell me what you want, Becca."

"More," she breathes. "I want more."

Gently, I move her panties to side and run a single finger between her slit. Her breath catches. So does mine. "Please," she whispers, the back of her head resting on my shoulder and both her hands gripping my forearm.

I slowly slide a finger inside her, my heart hammering against my chest—hoping to every fire trucking thing in the world that I'm doing it right. Her nails dig in, her entire body tensing when I replace one finger with two.

She moans, her hips gliding back and forth, meeting my hand thrust for thrust. "Holy shit, Josh."

I involuntarily lift my hips, pressing harder against her.

"Please don't stop," she says, one of her hands moving to her breast and squeezing gently.

"Fuck, Becca. I couldn't stop even if you asked me to."

Her eyes drift shut when I push the top of her dress down, and then her bra, and when I cup her bare breast, she jerks forward, her legs squeezing my hand between them.

Then her hips find a rhythm and my fingers follow. So does my cock against her ass. I kiss the back of her neck and pinch her nipple lightly. "You're so fucking wet, Becca. So fucking perfect."

She moans, then faces me quickly, her eyes wide. "Kiss me."

I do as she says, and a moment later she tightens around my fingers. Her moans start low, and get louder with each thrust. "Fuck, Josh, I'm gonna…"

"Fuck."

"I'm gonna…"

Her eyes squeeze shut, her sex pulsing around my fingers as she pants out my name, over and over, all while she shudders in my arms. I kiss her neck, her jaw, her mouth. Tiny, quiet moans escape her lips until she finally relaxes, her breaths heavy, mixed with mine.

"Holy shit," she says, pushing my hands away.

Then she stands up, her dress completely disheveled. Her eyes are hooded, filled with lust. "I've wanted to do that for so fucking long," I tell her. And something switches in the way she's look at me.

In a single move, she takes off her dress.

And then her bra.

My hands reach out, my gaze on her tits. Her hands circle my wrists and lead me to the places I've only dreamed about. I squeeze them gently, licking my lips and taking her in. "You're so fucking perfect."

Her chest falls with her heavy exhale before she steps forward and leans down, her fingers curling in the band of my shorts. My eyes stay on hers and I push back all my insecurities, all my questions, and lift my hips so she can free me.

I *needed* to be freed.

She smiles softly, her gaze on my junk and then, still facing me, she sits down on my legs—legs that tense as soon as her soft hand curls around my cock. My mouth finds her nipple, licking and sucking while she strokes me and I know I'm not going to last. It's been a long fucking time.

I move from one nipple to the other.

"Is this okay?" she says, her voice husky and sexy as fuck.

"Yeah, baby." I want to say that it's better than okay—that it's perfect, just like her, but there are so many better things I'd rather be doing with my mouth. Like suck hard on her nipple —making her back arch and her hand tighten. She starts to stroke faster and my hips thrust forward. I grab a handful of her butt and bring her closer to me—which is a huge mistake because now my dick's pressed against her wetness—the only thing separating us is the thin fabric of her panties. Her free hand combs through my hair and tugs lightly. I pull away from her breast and look up at her, right into her eyes. She starts to grind against me while still stroking and I can feel the wetness soaking through her panties and onto... "Fuck, Becca, I want inside you so bad."

Her head lolls back, her groan loud.

Then she releases me and scoots back before standing up.

And for a second I think it's over—that I fucked up and I'm going to live the rest of my life with blue balls.

But then she spreads my legs apart and drops to her knees in front of me—smiling, right before she takes me in her mouth.

Swear it, if heads could explode, mine just did.

My head throws back, my eyes unfocused as I stare at the ceiling trying to breathe through and prolong the pleasure she's giving me. Then she does something that pretty much seals the deal on her perfection—she takes my hand and places it on the back of her head and I shit you not, I go blind.

Legit, certifiable, blind.

All I can see are flashes of white.

My legs tense, my cock pulses, and a few seconds later I'm warning her and tugging on her hair for her to stop. She won't. She just doubles her efforts and I bite down on my lip to stop myself from screaming because it feels too fucking good to be true. She looks up at me through her lashes and that's all it takes for me to come. I close my eyes, partially because I can't help it, but also because I'm too ashamed to see what the outcome of over three years without sex could possibly be.

Her hands are gentle as they settle on my legs. "Are you okay?" I think she says, but it's hard to hear her over my heavy pants and my pulse pounding in my ears and the sounds of triumph running through my head.

Trumpets.

I hear trumpets.

"I'm blind and I can't feel my legs."

CHAPTER 19

JOSHUA

When Becca had to cancel our date because an old friend was coming to visit her, honestly—I was a little disappointed. But she said she couldn't do much about it—that it was kind of a surprise. She didn't give me any more information. In fact, when I'd asked her about it, she seemed to get even quieter than she normally was and when my curiosity peaked and I asked if it was a guy—an ex-boyfriend or something—she snapped.

Then I told her she was being evasive about it all and that I had to assume something was going on. She apologized quickly but still didn't offer up anything more.

But, my disappointment and curiosity turned to full-blown intrigue when Chazarae's car pulled into the driveway on the Friday afternoon of what should have been our date night. When Becca had said "friend" I had assumed a friend from high school—not the thirty-something-year-old blonde woman who's stepping out of the car.

I watch from my living room window as she gets her luggage out of the trunk and drags it behind her, her free arm linked with Becca's as they make their way into the house.

She must've been some friend if Becca was letting her touch her.

I fake a smile when Becca looks up and sees me, but she quickly averts her gaze and nods at whatever her "friend" is saying.

Stupid—that's pretty much how I feel, because a part of me thought—hoped even, that Becca would want to introduce me to her friend—a friend who might help me understand who Becca is—or *was*—before she moved here.

Clearly, I was wrong.

And honestly, it fucking hurts.

With a sigh, I look behind me at Tommy. "You ready to pack your bag?"

"Where go?"

"You're staying at Kim and Robby's for the weekend." We'd already planned it and I *thought* I'd be busy with Becca and her "friend" so I didn't want to cancel, just in case.

I fake another smile, this one for Tommy. "They have so many things planned for you. You're going to have the best time."

"You, too?" he asks.

"No, bud. Just you." ...while I stay home by myself, wondering what the fuck is happening with Becca.

An hour later we step out and I almost freeze in my spot at Becca and her friend sitting on the porch steps talking quietly.

"Can I bring my skateboard?" Tommy asks, pulling me from my daze.

"Sure, buddy."

The second we've climbed down my stairs, he runs toward them—where his skateboard is—and as soon as Becca sees him coming, her eyes widen and her face flushes.

"Hi Becca," Tommy shouts, stepping between them.

Becca smiles, but it's cold. Distant, almost.

Tommy grabs his board. "Bye Becca!" he shouts, running toward my truck. I lift him in his seat, my back toward Becca. I take my time, silently buckling him in, hoping that she offers something. Anything. A greeting, an introduction, any form of acknowledgement that I exist in her life. Because up until this point, I was sure I played a pretty big part in it.

But she doesn't do any of those things.

What she does is hurt me.

And that hurt is something I carry with me all the way to Robby's house.

"You all good?" he asks.

"Yep."

"Sucks Becca cancelled."

I shrug. "It is what it is."

He crosses his arms and leans against the doorframe, his brow bunched as he eyes me down. "You want to hang out here for a bit?"

"Nah." I shake my head.

"What are you going to do?"

"Skate."

I don't skate. Not right away. I do what my instincts tell me not to—I go home and give her time.

One more chance, I tell myself.

Maybe she just doesn't want to be rude to her guest—give her time to settle before she makes the introductions.

They're no longer outside when I get home so I busy myself cleaning the house from top to bottom—something I can only do when Tommy's not home. I take out the trash, and that's when I see them, walking arm in arm up the driveway and right toward me.

I stop in my tracks, my eyes on Becca, but she won't look at me.

Her friend waves.

I wave back.

"I'm Olivia," her friend says.

I wait for Becca to speak, and when enough time passes and all she does is turn away from me, I finally reply, "I'm Josh."

Becca clears her throat and for a second, I actually get excited. "Josh lives over there," she says, pointing to my apartment.

That's it.

That's all she says.

She drops her gaze, her thumb going between her teeth and her eyes squeeze shut. Olivia's hand circles Becca's wrist. "Becca," she whispers, her voice calm but firm.

Becca releases her thumb but doesn't open her eyes.

"Well…" I push back the lump in my throat and speak through the sinking of my heart. "Have a good weekend. I'll see you around, Becca." I walk past them and drop the trash in the can. I don't bother going back to my house. Instead, I get in my truck, wait for them to get the fuck out the way, and I skate.

Because skating is the only thing in my life that's never disappointed me.

CHAPTER 20

BECCA

"He seems nice," Livvy says, looking over her shoulder as Josh reverses out of the driveway. "And he's cute."

"Excuse me," I tell her once we're in the house.

For the next fifteen minutes I hide out in my bathroom, my sobs silent.

I don't respond to the knock on the door. I know who it is. And she already knows something's wrong, even if I try to hide it. Because she knows *me.*

She knows me better than anyone. Even Josh.

"Sweetheart, open the door."

I unlock the door, wiping my eyes as I do.

I can't speak. And right now, I don't want to.

"You bit your thumb when Josh was there."

I sniff back a sob but don't respond.

"Becca, please be honest with me. Are you and Josh…" She breaks off on a sigh before continuing. "Are you having sex with him?"

I shake my head but I can't look at her. "Not yet," I whisper.

She inhales a sharp breath and starts to speak but I cut her off. "It's not like that, Livvy. You have to believe me," I plead.

She closes the door behind her and folds her arms over her chest. The air in the room's so thick I can barely breathe.

"Why didn't you say something earlier? Or when he introduced himself?"

"Because I don't want you to be disappointed in me."

"Becca…"

I look up, letting my tears fall freely now. "I know how you feel and I know what you're going to think, but I swear it's not the same…" I hold a hand over my heart, unable to breathe through the pain. "I'm in love with him."

"Oh, baby," she whispers, taking me in her arms.

A sob bubbles out of me, followed by another, and another, until I'm crying in her arms. I cry so hard I fall to my knees, completely overwhelmed by my admission and my fear and my shame, and my *love.*

"Does he know about your past?"

"I can't…"

"Does he at least know about your future?"

I shake my head.

"It's just going to make things worse the closer you get," she says, like I don't already know that.

I try to push her away. "I can't. I don't want to!"

"Okay," she says, trying to calm me.

She tugs on my hand, pulling my thumb out of my mouth. I hadn't even realized I'd been biting it.

"It'll be okay, Becca. Everything will be okay…"

Olivia sets herself up in the guest room while I stare out my bedroom window waiting for Josh to come home.

Minutes turn to hours and by the time he pulls up at four in the morning—my thumb's completely numb from the aggressive onslaught, not just from the physical pain I'd caused, but from my shame.

My regrets.

And most of all, my past.

CHAPTER 21

JOSHUA

I see the handle on my front door turn for the third time while I stand behind it, fighting a war in my head trying to decide what the right thing to do is. I've been hiding all day, skating the hours away at the half-court because I didn't want to face her. "Josh?" Becca says, her voice barely audible. She knocks again.

I curse under my breath and finally open the door, just enough to slip outside and close it behind me. For the first time since she moved here—I don't want to see her and I sure as hell don't want to be near her.

I keep my head lowered, my hands in my pockets, and I wait for her to speak—too afraid of what will come out if I do it first.

She takes a step back, then shuffles on her feet.

The silence between us so fucking deafening I almost turn around and go back inside. But then she speaks, and what she says makes me wish I had. "Where were you last night?"

I sigh, shaking my head slightly. "Is your friend gone now?"

"Yes," she whispers.

"So it's cool for you to acknowledge me now?"

147

"That's why I came here…"

Finally, I look up at her, but she's looking down at my feet, just like I had been. And I can feel it—the wall slamming between us. "You know, one of my biggest fears in life is that Tommy's going to grow up being ashamed of who he is because of *me*. Because I couldn't keep it in my pants and that's how he came to." I sniff once and push down the hurt she'd caused. "The thing is—it's not me who's going to make him feel like that, Becca. It's the people around him who are going to judge him, who are going to belittle him, and who are going to make wrong assumptions about *him*. And it fucking destroys me to know that *I'll* be the cause of that." I lean against the door, my emotions making me too weak to stand. "So I try really hard to give him a life that's better than all those shitty judgments. And when he starts school and has his friends over, I don't want them to see the struggle that'd been his life—the struggles I've tried so hard to hide, the ones I've overcome to be who I am." My voice strains against the pain of my words but I push forward, because she needs to know what she did and how much she hurt me. "I just want them to see me—a dad who'll do anything for his kid. But people are assholes and they'll choose not to see that. It's going to be hard enough for him to make friends—not because he's not an amazing kid—because he is, Becca, and you know that—but because the other kid's parents are going to look down on him because of *me*. And as much as it isn't fair—as much as I wish it weren't the case—it's the truth. It'll be hard for him to have friends over because of the stigma that comes with being a male looking after kids—and that's going to be hard on him. I know that. And I don't want that for him." I clear my throat, barely able to speak. "I don't want to have to hide who I am and what I've made of my life. I just want to be respected. That's all. I know it isn't always going to happen and I expect that." I look up at her now, right into the eyes that had me falling for her from the first moment

I saw her. "I just never expected that it'd be you—that you'd be the first to make me feel like that."

Her eyes fill with tears as her mouth opens, but I don't give her the chance to speak.

"Take care, all right?"

Her eyes widen, but she doesn't speak.

She doesn't make a move.

She just blinks, causing her tears to fall.

And it takes everything in me to not reach out.

To not touch her.

To not wipe away the tears so I can see her beautiful emerald eyes.

Then she nods once, her thumb in her mouth before turning away.

She leaves.

And I let her.

My eyes snap open when I hear Becca's name. For a second I think I'm dreaming but I'm not, because it's Chazarae's voice and she's screaming. "Becca! Stop!"

I throw on my sweats, forget the shirt and, faster than I thought possible, sprint from my apartment to her house. I try to open the door, but it's locked. "Chaz!" I shout, banging on the door.

"Becca! Please stop!" I hear, and I instantly know there's no chance she can hear me. Through the darkness of the night, I feel around the top of her doorframe looking for the spare key. When I find it, I use it and run straight up the stairs.

"Please, Becca!" Chaz says, but she's not shouting anymore. She's crying, pleading.

Becca's the first thing I see when I run into her room, she's in the corner; her eyes squeezed shut and her legs kicking

149

widely. Her thumb's in her mouth again while Chazarae hovers above her.

"What happened?" I rush out, moving Chazarae out of the way.

"Josh," she cries, her hand wiping the blood from her mouth.

I ignore Becca for a moment and hold Chaz's face in my hands. Blood mixed with tears cover her chin. "Did she do this?"

"She didn't mean it," she sobs. "I should've known better. I shouldn't have touched her when she's like this."

"Like what?" I ask, looking back at Becca. Her eyes are still closed, but that doesn't stop the tears from falling. She's rocking back and forth, her free hand covering her head.

I drop to my knees and hesitate, just for a second, before touching her.

She squeals, her cry so loud it makes my ears ring.

"She's having a nightmare," Chaz cries. "I can't snap her out of it."

"Becca," I whisper, but it does nothing. As gentle as I can, I touch her bare leg, trying not to spook her. She kicks out, her foot finding my knee.

"Stop," she cries.

And everything inside me turns to stone. *What the fuck happened to her to make her like this?*

"I don't know what to do." Chazarae sobs, her hand on my shoulder.

"Becca. Baby, I need you to wake up." I try to shake her shoulder but all it does is make her flinch, make her kick, and make her cry harder.

She grunts loudly and bites down harder on her thumb.

"What the hell's she doing?" I ask, but it's not really a question. At least not one that warrants an answer.

She kicks again, only this time I see it coming. I grab both her ankles and hold them together. She resists, using every bit of strength she possibly has to try to get out of my hold. The adrenaline pulses through me, beating wildly in my ears. "Becca."

"She won't hear you," Chazarae cries while I quickly pick up Becca, one arm behind her knees, the other around her back. I carry her to her bed and rock her like a baby.

She fights.

With everything she has.

She fights me off of her.

"Becca," I whisper in her ear, "It's Josh." I wipe my tears caused by my guilt against her shoulder—because as much as I don't want to admit it, I *know*. Deep down, I know I caused this.

I caused this beautiful, fragile girl to break.

A girl I'm pretty sure I'm in love with.

I hold her tighter, pressing my lips against hers, and I ignore Chazarae in the room.

And I break.

Just like her.

"Baby, please. I'm so sorry." I run my hands up and down her legs, my mouth on her cheeks, kissing her tears away. "Baby, please, wake up," I cry.

And slowly, I feel her body relax beneath my touch—her cries fading to whimpers.

I lick her tears off my lips and try to slow the beating of my heart. Carefully, I grasp her wrist and try to pry her thumb away from between her teeth. She bites down harder. So I do the only thing I can think to do. I turn to Chazarae. "She's okay, she's coming to. Can you just—I need—"

"I can't leave her like this," she says, her voice hoarse from all the crying she's done.

"I'll stay with her. I won't leave. I just need you to trust me."

"Josh," Becca whispers, and Chaz and I both sigh, relieved.

Chaz asks, "Is Tommy—"

JAY MCLEAN

"He's not home. I promise you, I'll take care of her."

Chaz nods and slowly backs out of the room, switching off the light and closing the door after her.

The moonlight from outside the window illuminates the room, just enough for me to see the outline of Becca's face. I kiss her lips, and then her thumb, all while I continue to rock her. "Baby, you need to stop." I try again to remove her hand but she resists. My hand drifts up her bare leg, to her waist, my thumb skimming her stomach. "You said I was your safe place, Becca. And I'm here. Please, baby."

I kiss her mouth again, hoping I'll somehow get through to her, and when her hand lands on my leg, fisting the fabric of my sweats, I know it's working. I open my mouth wider, my tongue skimming the corner of her lips.

Her breathing slows.

So does mine.

"Josh," she says again.

And I kiss her harder, taking her bottom lip between mine as I slowly reach for her hand again. With tear stained lips, I kiss her with everything I have until her entire body relaxes against mine. Then she parts her mouth, her tongue swiping along mine and I pull her hand away, linking my fingers with hers. My thumb grazes against her thumb, feeling every single bump and dip caused by her teeth.

She whimpers as she returns my kiss, and with each second that passes, the kisses turn more passionate, more needy, more desperate. "Make it stop," she whispers, her mouth still on mine. "It hurts too much."

"How? Tell me what to do," I say, my desperation matching her kiss.

"Touch me. Please, Josh. Just touch me. Make it stop."

I pull back slowly, my eyes on hers, open for the first time since I came in. She chokes on a single sob—one that should break my heart. But when she whispers my name and cries, "Please, I need you," it has the opposite effect.

It repairs it.

And for the next hour, I do what she asks. I touch her. Everywhere. My hands, my mouth, everything. Until every single inch of her has felt my touch and her cries of desperation turn to moans of pleasure.

We do everything but have sex—because sex with her is something I don't want to regret. And when her body shudders under my touch, my lips between her legs, and her hands gripping my hair—that's exactly what I feel.

Regret.

Not because of what we've done.

But because I caused it.

I should've let her talk when she was at my door.

I should've given her a chance to explain.

But my pride out won my sense.

And now we were this—whatever the hell *this* is.

I move up her body, my mouth dragging along her sweat coated skin. I continue to kiss her neck, her lips, her cheeks, her eyes, her tears.

"I'm so sorry," she whispers.

"Me, too, Becca." I sigh. "Me, too."

Her fingers comb through my hair while I roll to my side, my head on her chest, listening to her heart thump against my ear.

"My mom—she was in the car with me. The one that crushed my throat."

I hold my breath, not wanting to move in case she stops.

"She died."

"I'm sorry," I whisper.

"Olivia was my high school counselor. I didn't know I had

any family and she took me in. Josh…" She tilts my head up so she can look in my eyes. "She knows stuff about my past. Stuff that made me hesitate to tell her about who you were to me. You have to believe me. It has nothing to do with you and everything to do with *me*. My past—it makes me… *this*. And I *hate* this," she whispers, breaking off on a sob. "You've seen me at my worse now. And I can't handle the pain of it—let alone talk about it. And I don't want my past to determine my future —and my future is you, Josh. That's all I can give you. I'm sorry if that isn't good enough for you."

Her chest rises and falls against my cheek, her eyes on mine. And I realize now, that she needs me as much as I need her.

I close my eyes and keep them that way.

Because I don't want her to see me holding back tears.

I don't respond yet. Because if I do—I'll tell her how I feel about her.

And she can't know either of those things. Because even though it feels wrong to be in so deep, so desperate, so dependent on our feelings—on each other—I don't want it to stop.

But the worst part? She'll *know*.

She'll know that I'm falling in love with her.

And that means she has the power.

The power to *destroy* me.

And if there's something I fear more than anything in the entire world—it's the aftermath of the damage we'll cause. Because it won't just be me caught under the fragments of it all, it'll be Tommy, too. And Tommy and I—we don't need any more destruction.

"Say something, Josh."

I push back those thoughts and give her a kiss, and with it, I give her my heart. "You're more than enough."

CHAPTER 22

JOSHUA

For the next few days Becca's quiet, and not just quiet in that she doesn't speak, but she's almost completely unresponsive. Even to Tommy. "I'm going to put Tommy to bed," I tell her, squeezing her hand before kissing it. "Can you hang back for a while?"

She nods, her gaze distant.

After tucking Tommy in, I sit down on the couch next to her. She hasn't moved. "Becca?"

She blinks.

I pick her up and sit her on my lap, her legs across mine. I place one of her arms around my neck, and hold the hand of the other. She doesn't seem to notice any of it. With a sigh, I rub my nose across her cheek and kiss her neck. "What's wrong, baby? Are you still worried about that night or something?"

Her shoulders lift—just slightly.

"You know it doesn't change anything, right? It doesn't change how I feel about you."

Finally, her eyes move to mine. "I'm so sad," she whispers, her voice shaky.

And my heart breaks. "Babe…"

She wipes her eyes on my shirt—the wetness from her tears soak through to my skin. "I don't know why, Josh. It's like… I'm here but I'm not. And I can't shake it."

"Well, you've stayed here every night so I know you haven't had any more nightmares. Is there something else going on?"

She shakes her head, a frown on her lips as she tries to hold back another sob. "I think I'm going crazy," she says. "Just being in the house all day waiting for you to come home… I don't know…"

I scratch my head, trying to come up with a way to help her. "You know Tommy's birthday's coming up and I wanted to throw him a party—but work's been crazy lately and I haven't had a chance to plan anything. I was going to ask if you could help me out."

She sits up a little higher—at least I know she's actually hearing me.

"It doesn't have to be big," I add. "Just family and close friends. He's never had a party before. I thought it'd be cool now that you're part of our lives… we can celebrate it together?"

The tiniest hint of a smile forms on her perfectly beautiful face. She nods; her arms around my neck squeezing me tighter. "I want to do it," she whispers. "But I want it to be a surprise, okay?"

When Becca said she wanted it to be a surprise, I was kind of confused, but I let her do it anyway. And now I know why. She isn't throwing Tommy a party as much as she's throwing me one. She's gone all out with skateboard themed decorations and a skateboard cake and even though the only people here are Robby, Kim, Hunter and Chloe and, of course, Grams, she put so much time and thought into every single detail. And while I can still see a hint of the same sadness she'd been carrying with her lately, she doesn't let it show. At least not to anyone else. She makes an effort to listen in on conversations—which is probably why her and Chloe take an instant liking to each other. Chloe talks. Becca listens. At one point, I even hear Becca speak—something about magnets. She also makes sure to capture every single moment with her camera. It's kind of sad that Tommy won't remember this—but I sure as hell will. I'll remember today for the rest of my life, because it's the first day since Tommy was born that I realized something.

Tommy and I—we have support.

But above that, we have *family.*

I come up behind her as she pins more images onto the collage she'd made filled with pictures of Tommy and me.

Her hand covers mine resting on her stomach. "Do you like it?" she whispers.

"I love it," I tell her. "I love everything about this day. You're kind of amazing, you know that? This… All of *this*. It means everything to me, Becca. *Everything.*"

She tilts her head up to look at me but I'm too busy scanning all the different pictures. The one of me in the hospital holding him for the first time. Me giving him his first bath. Me with him sleeping peacefully on my chest. Him sitting on a skateboard with a hood over his head and his first pair of sunglasses with me behind him taking the picture. There had to be over a hundred pictures. Each one of just me and my son. I let out a nervous laugh. "You've got me in every single one."

She doesn't answer for a while, so I finally look down at her. She's already watching me, her lips pulled down to a frown. Then she reaches up and cups my face. "Well, yeah, Tommy's three years old today, that means you raised him for three years. *You.* And you did an amazing job because look at him," she says, pointing to the pictures. "Look how beautiful he

157

is. How happy he is. You did that, Josh. You gave him a life worth smiling about." She pauses a beat. "We're not just here to celebrate Tommy's birthday. We're all here to celebrate *you*."

∽

"I tired. I go bed," Tommy says through a yawn, standing up from the couch.

I stand up, too. "You sure, bud? You don't want to watch the end of the movie?"

He shakes his head.

"All right, I'll come tuck you in."

Raising a hand, he says, "I'm free. I go nigh nighs by my own now."

A chuckle bubbles out of me as I sit back down. "Okay then."

"Fank you for my party."

"That was all Becca, Tommy. She did it all."

He steps forward, his arms tight around my neck. "Good night, Daddy, I love you."

"Aw. I love you, too, bud."

He releases me and hugs Becca. "Good night, Mommy, I love you."

Becca tenses, her eyes wide.

I hold my breath, my mind racing and I try come up with a quick explanation, or at least a response. "Um, no, Tommy…" I grab his arm and gently stand him in front of me. "Tommy, Becca—she's not your mommy."

His eyes lock on mine, so innocent and pure, and he just stands there waiting for me to give him the answers he needs but the words are caught in my throat and I can't—"Where's my mommy, Daddy?"

I look at Becca. "Can you give us a minute?"

CHAPTER 23

BECCA

It should be impossible to feel so much at once.

Love.

Hate.

Envy.

Despair.

Sadness.

Guilt.

Yet here I am, sitting on the steps just outside their door, and I feel all of it. It's like a weight pulling down on my heart and the only thing I can do to survive is breathe.

Through the pain.

The excitement.

The longing for something that isn't mine.

That never will be.

Inhale.

Exhale.

My phone buzzes in my hand, pulling me from my thoughts.

Joshua: Are you able to come back?

Becca: I'm just outside on the stairs.

A moment later he steps out, his hands in his pockets and his eyes on mine. "You waited for me?"

With a shrug, I say, "I figure you might need to talk." I wait for him to sit down next to me before asking, "How did it go?"

He leans forward, his elbows on his knees and looks up at the stars—the stars that were once so bright now dim because of my emotions. He clears his throat before speaking. "It was hard."

"I'm sorry."

"I knew that at some point he'd ask. I've thought about it so many times—everything that I would say to him. But to actually say it…" He inhales sharply. "I think it's more that I don't really have an answer for him. I wanted to tell him that his mom just wasn't around, but that she still loved him… and I couldn't even do that because I don't know if it's true. And I'm scared that it's something he's going to feel for the rest of his life. He's going to wonder where she is and why she doesn't *want* him. I think that's what I worry about the most; that he's going to think less of himself, and less of me, because of *her*. And I don't want that for him."

I hug his arm to my chest and kiss it once. "I know, babe."

"I'm sorry, Becca," he says, and I pull back surprised.

"Why are you sorry?"

"Because I froze when he said it to you. I should've said something then and there. I don't want you to think I'm not happy he thinks of you like that—like you're his mom—because to him, you're the closest thing to one… I just don't want to confuse him and I think that's what's happening—especially with you spending the night and us kissing around him and—"

"So you want to stop doing that—"

"No," he cuts in, "That's not why I'm saying it. I don't really know what I'm saying. I guess I just wanted you to know that if there was someone in his life that I'd be proud to call his mother, it would be you."

I choke on a sob and release his arm. "I can't be his mother," I whisper.

I can't be anyone's mother.

Ever.

CHAPTER 24

JOSHUA

Chazarae's eyes lock on mine and I can feel the beads of sweat building across my hairline. I wipe my palms against my jeans, my heart beating so hard I'm pretty sure it's about to crack a rib. Vomit rises to my throat but I push it back quickly and swallow my nerves. "So... it's just... I mean... we've gotten close lately—Becca and me. Not you and me. Me. You. Just..."

She quirks an eyebrow; her jaw tense.

I determine right then and there that she might possibly be the scariest old lady in the history of old ladies.

"Um... so I wanted... She's been sad and—"

"What?"

"I mean Becca..."

"I know you mean Becca. She's been sad?"

I nod. "And I-I-I wanted to do something to make her not so sad... so I was wondering if-if maybe you would mind if I could take her away somewhere... she doesn't know. It would be a surprise."

"What are you asking, Josh?"

"Uh... just your permission I guess."

She eyes me sideways. "Oh, jeez. That's it? You've spent the night at our house, she stays at yours, and you're asking—"

"We haven't had sex!" I blurt, because I'm an idiot.

"Josh," Chaz says through an exhale. "You almost gave me a heart attack."

"What?"

"I thought you were going to tell me she's pregnant."

I puke.

In my throat.

Just a little bit.

I hadn't told Robby that Becca and I had spent every night together since the weekend she canceled our date, so when I asked him if they could take Tommy for the night, he had questions. Of course. And lots of them. The questions turned to advice and the advice turned to ridicule. And because, apparently, my uncle's twelve, his biggest advice was to rub one out right before we left for the big night. And, because my uncle—who's apparently my friend—has a big mouth, he told his wife all about it. Kim showed up the night of my and Robby's great debate with a box of condoms; one hundred and forty-four of them. Then proceeded to give me a speech on what women want and expect in the bedroom—this speech consisted of, but was not limited to; touching, biting, caressing, and something about ice-cubes that I was too grossed out to listen to.

The second I open the door to our hotel room and we step in, my insides turn to stone and all the shitty advice I'd been given cause an epic amount of mayhem in my mind. Becca stands in front of me, her hands clasped together, her eyes on mine, expecting me to make the first move. So I do. I throw her on the bed, climb on, devour her mouth and start dry humping her leg. Surprisingly, she does the same. We roll around on the huge king-sized bed, our hands everywhere all at once and at some point she manages to take my shirt off without me realizing. We roll around some more until we fall off the bed with her landing on top of me, knocking the wind out of my lungs. "Sorry," she mumbles, and we continue. A moment later she's beneath me and her dress is off and she's fumbling for my belt and I wonder why—*why* in all the advice given to me were the words, *Don't wear a belt. It's awkward as fuck!* never spoken.

Her eyebrows draw in and she pouts as she tries, in vain, to loosen the belt. Then she curses under her breath and her eyes lift from the belt to my face. "I…" she trails off.

"You what?" I pant.

"Is this… I don't know. Is this weird?"

"You want to stop?"

She grimaces slightly and nods.

"Thank God!" I yell, letting her out from under me.

She sits with her ass on her heels and bubbles out a laugh— one I haven't heard in a long time. "I'm sorry."

"No. Please, don't be sorry." I move so my back's against the bed and yank on her hand to bring her closer to me. "I think maybe we, or at least me, hyped up the sex thing so much in my mind and everyone made a big deal out of it—"

She gasps. "Who's everyone?"

"No. Just Robby and Kim. They gave me all this stupid advice and a ridiculous amount of condoms it made me so nervous and I almost felt like if we just get it out of the way it wouldn't be so bad. But that's not why I brought you here. I just wanted some time with you, you know? Away from the everyday mundane stuff."

"One," she says, "I'm glad about the condoms even though *I'm* protected, I'm sure *you* want that piece of mind. And two: *I* get it. Completely. And thank you for thinking of me. I think I really need this."

"Good, babe. I'm glad. And also—I'm starving."

"You want to head out or get room service?"

"Room service," I tell her. "I don't want to share you with anyone tonight."

We order food and when it comes, we set ourselves up on the table in the corner of the room and dig in. "I feel so grown up right now."

"You are grown up," she says.

"Sometimes. When I'm in Dad mode I am, but I've done some stupid, immature shit," I admit.

She rolls her eyes. "Like what? Let Tommy go to bed without eating his vegetables?"

I lean forward. "You think you know me?" I joke.

She smiles. "Seriously. Like what?"

"I don't know." I shrug. "Like get drunk and smoke weed."

"You smoked weed?"

I nod. "Don't judge me."

"No judgment here, but why'd you stop? Me?"

"No." I set my fork on my plate and lean back in my chair. "The last time I did, I was with Hunter and Chloe, and the cops busted us."

"You got arrested?" she almost yells.

"Almost. You know how they say your life flashes before your eyes right before you die? It was kind of like that and all I could see was Tommy and what would've happened if I'd been caught. I remember fearing that they'd take him away from me because I was irresponsible and Hunter—he must've seen the fear because he took the bag from me just as the cops walked up."

"He took the blame?" she asked, her eyes wide.

"He would've if Chloe didn't step up."

"So Chloe copped it?"

"Yeah."

"Why?"

I lean forward now, my forearms resting on the table. "Chloe—she's had a complicated life. Before Hunter came along she kind of chose to be invisible. She took the blame for me because she didn't believe she had anything to lose. I had Tommy, Hunter had his Duke scholarship and she—she had *the road.*"

"What's the road?"

"It's nothing," I say, but my words come out harsher than intended.

Becca eyes me sideways and clears her throat. "It's obviously something."

"I don't know, Becca. I don't really like talking about it."

"I'm so confused right now."

I rub the back of my neck in frustration, but her eyes stay on mine.

"What does Chloe's road, or whatever, have to do with you?"

"It's not—" I break off with a sigh and try to piece together my thoughts. "So Chloe had this plan after she graduated, she'd just take off and hit the road and never look back. Like I said, her life was complicated and, if you ask me, she was running away. And Hunter—he just dropped everything—forgot everything else, and left with her."

"So, you're mad at Hunter for leaving?"

"No. I'm jealous of Hunter for being able to do that," I finally admit. "I'm bitter because he could so easily just drop everything and follow his heart." I pause to take a breath, my mind reeling. "And I can't," I blurt out.

"But why would you need to?" she cuts in. "I get that having

Tommy means you can't just go on some random road trip but why? Was there a girl?"

"I don't mean a girl," I assure her. "I mean skating."

"Oh."

"Becca, please don't get me wrong. It's not that I don't love Tommy or that I wouldn't move heaven and earth for him because you know me, and you know I would," I rush out. "It's just I think about Hunter leaving and I get jealous and bitter that he could just do that—without a single care in the world. And I hate that I feel that because he's my best friend and I'm happy for him. But sometimes I wonder, you know? Sometimes I go out there and skate till my feet hurt and my cheeks are numb from the pressure of the wind around me and I miss it. I'll keep missing it. And I wonder if I'm any good at it—like, good enough to compete. But then I remember Tommy and remember that's not my life or anything close to it. And I get angry and then afraid that that anger will show one day when I look at Tommy and that's the last thing I want."

"Josh…" she whispers, her voice laced with pity.

"It's nothing," I lie.

"Where was Tommy when Chloe got arrested?"

"I think he would've been with Natalie's parents."

"What?"

"Yeah, they take him once a month for the night."

Her brow bunches. "I just—I mean…you've never once mentioned it. Has he been there since you and I—"

"He hasn't been there for a few months. They're on a six month cruise or something at the moment."

Her eyes narrow.

"Is this a problem for you?"

"I don't know," she says, her gaze lifting and locking on mine. "It just seems strange that you haven't brought it up. All this time I thought you had absolutely no connection with Natalie and now this. You'd think you'd tell me, right?"

"It just hasn't really come up."

"Josh," she says incredulously. "We've spent all this time together and you never once thought to mention that Natalie was still part of Tommy's life? Even if far removed, she's still there. And she's Tommy's mom and your ex and…" She sighs. "Never mind. Eat your food."

After our meal, she grabs her camera and starts taking pictures of anything and everything. From the view out on the balcony to the tiny soaps on the bathroom sink. She hides her smile behind the camera as she takes shot after shot of me goofing around trying to make her laugh. It works—and her laughter is a sound I'd spend my entire life craving. "You're such a dork," she whispers, climbing onto the bed and fluffing the pillows against the headboard.

I take it as my cue and sit on the bed, my back against the headboard and my legs spread waiting for her to join me—something we do almost every night so she can show me the photographs she'd taken that day. After getting up and grabbing her camera bag, she positions herself in front of me, but not close enough. I grasp her waist and pull her into me, my chin on her shoulder as she flips through the images. "I think you've got close to a thousand pictures of me."

She smiles. "And it's still not enough," she says, reaching up and running her fingers through the back of my head.

"Do you have a favorite photo you've taken?"

"Of you, or ever?"

"Ever."

"I have two," she says.

"Can I see them?"

She turns in my arms, her gaze right on mine. Then she sighs. "I only have one here."

"So show me."

She inhales a huge breath before going through her bag and pulling out a memory card. She sits opposite me now, changes the cards over and starts flicking through the pictures. I keep my eyes on hers trying to read her expression. Occasionally she'll chew her lip and look up at me, as if she's nervous to show me. Her shoulders drop when she seems to find the one she's looking for. Almost hesitantly, she turns the back of the camera toward me. It's a picture of me skating. I'm in the air, on top of the pipe grabbing the board. It looks just like any other skate shot. "You take hundreds of photos a day and you're telling me this one's top two?"

She nods slowly. "It's not about the photo," she whispers, "it's about the content."

"Because it's a picture of me?" I ask incredulously.

"No, Josh. Because it *is* you. In that moment, I captured who you are—what you love and what makes you happy… what sets you *free.*" She clears her throat and takes the camera from my hand and places it on the nightstand. Then she climbs over me, straddling my waist. She runs a finger down my chest, her head tilted to the side, her eyes following the path she's creating. "When I was fourteen, I went on this field trip. I don't even really remember where it was. I just remember being the only kid there who didn't have a phone or a camera. Olivia was there—and she saw how left out I was because of it. She let me use her SLR. It was the first time I ever held one. She walked me through the basic steps and soon enough I was more interested in the camera than the actual field trip."

She's giving me a piece of herself—a piece of her past—something I've wanted for so long. So I stay silent, letting her speak.

"I don't really know why but Olivia let me borrow her camera for the rest of the week. That camera, it was like your version of a skateboard. I'd take it everywhere with me and snap away at anything and everything, probably like how you'd skate anywhere and everywhere."

I link my fingers behind her back and continue to watch her, smiling at the thought of her at that age doing exactly what she's describing.

"There was this one picture I'd taken of this homeless man. The clouds had just formed together to hide the sun and the atmosphere had turned this eerie gray. I took the shot just as the first clap of thunder sounded and he was looking up to the skies, his hand out, palm up waiting to feel the rain descend. It wasn't until I got to school and Olivia and I looked at it on the computer that I saw a bead of water had splashed against his forehead… and his eyes, I'll always remember the first time I saw his eyes. They were so dull, so lifeless, so hopeless. And I remember this ache in my chest when I reached out to touch the screen. I traced the lines on his face, the wrinkles that donned him, and I thought that it was horrible that his eyes held such lifelessness; because those lines—each crease on his face—they told a story. Good or bad. There was a story behind this man and I wanted to ask him about every single one." Her voice turns to a whisper. "And with my hand on my computer screen and my heart racing, I knew it. I'd fallen in love with something. I'd fallen in love with photography and the ability it had to capture a split second moment and evoke something emotional out of me. And if I could do that for the rest of my life—capture moments that made me question *life*—then that's what I wanted to do."

I stare at her, silent and unblinking. Then, finally, I lean forward and kiss her shoulder. "Your perfection is over-whelming."

She laughs a little and places her hands behind my neck before leaning back. "When did you know?"

"Know you were perfect? The first time I saw you step out of your grams' car—"

"No." She smiles. "I mean, when did you know you were in love with skating?"

I release a heavy breath, feeling the weight shift and tighten in my chest. I look back up at her; past the frown on her lips, the freckles on her nose, to her eyes, waiting for me to give her a piece of me. "I was fifteen," I tell her. "I'd snuck out of the house while my parents were asleep and went to the skate park. There was no one there, just me and the moon and the stars. I was there for hours, fooling around, excited that I had the place to myself. I didn't do anything special, or miraculous or land some epic trick or anything. I was just skating for the sake of skating. And I remember standing on edge of the coping, my foot on the tail of the board, and just breathing in the night air, and I looked around me with nothing but ramps and posts and my private concrete playground." I laugh once, remembering the moment. "My mom texted me and it said *'Don't wake your dad when you come home. Leave your board in the garage.'* She knew where I was and what I was doing past midnight on a school night and she didn't really care. I leaned my weight at the front of the board and flew down the pipe. I promised myself I'd only be a few more minutes, but the minutes turned to hours and when the sun started to come up I knew I had to go home. So, I attempted one more trick and I got to end of the pipe and my board left me and I was in the air and the sun was this perfect orange coming up from the horizon and I think that's when it happened. While I was in the air, my board somewhere beneath me and the wind surrounding me and I just... it was a split second, you know? But in that moment, I had no fears... nothing holding back. Just the sun rising letting me know there was a new a day. A clear future. And it was that feeling I fell in love with. Being weight-less and free. Being *airborne*."

"Airborne?"

I nodded. "Yeah. Airborne."

She returns my nod, her mouth slightly parted and her eyes right on mine. She starts to speak, but cuts herself off. This happens twice before she finally says, "Have you heard of SK8F8?"

"Of course I have. Why?"

"You know there's a comp in a few months. It's open registration."

I sigh, frustrated, and lean back on my arms, my head tilted back, my eyes focused on the ceiling.

"I'm sorry," she says, "I know the heartache you associate with skating and I'm being insensitive. I shouldn't have brought it up."

"Yep."

"It's just that you said yourself that you want to know if you're any good. And you have the chance to do that. Josh…" She cups my face and makes me look at her. "It just breaks my heart to hear you talk about something with so much passion and love and know that you feel like you can't have it. Who's to say you can't? It's different now, right? Tommy's older and you have me and Grams and your aunt and uncle. Why not try? Why not see if you're good enough?"

"Becca…" I warn.

"I know. I'll shut up."

"Good."

"Just one more thing. I promise," she rushes out, her eyes wide. "When Tommy's older and he somehow finds out about your skating—because he will—what are you going to tell him? That *he's* the reason you quit? I mean the fact that you're going to have to admit you're a quitter is one thing, but then you're going to make him feel guilty that it's his fault." She cringes as soon as the last word leaves her.

"Are you trying to guilt me?" I ask, unable to contain my smile.

She shrugs. "Is it working?"

I stare at her, right into her emerald eyes, and my heart has never felt so full of promise. "Fine."

She covers her squeal—or at least her version of a squeal—with her hand. "Because I guilted you into it?"

"No." I move beneath her to get more comfortable. "Because you asked me and I'm pretty sure I'd do absolutely anything you asked." I grasp her waist and shift her higher slightly. She's still in my shirt and I'm still shirtless and she looks… she looks like Becca. *Perfect.*

"Thank you, Josh. I know it doesn't really involve me but I feel like I'm part of it."

"Of course it involves you, Becca. You're giving me the courage to *coast.*" I lean in and kiss her softly. "Thank you for caring about me. And I'm sorry for not telling you about Natalie's parents. I should have. I'm just dumb with stuff like that."

"You're not dumb. Stop it. It's not like it changes anything."

"I never thought I'd find someone like you. Someone who'd put up with me having a son and wanting to be part of both our lives. Why do you do it, Becca?" I ask, my heart pounding against my chest.

"Because, Josh. You and Tommy…" She places my hand over her heart. "…you own me in here." And even as I feel her heart beat against my palm, I wonder if she knows that she just made mine stop.

All my words anchor somewhere between my heart and my throat. Maybe it's because deep down, I know nothing I can ever tell her will be worthy of how I feel—that even though she thought my love and my passion were skating—she has it wrong.

It's her.

She must sense what I'm feeling, because a slow smile spreads across her lips. "I know," she whispers. But she doesn't. She has no fucking clue. She can't possibly.

I press my lips to hers, trying, *hoping,* that it's enough, that somehow, through a single kiss she'll be able to feel it: how much she means to me. How much I appreciate her. How much I *love* that she didn't just want *me*. She wanted *us*. All *three* of us.

Her fingers tighten in my hair and she presses firmer, rocking her hips into me. We break the kiss just long enough for me to remove her top, and when her hand covers my heart and she breathes out my name, I know what'll happen next… I know we'll give each other a piece of ourselves. Not just physically, but in every way possible. And when I flip us over; her lying on her back with me on top of her and I push into her for the first time, watching her eyes roll back and feeling her fingers dig into my back—I know it.

I *feel* it.

She's disintegrated my armor with her existence, and now she has all of me.

Every single part.

I let her see *me.*

I let her love *me.*

And I let myself believe, just for a moment, I understood *why.*

CHAPTER 25

BECCA

"Wow." I clutch the covers to my chest and try to catch my breath.

"Sorry," he murmurs kissing my shoulder. I face him just as he smiles against my skin.

Turning to my side, I run my finger across his forehead to move the hair caught in the sweat across his brow. "Why are you sorry?"

"About the first time."

A giggle bubbles out of me. "You made up for it the second and third."

"Yeah?" he asks, his cheeks darkening with his blush. "I hope so."

"You did. Trust me."

He moans from deep in his throat and places his hand on my waist, drawing me closer to him until our bare chests meet. His mouth connects with my neck and moves down to my collarbone. "This is going to sound so weird," he mumbles, lifting his gaze a little. "I really wish I had people around to show you off to."

"Like a prize?"

He nods through a laugh and holds me tighter. "Exactly like a prize."

"What would you say?"

"I don't know." He moves back slightly and rests his head on my pillow. "I'd probably just shout that this really hot girl let me have sex with her."

I shake my head. "You're such a dork."

"I'm kidding." He rolls over onto his back and holds his arm out, indicating for me to rest my head on it—which I do. "You know there's never been a time since my parents disowned me that I'd ever wished it were different. I never wanted them to change their minds or to come knocking on my door begging for forgiveness. But right now, I wish it were different."

I lace my fingers with his and kiss his hand. "Why?"

"Because I'd want them to meet you. I'd want them to know that even though I've made mistakes in the past, that I'm still loveable. That if *you* can find a way to care about me—then they should be able to, too." His voice cracks and after clearing his throat he adds, "It's not just that, though. I think they'd really like you, Becca."

"Yeah?" I ask, unable to control my smile. "You don't talk about them often."

"I don't really have anything to say."

"But you have to be mad at them, or at least like—"

"I was," he admits. "I used to be really angry and bitter and when that faded, I was just confused. It's not like I came from a bad family. They were both active in my life. They supported my skating, encouraged it even. I don't know... it's like out of all the things I could do to fuck up; getting a girl pregnant was where they drew the line. The point of no return, you know? Yeah, they went to church and it was against their beliefs, but really? To not even try? It doesn't make sense. And it's not like they sat down and tried to talk to me about it, they just shut me out completely. The worst part is I still see her—my mom. I see her around town and at the store or whatever and she looks at me like I'm some kind of disease. I mean, I get that she's disappointed and hates me... but her own grandson? She won't even look at him. I doubt she'd even know his name, and if she does, she didn't hear it from me. She won't look at Tommy. Won't even acknowledge his existence. Who does that, Becca? Who the hell can turn away their own grandchild?"

The same ones who turn away their own children, I want to tell him. But I don't. Instead I say, "I'm sorry."

He shrugs, but his mind's elsewhere.

"What's your dad like?"

"He's... proud, I guess."

"Of you?"

"No. Of himself and his life. He was a good dad, don't get me wrong, but he's always been stubborn and hated being wrong. Like, he and my uncle Robby are stepbrothers. My grandma remarried and treated Robby like her own. Robby's dad was successful and came from a line of wealth. That's where Robby got the funding to start his business. But my dad? He won't take a cent of it. Even when dad went to college and it was all set up and paid for, he worked to pay it back as soon as possible. He'd never pay for anyone to come to the house to fix things—he'd always spend hours on weekends trying to do it himself. Even though there was trust fund money for Dad, he wouldn't touch it... as if it was dirty money or something." He shrugs. "I don't know. He's just stubborn and stupid."

"Do you miss them at all?"

"It's kind of irrelevant, right?" he says, kissing the tip of my nose. "It won't change anything."

I wake up before he does and I watch him sleep. With his eyes closed and his mouth parted slightly—his bottom lip quivering with each exhale of breath—I've never seen him so at peace, and even though the permanent lines between his eyebrows can't hide the constant worry that falls on his shoulders—he's never looked so weightless before. When every single part of me aches to kiss him, I creep to the bathroom, brush my teeth, and then silently sneak back in his arms. "Wake up," I whisper, lightly kissing his bottom lip.

His mouth forms into a smile against mine—his hand finding my waist and gently pulling me to him. One eye opens and then closes quickly. He groans quietly—his voice hoarse from sleep, and rests his head on my chest. Holding me tighter, he mumbles, "Please tell me this isn't a dream."

I run my fingers through his hair. "It's not a dream, baby."

"Sure?"

"Positive."

He's silent a moment, and just when I'd assumed he's fallen asleep, he mumbles, "Good, because I have to tell you something…"

"Yeah?"

"Yep." He moves up a little and presses his lips to my bare shoulder. "I'm kind of crazy in love with you, Becca." Then he jumps out of bed before I can respond. "And I need to go potty."

"What kind of jerk declares their love for someone and then announces a potty break!"

He simply laughs as he closes the bathroom door behind him, all while I sit there, my heart pounding and my emotions forming a puddle in the pit of my stomach. I open my mouth, the words *I love you too* on the tip of my tongue.

I wait for minutes that feel like hours and when he finally reemerges from the bathroom—his hair and lips wet and his entire body still drunk from sleep—I sit up and pull the covers over my bare chest.

He smirks, his eyes focused on mine and I self-consciously tighten my hold on the sheets. "So…" I say, shrinking under his gaze. "Did you want to order breakfast… or…"

He settles his palms flat on the bed, his arms outstretched as he leans forward, his face less than an inch from mine. The muscles in his forearms and shoulders flex with his movements —movements that intimidate me and cause my breath to catch. *"Or…"* he answers, taking my bottom lip between his. He pulls back slightly. "Definitely *'or'.*"

We "or"ed until we we're forced to stop and when we're satisfied, he holds me to him, his thumb grazing up and down my arm. "When I was a kid," he says, pausing to kiss the top of my head, "my dad made me this skate grind rail. I had no idea he was doing it but the look on his face when he saw my face was just… it's how I try to remember him, you know? Anyway, that weekend Hunter came around and we spent every second messing around on it. His dad kept calling on the Sunday afternoon telling him he had to go home. I stayed out there until my mom made me go inside for dinner. I couldn't sleep that night. I couldn't stop thinking about it. And I hated that I had to go to school the next day and be away from it. I remember thinking that I wished I lived two lives. The skating and the reality, and I wished I could live them both at the same time. I hated school for so many reasons but mainly because it took me away from something that made me so happy… something I loved.

"I have that feeling now, Becca, with you in my arms. You're the reality I want and now I have to go back to real life where I'm going to be away from you. And even though I miss Tommy and I know that I see you every day, it's not the same. In this room, within these walls, you've given me a better reality. A greater existence."

"Josh?"

"Yeah?"

"I'm so deeply, insanely, desperately in love with you."

"Yeah?" he says again, neither of us looking at each other.

I nod against his chest.

He reaches to the nightstand and grabs my camera, then proceeds to take a shot of us lying exactly how we are. "There's absolutely nothing to question about what I just captured. It's perfect. *This* is perfect."

CHAPTER 26

JOSHUA

Sometimes the most basic of moments become your most treasured memories. Like the time Tommy got on a skateboard for the first time and just stood there, not knowing what to do. He looked up at me with those clear blue eyes and said, "What now, daddy?"

I showed him where to place his feet and how to kick off the ground. He rolled for two feet before stopping and throwing his arms in the air. He shouted, "I just like Daddy!" And I laughed at the time, but now I look back on it and wish I'd paid more attention to every detail of that moment—what he was wearing, what the weather was like, what time of day it was.

So now, as I wait for Becca and Tommy who are getting ready to perform some kind of show they've apparently been working on for me, I try to remember everything. I look at the time; look at the orange of the sky outside. I try to memorize the sounds of their loud unrestricted laughter coming from Tommy's room. But most of all, I try to bottle my emotions, not to contain them, but to savor them. I try to remember the excitement and the acceptance I feel and *the love.* There's *so* much love. Not just the love I *have* for them, but the love I feel *from* them.

His bedroom door opens and Becca sticks her head out. "Babe! Can you move the coffee table to the side?"

After a nod, I do as she asks.

"Ready, Daddy?"

I sit on the couch and clap my hands together. "I can't wait!"

A moment later they charge out of his room and my head throws back with laughter. "You guys look ridiculous!" And it's not a lie. They're both wearing bed sheets around their necks as capes. Becca has a pile of my hats on her head and Tommy has a metal strainer on his. Tommy's in the brightest clothes he owns, but they're on backwards and inside out and in the wrong order—he's wearing his underwear on the outside of his pants, but the absolute best part, is that Becca's the same. Only she's in my clothes. My boxer shorts on the outside of her leggings and close to ten different layers of the ugliest items she would've found in my closet. And they're holding spoons. "What's with the spoons?" I laugh.

Becca shakes her head at me trying to contain her own cackle. "We are The Spoon Loving League," she announces, and indicates to Tommy, letting me know it was his idea.

Tommy puts one hand on his hip, the other holding the spoon in the air and as loud as he can, he yells, "I am Captain LoonySpoon!"

I wipe the tears from my eyes caused by my laughter, and look at Becca. "And who are you supposed to be?"

Her gaze drops and her shoulders lift, then she mumbles something incoherent.

"What was that?" I ask her.

Tommy answers, his voice just as loud as earlier. "I am her leader. She is Officer PoopSniffer."

I contain my laughter, just long enough to get out, "I'd like to hear Becca say it."

She looks up, her glare in place, which just makes me smile wider. "I am Officer PoopSniffer," she murmurs.

"Sorry, I couldn't hear you."

She huffs out a breath. "I wanted to be DesertSpoon but Tommy—"

"Captain LoonySpoon!" he cuts in.

She smiles. "Captain LoonySpoon wouldn't let me."

"And what are your powers?" I ask.

Tommy hits his helmet/metal strainer with the spoon and Becca goes flying back, pretending to fall on the ground.

"Did you feel it, Daddy?" Tommy asks, his eyes wide with excitement.

My eyes move from Becca to him. "Feel what?"

"The force field."

"Oh!"

He does it again, and this time I pretend to be affected by it. "Those are some awesome powers," I tell him. "What are Becca's powers?"

"She can smell poop from far away."

Becca starts to get up but before she can there's a knock the door. Her eyes widen.

"Open the door, PoopSniffer," I say.

She stands up and looks down at her clothes, then crosses her arms. "No way."

Tommy chimes in. "I am your leader so open the door, PoopSniffer!"

I get up and squeeze Tommy's shoulder as I pass him. "I was just kidding, Tommy." I open the door, my eyes still on him. "We shouldn't talk to Becca like that." Then I turn around and come face to face with Robby and Kim. "Hey. I didn't know you guys were coming over." I open the door wider. "Tommy, Uncle Robby and Aunt Kim are here."

He sidles up next me. "I am Captain LoonySpoon," he shouts.

But they don't react. They just stand there, their expressions identical. There's no hint of smile, no form of happiness to see us. "What's going on?"

Kim's eyes move from me to Tommy, and I can tell right away that something's wrong because her eyes cloud with tears but behind that, I can see the pity.

I suck in a breath and hold it, my mind racing with a thousand scenarios. Then I hear it—*my name*—coming from a voice I hadn't heard since just after Tommy was born. I square my shoulders, my glare formed and directed at Robby. "Why?" I whisper.

"Sorry," he says, stepping to the side.

Time hasn't changed her. She looks exactly like she did the last time I saw her; with tears in her eyes and a pleading look on her face, and instantly, I'm pissed—at Robby for bringing her to *my* home, and at *her* for looking at me the way she is… for coming here and ruining a perfectly perfect moment.

After three years of no contact, I do my best to not let the anger show. "What the hell are you doing here?"

But it's Robby who answers. "Your mom and I—we need to talk to you."

"You see me every day, Robby. If you needed to say something you could have," I clip. "You didn't need to bring *her* here. This is my house. My *home.*" I look over at my mom. "This is where I've set up a life with my son. *Your grandson*—just in case you forgot he existed."

Becca's hand brushes against my back as she squeezes past me and picks up Tommy. My gaze drops and I wait until Becca's carried Tommy down the stairs, my heart thumping hard against my chest, and when I hear her front door close and I know she's taken him away from the destruction I know is about to occur, I look back up at my mother, my jaw tense and every single muscle in my body aching to slam the door in all their faces. I cross my arms and ball my fists. "I'll ask you again. One last time. What the fuck are you doing here?"

CHAPTER 27

BECCA

---

haunt

    verb

    be persistently and disturbingly present in (the mind).

I watch from the living room window as Josh crosses his arms over his chest, his face red and his eyes flaming with anger. The same anger I'd heard in his voice—the same voice that made my insides turn to stone and I knew that whatever was happening—I needed to save Tommy.

Josh stands opposite the woman I assume is his mom as his shoulders slowly drop and the anger in his eyes fade. His mouth parts and he nods once, opening the door wider for them.

"What happened?" Grams asks from behind me.

I turn to her. "Josh has some visitors, I guess."

"Can we play in your room?" Tommy asks with a smile. I

take his hand and lead him upstairs, wondering if he has any idea that his life's about to change. Because I do. I can sense it.

I keep an eye on the time, watching the minutes turn to hours and nothing. Not a phone call. Not a single text. I give Tommy a bath and start to get him ready for bed. Just as I finish dressing him and get him settled in my room, there's a knock on the door. "I'll be back. Stay here, okay?"

Josh stands with his hands in his pockets and his head lowered. I look over his shoulder and notice that Robby's car is gone.

"What happened?" I ask.

"Nothing. Is Tommy still up?"

"Yeah, he's in my room watching TV."

"Can you get him?"

"Is everything okay? You guys talked for a long time."

He sighs, seemingly frustrated by my question. "Everything's fine, Becca. I just really don't want to talk about it. Not now and probably not ever."

"Josh—"

"Can you just get my son, please!"

I clear my throat, hoping the strength of my voice hides my weakness. "I think maybe Tommy should stay here tonight."

"You know what I think?" he snaps, pinning me with his glare. "I think maybe you should keep your opinions to yourself."

My stomach drops, so does my gaze, and it stays that way as I run upstairs, get Tommy and bring him back down.

Once they're gone, I take myself up to my room and into my

bed, where I do something I'd spent the majority of life doing—I cry my silent cries and wear my silent tears.

But I don't question any of it—because if there's anyone who knows how quickly things can change—how someone's love can turn to anger in the blink of an eye—it's me.

I hear her voice. It echoes in my mind. *"He doesn't love you,"* she says over and over. After an hour of crying into my pillow, I start to believe her. *"No one can love you like I do,"* she haunts.

My phone rings.

It's Josh, of course. I reject the call and a second later a text comes through.

Joshua: I'm at your door. Please, Becca.

I gather whatever strength I have left, wipe my stupid tears, and meet him outside. His hands are in his pockets again and his head's lowered. I do everything I can to hide any proof I'd spent the last hour crying over him. But it doesn't work because after he inhales sharply and slowly lifts his gaze to mine, he whispers, "Fuck," and then reaches up and cups my face, tilting my head back so he can look at me. "Did I do this?"

I turn away from his touch and away from his sympathetic eyes.

"Becca, I'm so sorry."

But I don't believe him because I'm mad and I'm hurt and like she said, he *doesn't love me.* Yet, when he touches me from my face, down my arm, and to my hand, I let him take it. I let him lead me away and up to his apartment, to his room, where he closes the door behind him.

"I'm so sorry," he says again, and I want to forgive him. But it doesn't take back how he made me feel, and how my fucked up mind responded to those feelings. "What happened?" I ask while he goes through his drawers and pulls out clothes for me to wear.

He sighs and drops his head as he sits on the edge of the bed. He stays silent while he hands me his boxers and I change into them, rolling the band over so they fit. He looks up now, and for the first time, I see the redness in his eyes and the puffiness that surrounds them.

He doesn't speak, though—just places his hands on my hips and slowly glides them up my sides, taking my top with them. I lift my arms, my eyes on his as he removes my shirt, and I just want to yell at him to give me something. *Anything.* His eyes drift shut and his arms circle my waist, pulling me to him. The roughness of his cheek presses against my bare stomach. "Don't, Becca. Not now."

I swallow loudly, the pain of what feels like rejection filters through every surface of my body and it hurts. It hurts so damn bad. But then he kisses me, just under my navel and I close my eyes and submerge myself in the feeling of his touch, of his kiss, of his mouth as it lowers. His fingers, warm, curl around my shorts and my underwear and he tugs them down, past my hips and down my legs until they're on the floor by my feet and I feel the cool air between my legs. He moves lower again and my eyes shut tight when I feel his lips against my mound. I choke on a gasp when his tongue, slow and wet, moves between my legs. He moans from deep in his throat and pulls back, his eyes focused on my chest; heaving as I struggle for breath. Then he reaches behind me, unhooks my bra and, with one arm around me and his free hand covering a breast, he pulls me over him as he lies down on the bed. He flips us until I'm on my back and he's on his side and then he takes my nipple between his lips while his hand's between my legs with two fingers inside me. I comb my fingers through his hair and move with him as he continues to kiss, suck, and lick down my body until he's on the floor. He stands up and chews his lip while his eyes slowly roam my naked body. Then he grabs my ankles, rough and demanding, and pulls them down until I'm on the edge of the bed. He drops to his knees; his palms flat against my thighs as he pushes them apart. My back arches as his lips make contact with my sex, my eyes wide, my vision blurred while his tongue, his mouth, his fingers, work me to the edge. I lick my lips, my mouth dry, my hands gripping the sheets beneath me.

"Let go, baby," he murmurs against me.

"Josh," I whisper, my eyes filling with tears. I want to tell him to stop, that *he* doesn't want this. But I know what it's like to want to feel something, *anything*, but pain. And I know that's what he's doing.

He doubles his efforts and within seconds I'm panting his name over and over. He pushes me over the edge as tears mixed with sweat trickle down my hairline. He waits until I'm settled before running his tongue up my stomach, between my breast, and up to my ear. "Flip over," he says, but his hand's already on my waist, guiding me to where he wants me. I wait on all fours while he opens the drawer of his nightstand and rips open the condom packet. I feel one of his hands on my butt, the other on my back as he pushes me down and then pushes inside me. His thrusts are fast, hard and painful. And I can no longer tell if he's using me, or if I'm using him, but either way we want the physical pleasure to help us forget the pain. So I let him take me, however he wants me. He leans down, his chest pressed against my back and his mouth on my ear. "I'm so sorry," he says, and I have no idea which part he's apologizing for. He slows his thrusts, his mouth moving from my ear to my neck, kissing me slow and soft.

And I remember why I love this, why I *crave* this… his touch, his kiss…

His hand's in my hair now, pulling tight and I grunt in response—pushing back memories of the last time my hair was pulled…

Then he kisses my shoulder, his fingers brushing the hair

away from my eyes so he can look at me—at the eyes he loves so much. "I love you," he whispers, and I forget the pain... the pain of his hands in my hair, the pain of how he spoke to me earlier, and I let the pleasure of his touch balance out the torture and the fear of my life.

CHAPTER 28

BECCA

---

sink

> **verb**

> **descend from a higher to a lower position; drop downwards.**

Days pass and Josh's mood doesn't change. He's distant and withdrawn and he does what I normally do—he uses Tommy as a distraction to not pay attention to me. Honestly, I doubt I'd even see Josh if knocking on my door and asking me to play wasn't the first thing Tommy does as soon as they get home. I don't spend nights. Josh doesn't ask me to. As soon as Tommy's in bed, I leave. He doesn't call. Doesn't text. We don't talk about what went on with his mom and we sure as hell don't talk about what happened with *us* that night. In fact, we don't really talk at all. Which is quite easy considering I've reverted back to the girl I was when I moved here; lying awake in bed every night with voices in my head, pulling me further and further back into the darkness.

. . .

Then one night, right after Tommy goes down, he asks me to stay—not with him—but to watch Tommy. I agree, of course, and watch from his window as he grabs his skateboard from his truck and rolls out the driveway. I wait for him to return and when two a.m. hits, I send him a text asking when he'll be home. After a half hour of no reply, I finally give in and fall asleep on his couch.

I startle awake when I hear the key turn in his door and he steps inside. He eyes me curiously as I sit up and wipe the sleep from my eyes. "Why aren't you in bed?" he asks, sitting down next to me.

I shrug.

Then he does something I've wanted him to do, something I've craved since that night. He touches me. He holds my hand, his eyes fixed on the connection. "Is it because of what happened in there?"

I shrug again, though he can't see me. So he faces me, his eyes right on mine. "Did I hurt you?" he asks.

I nod.

"Physically?"

I shake my head and point to my heart.

He releases a breath and my hand at the same time, but he doesn't pull away, he grabs my legs and puts them over his, turning my entire body to face him. His hand's on my neck now, gently stroking my cheek. "I'm sorry I hurt you," he whispers. "And I'm sorry I've been pushing you away, Becca. I just don't know how else to handle this. I know it's hard for you—the fact that I'm not willing to talk about it yet—and I'm sorry for that, too. But I needed time, I needed to skate and to clear my head. I thought about a lot of things tonight." His dark eyes glaze with tears and he swallows loudly, his head tilting forward and his voice softening. "Mainly about you and the fact that you're the only constant in my life right now. I was a dick to you and I know I've been treating you horribly the last week but I just… I need you to be patient with me. I'm going to make mistakes—a lot of them—and I'm going to fuck up, especially when it comes to you and me because I'm not used to thinking about anyone or anything but myself and Tommy." He sniffs once and looks back up at me. "I don't want to lose you, Becca. I *can't* lose you. So if I hurt you, I need you tell me. If I fuck up, call me out on it. The last thing I want is for you to walk away without me knowing *why*. If one day you realize you're only here for Tommy and not for me and you want to walk away, then I have to let you, but I at least want to know that I did everything I could to make it right before letting you go. But *please* don't do that, Becca. *Please* don't leave me." His voice breaks with the desperation in his words. He holds my face in his hands, his gaze searching mine. "Please," he begs.

I kiss him once, twice, and by the third time, he starts to kiss me back. He kisses away the pain and the hurt. Not with his touch this time, but with his words, his despair and his declaration.

I stand up, take his hand, and lead us to his room, where we climb into bed, our arms wrapped around each other, my face on his chest, his hands in my hair and our hearts beating as one again.

"I love you, baby," he whispers, kissing the top of my head.

"I love you, too."

For the next few days, things go back to normal. Or at least a version of normal that's enough to not make me sink into myself. Josh works and some nights he leaves and skates for a few hours, or at least that's what he tells me. Of course I wonder. Every insecure part of me questions what he's doing, who he's with… if there's someone else he's seeing. And then I remember what he said and I know it can't be true.

Right?

Josh's truck pulls in and the second Tommy's free he comes charging up to me waiting on the porch steps with my camera ready. I told him we'd spend the evening taking pictures—all of him.

He's such a little poser.

He sits down next to me—his hand on my leg. "What doing?"

"Just clearing some space on my card so I can get more photos of you. Hey…" I face him. "I'm pretty sure Grams has a new costume for you."

His eyes light up. "Wardrobe change?"

"Yeah, bud. Go inside. We've been waiting for you to get home."

He's up and on his feet in no time, opening the door and shouting, "Ma'am!" right before the door slams shut.

I look up at Josh who's standing by the mailbox; he's looking at a letter, his eyebrows drawn. Slowly, he looks at me, his lips pressed tight.

I stand up nervously and wait for him to make his way over to me. "You got a letter," he says, handing it to me.

The Washington University logo is the first thing I see and I can't help but smile.

"St. Louis?" he asks.

My smile drops when I look back up at him.

He's angry again.

"You never mentioned a word about it before. Is that—I mean, are you going there?"

"It's complicated," I tell him, my voice cracking. "It's still kind of… up in the air at the moment."

His eyes thin to slits. "So that's what this is? You take a year off before college, live with your grandmother, fuck some guy because it's convenient and then take off?"

"What? Josh. No."

"Then what is it, Becs? You didn't think it was important to bring this up?"

"It wasn't confirmed… and you knew, right? You knew I wasn't staying here forever."

He crosses his arms, his head moving from side to side while he stares me down. "I've let you keep your secrets. I've held you through your bullshit nightmares—"

"Josh!" I indicate to the front door, hoping Grams can't hear this conversation. I don't want her hearing how he's talking to me. That he's pushing me down. Making me weak.

He lowers his voice. "You should've fucking told me, Becca. You should have at least given me that."

"Yeah, well you also told me to tell you if you were hurting me. And you are."

"Yeah!" He's back to yelling now. "And I also fucking begged you not to leave me. Yet here you are, Becs, leaving me."

"What's going on?" Grams snaps from behind me. I stare at Josh. He stares back. Neither speaking. Then his phone rings, breaking the silence. He shoves his hand in his pocket and pulls it out, then turns away from me when he must see who's calling. Tommy's next to me now, dressed in his cowboy outfit Grams had bought him.

"I have to go," Josh says, walking backward to his truck. "I'll be back soon. Can you watch Tommy?"

I nod, even though I'm angry and hurt and blink away the tears before looking over at Tommy with the fakest smile I've ever had to fake before. "You ready, Cowboy?"

CHAPTER 29

JOSHUA

"So there's nothing else we can do?" I ask the doctor while my mom sits next to me, her head bent, her shoulders shaking with each sob.

"No," the doctor says. "Unfortunately not."

I look at my mom. "Sorry," I tell her, because I don't really know what else to say in this situation.

Mom says, "Thank you for trying, Joshua. I appreciate it."

"Is he here? In the hospital, I mean."

Doc stands up, pushing his chair behind him. "I'll give you a moment," he tells us. "I have another appointment in ten minutes though."

I nod.

My mom waits until he's left before partially turning to me. "He is. But he doesn't want to see you."

"What?"

"You know him, Josh. He's too proud for his own good. It has nothing to do with you."

"That's bullshit, Mom."

She cringes. "I know. And please remember—this stays between us."

CHAPTER 30

BECCA

When you spend your whole life faking happiness, it becomes a second emotion. Somewhere between fine and anger and hurt and content and satisfied. But really, it's just feeling numb, only you carry a smile with it.

I answer the knock on my bedroom door. Grams looks over my shoulder at Tommy playing with his blocks on the floor. "I'm going to Bingo." She smiles sadly and places her hand on my cheek. "Are you going to be okay?"

I nod.

"Becca, if he's not treating you right—"

"He is. He's just distracted and going through some stuff at the moment. And he's right, I should've told him about St. Louis."

"I love Joshua, please don't get me wrong. But I feel like you're making excuses—"

"I'm not," I tell her, pushing back the tears pricking in the back of my eyes.

"Okay. I just worry is all."

"I know, Grams. But seriously, there's nothing to worry about. We'll work it out."

. . .

I close the door and turn back to Tommy, who's in my closet now, pulling out the skateboard we've been working on. He looks up at me with the board in his hands and grins from ear to ear. "Daddy secwet present?"

"You want to do some crafting?"

He nods enthusiastically and I can't say no. I get down on my knees and pick up the shoebox filled with pictures of Josh skating. Pictures Josh has never seen before. And then I lay out the glue and scissors and everything we'll need, just like we've done so many times before.

Tommy's attention span doesn't last long and when he starts rolling around on the floor, licking the carpet, I know it's time to find something else to do. "Let's get you a snack," I say, and he jumps to his feet and runs out the door before I can even stand up. I chase him out of the room and try to grab him before he hits the stairs. But I'm too late, and by the time he's on the third to last step, he turns to me, smiles, and then he jumps.

And the rest is a blur.

The thud as he lands on his side.

The screams that leave him.

The cries as I try to soothe him.

All while he's holding his arm to his chest.

I call Josh, my heart pounding.

He doesn't answer.

I call Grams.

Straight to voicemail.

I call Robby, but he doesn't answer either.

So I call an ambulance because I don't know what else to do.

Tommy's cries are loud.

Mine are silent.

The nurses at the hospital ask a million questions, all while I hold Tommy in my arms. And if there's one sound I hate more than anything in the world, it's the sound of a constant dial tone and the standard voicemail that means no one's going to answer. I call Josh thirty-four times as I pace the hospital waiting room, desperate, worried, and afraid.

I run between the waiting room and Tommy's room while they put a cast on his arm, tears flowing, stomach in knots. At one stage, a nurse approaches, asks if I'm okay and offers me water. "I don't need water!" I shout, but my voice cracks and nothing comes out. I continue to dial Josh's number and after what feels like an eternity, he finally calls back.

"What's wrong? What happened?" he rushes out.

"Josh! I've been calling you!"

"What happened?" he asks again, louder this time, but I hear his voice twice and I swear I'm fucking losing it. I feel faint, like I'm about to pass out. "Becca!" he shouts, clearer, louder. So loud it seems to echo.

Then I feel a hand on my arm and I flinch, shaking it off. "Josh, I'm at the hospital!"

The hand grips my arm tighter and spins me around and all of a sudden Josh is standing there. His heavy exhale hits my face, his eyes wide in panic. Then he seems to stop breathing. So do I. He looks around, his gaze frantic. "Where's Tommy?"

"I'm so sorry!" I cry out.

"Where is he?"

"Room 203. His arm—" He's off before I can finish, ignoring the shouts from the nurses as he pushes past them and through the ER doors.

I feel hands clasp my shoulders and the fear of someone else's touch is completely overshadowed by the fear of what's happening to Tommy.

And what's going to happen to Josh and me.

"He's going to hate you," the voice in my head says. And then

she laughs—an evil, sinister laugh that turns everything around me *black.* I get led to a chair and guided to sit down. And then I break. "I didn't mean it. I should have watched him closer. I didn't mean it," I keep saying, my voice a whisper. The words meant for *her.*

An older couple rushes through the doors and marches straight to the nurse's desk. "Thomas Christian," they say, and then they, too, go through the doors.

I sit and I wait for Josh to come out. To yell at me. And I gear myself up to take it all.

After way too long, he finally emerges—his jaw clenched and his chest out. I stand slowly, waiting for him to make his way to me—to tell me that he hates me and he never wants to see me again.

He's two steps away when someone shouts his name.

Our eyes switch to the blonde girl running toward him, tears mixed with mascara streaking down her cheeks.

"Is he okay?" she asks, and I look over at Josh.

All color has drained from his face and he just stands there, mouth open, eyes wide.

Static fills my ears and everything inside me goes still—like a light switching off in my soul.

I know who she is.

Even before I see her eyes—the same eyes as Tommy's.

Even before she cries out her son's name and falls forward onto Josh's chest.

And I know who she is, even before she wraps her arms around him, her fingers curled in the back of his T-shirt. "Shhh," he comforts. "It's okay. Everything's okay."

And I know it now.

Where he's been going late at night.

Where he's been rushing off to.

All his secrets are revealed.

But worse? I *know.* I can feel it with every fiber of my being. It's all over.

All of it.

I know it even before he hugs her back, his eyes drifting shut.

Then he inhales deeply and lets out a breath with a single word: *"Natalie."*

I catch a cab home, my mind in a daze. I don't go into the house. Instead, I sit on the porch steps, phone in hand, and I wait. I can't stop crying. I can't stop shaking. And I can't stop the puke that rises from my throat and ends up in Grams's rose garden. *Twice.*

An hour later, he pulls into the house, his eyes catching my figure as I stand up and wait anxiously for news that Tommy's okay. The interior light of his truck switches on and he steps out, eyeing Tommy who's fallen asleep in the back seat. He seems to sigh, or let out a frustrated breath… I can't tell.

"Is he okay?" I ask, my voice hoarse from all the crying and puking I'd done.

Josh shakes his head as he walks toward me. "What the hell happened, Becca? I left you with him for less than an hour and you broke his arm?"

"I'm so sorry."

He shakes his head again, his eyes on mine. "Do you know how much that five minute ambulance ride is going to cost me?"

"I didn't know what else to do," I whisper.

"What happened?"

"He ran down the stairs and I couldn't keep up and—"

"He's three, Becca, you can't leave him…" he trails off when headlights shine on both of us. The engine of the car switches off and all of my worst fears hit me at once. Natalie steps out; one perfect leg after the other. She stands to full height, eyeing her surroundings and flicks her hair over her shoulder. Then she walks to the trunk of her car, pulls out a suitcase, releases the handle and drags it behind her as she starts walking toward us. "Is he okay?" she asks.

Josh nods. "He fell asleep."

Natalie's eyes moves from Josh to me—bright blue, just like her son's. "You're the one who was meant to be watching him?"

"Yes," I whisper, looking between them. "I'm sorry."

"You should be," she says, arching her eyebrows.

"Natalie," Josh says, shaking his head at her. I wait for him to say something else and when enough time has passed and I know that he's not going to defend me, I run into the house and up to my room, trying to silence my cries into the pillow so he—she—*they* can't hear me.

Grams comes home and up to my room.

I can't hide my cries from her.

"What happened, baby girl?" she asks, her hand soothing against my hair.

I tell her everything. The broken arm. The hospital. Josh. I struggle, so badly, to tell her about Natalie. But I do. And before she can respond, I get a text from Josh.

Joshua: I'm at your door. Can you come out?

"Maybe say no this time, Becca. Give it some time for things to cool off. You're both not thinking straight and someone's going to say something they'll regret."

I shake my head. "I'd rather hear it now."

Josh leans against the porch railings, his phone in his hand. He doesn't look up when I step outside, not until he's tapped a few buttons and puts the phone back in his pocket. I shut the door behind me and lean against it, eying Natalie's car in the driveway. "So that's where you've been?" I ask.

"What are you talking about?"

"All the late night skating to clear your head..." I choke on a sob and do my best to speak through it. "You've been seeing Natalie?"

"What?" his gaze follows mine. "No. Shit, Becca. What the fuck kind of person do you think I am?"

I shrug. "It makes sense. She's there..." I point to his apartment. "I'm here. And you're... I don't even know where you are lately."

He sighs dramatically and tilts his head back. "What the hell are we doing, Becca?"

"What do you mean?"

"I mean, apart from what I know about you since you've moved here, I don't know anything else. You're a complete stranger to me. And you've taken Tommy and me on some kind of joy ride where you plan to get off and we're supposed to just... You should've told me about St. Louis."

"I'm sorry," I tell him, unable to look at him. "You should've told me about Natalie."

"I didn't know about Natalie! There *was* no Natalie! Fuck, Becca. I saw her at the same time you did. She just showed up. And it's completely irrelevant when it comes to what you've done to us."

"What *I've* done to *you*?"

"Yes, Becca. You screwed us over. You used me to help you stop feeling whatever you were feeling and you made me fall in love with you!"

Tears stream down my cheeks, the pain of my heartbreak greater than any pain I've ever felt before.

Physical.

Emotional.

All of it.

He adds, "When do you plan on leaving?"

"It's not up to me," I say quietly.

"What the hell does that mean?"

"I don't know what you want from me!"

"How about we cut the secretive bullshit and start with the truth?" he shouts.

"Why are you yelling right now?"

"Because I'm pissed, Becs. How can I not be? You know how I feel. You can't just keep going on acting like what you're doing isn't wrong."

"You knew I was leaving!"

His entire body tenses. "So you're still going?"

"Josh…"

"I just don't see the point of this. Of any of it. You go and you leave Tommy and me behind, lost in the wake of your destruction and you think that's okay?"

"So you're breaking up with me?"

"Are we even really together?"

"You know I love you, Josh."

"And yet you're still leaving, *Becca*."

I turn and face the door, my tears falling fast and free while I close my eyes—submerged in the pain of heartbreak. "I'm gonna go."

"Fine! Go. What difference does it make? You do it now or you do it whenever the fuck you want to. What do I care?"

His apartment door opens and we both turn to the sound. Natalie stands in the doorway. "Josh, where are your towels?"

Josh faces me and ignores her. "If you have something to say, say it now."

I look over at Natalie, and back at him, and I think about Tommy. *My best friend.* The boy with the smile just like his father's. But as I look at Josh now, I realize how long it's been since I've seen it on him. And I know that I'm the reason for it.

I think about his confession—about wanting Tommy to have both his parents. And I remember his words—that he'll always love *her*.

So.

I stay silent.

And I go into the house and back up to my room, where *silence* becomes my new best friend.

CHAPTER 31

JOSHUA

Natalie enters the bedroom after her shower and sits down next to me on the bed. "What a crazy homecoming."

I stay quiet, not knowing what to say.

"I know this is weird for you, Josh, and I get it. Obviously we need to talk. That's why I came home. But when I called my parents to tell them I was here and they said that Thomas—"

"Tommy," I cut in.

"Right." She exhales loudly. "When they said Tommy was in the hospital, I drove straight there and I just... I mean, I was going to ease into things, you know? I was going to come back and talk to you and hopefully maybe earn a little of your trust back and see how you felt about me seeing Thomas—I mean *Tommy*—again. I just want to be part of his life, and yours, and..."

She keeps talking but I can't hear her, not over the blood rushing through my eardrums. "We can talk about it tomorrow." I stand up and grab a pillow off the bed. "You can sleep in here. I'll be on the couch." I turn to leave and out of habit, I glance out the window. And I regret it the instant I see her emerald eyes staring back at me. They're not the same though. They're lifeless, dull and dark.

CHAPTER 32

BECCA

Days pass.

Natalie stays.

I dedicate my life to staring at my wallpaper.

I can't even look at Tommy.

Not after what I did.

I don't look for Josh.

And I *definitely* don't look for *her*.

CHAPTER 33

JOSHUA

Days turn into weeks and nothing changes. The seconds tick by and the world exists without me ever really taking part in it. Natalie stays with us, sleeping in my bed while I take the couch. At first I was afraid to tell Hunter that she was back—that she was here with us. I was afraid of his reaction... of his judgment. I expected him to ask what the hell I was doing or why I let her in so easily. But what I didn't expect was for him to understand. And when I told him that he simply said, "It's what you've always wanted, right? I mean you always said that if she came back you wouldn't turn her away. Is Tommy happy?"

"Yeah," I'd told him, because he really was. He seemed happy to have two people in his life who genuinely loved him. And Natalie—she did. It may have taken her three years to realize that, but it was clear by the way she looked at him. By the hundreds of questions she'd ask about him—about his past and my plans for his future. Even the little things like how he likes his sandwiches cut. The questions only went one way. I never asked her about what she'd done in the three years she was away. I didn't care. And to be honest, I didn't really care about her at all. The feelings I'd had for her three years ago were no longer there. Natalie—she never really loved me. I don't think I ever really loved her. And I know that because while I lay on my uncomfortable couch every night, my son in one room and his mother in the other, all my thoughts are filled with Becca.

I find a letter in the mailbox. Hand written with my name on it —no stamp. No address. I open it quickly and pull out the check for a thousand dollars.

I knock on her door. "Becca!"

She answers, her eyes lowered.

"What is this?" I ask, waving the check in her face.

Without responding, she attempts to close the door in my face. I block it with my hand.

So she just stands there—one hand on the door, the other at her side.

"Becca."

Then she looks up and my heart breaks and nothing makes sense anymore. *Nothing.* Her eyes, filled with tears, are surrounded by darkness. Her nose is red. Her hair's a mess. And she's looking at me like she's not seeing *me.*

As if I'm a stranger.

I didn't want any of this, Becca, I want to tell her.

But I can't.

So I don't.

I ask, "What's the money for?"

She points to the back of the check and I flip it over.

Ambulance.

I look back up at her. "I see you've gone back to not talking… even to me?"

She shrugs.

I sigh. "Becca, I didn't mean what I said. I was just upset... how did you even get this much money?"

Her gaze drops again, and just when I think I'm not going to get an answer, I see her hand move, almost like she doesn't realize she's doing it. Her thumb spins against the ring on her index finger—the ring *I* gave her.

Both my hands grip my hair when realization sets in. "Holy shit, Becca. Please don't tell me you sold your camera!"

She looks up now, her tear soaked eyes pinning me to my spot. She blinks twice, the tears fall, and I reach out to wipe them away.

But she flinches.

She flinches away from *my* touch.

Then she sniffs, the only sound I've heard from her in days, and closes the door in my face.

And I hate everyone and everything and most of all, I hate myself.

Thanksgiving comes. I drop by my parent's house. Dad doesn't acknowledge me when I enter and the rest of the time is spent with him staring at the wall and me staring out the window.

We don't talk.

We never do.

Natalie has made herself nice and comfortable, decorating and rearranging furniture exactly the way she likes it. She likes owls, apparently. I didn't realize how much I hated them until my house was filled with them. But she cooks and cleans and she does everything a mother's supposed to do, and Tommy— he loves having her around.

I kick the dust off my work shoes and slip them off at the front door before I enter my house—or at least what used to be my house. The aroma of whatever Natalie's cooking floods my senses the second I walk in. "Hey Momma!" Tommy says, running toward her. I hate that he calls her Momma—that it took me almost a year to get him to say Daddy and she just gets to be called that. Apart from the seven hours in labor, she hasn't earned the name. Not even a little bit.

From the kitchen, Natalie looks at me and smiles; her blonde hair up in a bun, wearing her stupid owl-patterned apron.

"What are you making?" I ask.

She answers with something I've never heard of and I tell her I'm taking a shower.

She cooks a lot—something different every night.

She can't cook for shit.

I don't tell her that, though. I sit at the table and eat the damn food because I don't care about it enough to start something.

I don't care about her stupid food or her stupid owls and right now I'm pretty sure I don't care about much of anything.

I get out of the shower, make my way to the bedroom and open the only drawer that Natalie's left untouched. I get dressed and sit on the edge of the bed, and that's when I see it —a skateboard in the closet underneath a bunch of Natalie's clothes. I get up and walk over to it, dropping down on one knee so I can pull it out and look at it closer. And then all the air, along with any sense of hope I've had, leaves me.

I carry the skateboard to the kitchen. "What's this?" I ask Natalie.

She looks up at me and smiles. "You weren't supposed to see it! That Becca girl dropped it off a few days ago with a note that said she was working on it with Tommy as a Christmas present for you. It's only half done so she gave it to me and said

I could finish it with him if I wanted." She shrugs and walks over to me, ruffling my hair. "She's got a whole shoebox full of pictures of you and Tommy. Looks like someone has a border-line obsession with you. I'd be careful of that one."

I look down at the board again.

"Are you going to eat?" she asks.

I lift my gaze. "Maybe later."

There are cars parked in our street and I can hear a bunch of old ladies laughing from inside their house, but it doesn't deter me. I raise my fist, hesitating only for a moment, before knocking on their door. I have no plan of what I'm going to say and absolutely no expectations of her reaction. The door opens and there she is, her hair down and her eyes wide and clear and emerald and perfect. God, she's *so* perfect.

She inhales sharply and drops her gaze and only then do I get enough strength to look away from her face and down her body and the dress she's wearing, modest but hot. Like always. Her chest heaves, matching my breaths—breaths that seem so loud in my head and before she has time to shut the door in my face, I tell her, "You look beautiful." And I know it's dumb to say that, but I don't want her to ask what I'm doing and why I'm looking at her the way I am.

She looks down at her hands, now patting down her dress and then back at me, and her eyes…

Her.

Eyes.

God, I miss those eyes.

She points to the skateboard still in my hand.

I blink, pulling me out of my trance. "Natalie said that you came over and—"

She nods.

"You can finish it with Tommy. He'd like that."

She shakes her head and pushes the door forward, her face half hidden behind it.

"Who is it, sweetheart?" Chaz calls out from behind her.

Becca opens the door wider and drops her gaze just as Chazarae stands next to her. Chaz doesn't smile at me like she always does. She guides Becca out of the way, as if I'm here to hurt her in some way. And for the first time since shit went down with us, I wonder how much Chazarae knows and I wonder what she sees that I don't. And worst of all, I wonder what she thinks about me. "Can I help you, Joshua?"

I clamp my mouth shut.

Chazarae sighs. "Okay. Well, we have guests," she says, "and I don't want to keep them waiting." She points to Natalie's car. "Maybe you shouldn't keep yours waiting either."

"Yes, ma'am," I murmur, gripping the board tighter and turning away from her. She grasps my arm just as I'm about to step foot off the porch. I turn back around in time to see her closing the door behind her.

"I think it might be best if you don't bother Becca anymore, Joshua. Tommy's always welcome here, but for now, while Becca is living in my house, I have to make her my priority, and I'm sorry. I really am. But Becca—she's been through enough already, okay?"

I clear my throat, and let my shame and my self-loathing consume me. "Yes, ma'am."

Instead of returning to my apartment, I go back to my truck and pull out my every day board, then I skate out of the driveway and through the darkness of the streets until the chill of the wind makes my face numb and my muscles ache and I know it's late enough that Tommy will be down and hopefully Natalie will be asleep.

She isn't, though.

She's sitting on the couch, a beer in her hand, staring down at her phone.

"I've been calling you," she says, before I've even closed the door.

I pull out my phone and see the thirteen missed calls from her.

"Where have you been?"

I hide my eye roll and walk to the fridge where I pull out a beer of my own. "Nowhere."

"Did you see that Becca girl? Are you guys, like, sleeping together?"

I lean against the fridge, my eyes on her. "What are you still doing here, Natalie? Why haven't you left yet?"

She sets her beer on the coffee table in front of her and gets up; her gaze lowered as she makes her way to the kitchen. "I told you," she says, still looking down at the floor. "I wanted to get to know my son."

"And you can't do that from your house?"

"I didn't know I was such a burden. You've never mentioned anything before." She looks up at me now—her insecurities and her doubts showing. "I don't want to leave but if you make me I can't stop it. I like being here, Josh. I like being with Tommy and I like being with you."

"You're three years late, Nat." I sigh. "I'm taking back my bed. And don't ever breathe Becca's name again."

CHAPTER 34

JOSHUA

Christmas morning looks like Toys R Us vomited in the living room. To say that Natalie went overboard would be an understatement. I have no idea where she plans to put all this stuff because it sure as shit won't fit neatly in my tiny apartment. Hopefully she'll find her own place soon and she can take all of her shit with her.

I'm too busy picking up wrapping paper from every surface possible so Natalie beats me to opening the door only seconds after the knock sounds. "Hi Becca," Natalie says, and I drop everything in my hands and bolt for the door. She nods at Nat and then takes a step back when I come into view. Tommy yells Becca's name and for some reason this makes her cringe. She hands Natalie a box and points to the name on it: *Captain LoonySpoon.*

"Who the hell is Captain LoonySpoon?" Nat asks. I push her out of the way and close the door between us. Becca's already two steps down the stairs when I grab her arm. "Becca, wait!" She stops in her tracks and slowly faces me.

Inside, Tommy's crying, screaming Becca's name.

"You can give him your present yourself, Becca." I try to settle my nerves. "You're allowed to see him. I'm sorry if I made you feel like—"

She shakes her head, cutting me off. Then grimaces as Tommy's cry for her gets louder. She looks from the door to me, and then points to her arm.

"His arm is fine. It's healing well. I told him the cast gives him super powers."

Her throat bobs with her swallow and she nods. She starts to turn away but the front door opens and Tommy's in Natalie's arms, crying Becca's name again. "I can't control him," Natalie snaps. She places Tommy on the ground and Becca gasps as soon he starts down the stairs to get to her. She lifts her hand, her palm up, and he stops instantly. Slowly, she looks between all three of us standing on the landing and I wonder what the hell she could possibly be thinking.

She probably thinks we're some happy family.

We're not.

She was.

She and Tommy and I—we *were.*

She climbs the steps until she's two down from him and bends down so they're eye to eye. She runs her fingers across his cast, her eyes filling with tears. And then she reaches out, her arms around him, her hug so fierce and so full of love that my chest tightens, the pain so overwhelming it forces a sob out of me—because, fuck, how can everything feel so right and be so fucking wrong?

Tommy pulls back slightly, his eyes on hers and his hands on her cheeks, wiping her tears. She doesn't flinch—not for him.

"You have a booboo?" he asks her and she nods.

"Where?"

She chokes back on her own sob, her eyes only for him. Then she points to her chest.

Tommy frowns and kisses the spot on her chest she just pointed to. "Daddy says kisses make all booboos better," he tells her.

I hold my breath.

She smiles sadly and taps her nose followed by her chest. He nods and throws his arms around her neck, squeezing tight. "I love you, too, Becca."

~

It's a hard emotion to explain—what it feels like to fake every single moment of your life. To breathe but to not exist. To smile but to not be happy. To nod and agree but to not really care. And some nights, I'd put Tommy down to sleep and listen to him speak and there'd be an ache in my chest and I didn't know why. So as I sit on the edge my bed, beer in hand, and listen to the fireworks go off around me—the cheers as hundreds of people bring in the New Year—I can't even find it in myself to look forward to the next day, let alone three hundred and sixty-five of them.

Natalie knocks on my door and lets herself in, because apparently this is her house now and she doesn't need permission to do anything. She's wearing one of my work shirts, which she uses to sleep in. Her legs, long and tanned and much more defined than when I'd been between them over three years ago, are bare as she makes her way over to me. She stops in front of me, her hands at her sides. "Happy New Year, Joshua."

I rub my eyes and try to fight off the effects of alcohol. "Yeah. You, too."

She steps forward, between my legs, and I don't stop her.

Because I don't care.

But when her hand reaches out and cups my face, my eyes drift shut and my breath leaves me in a shudder. She lifts my chin with her finger and I keep my eyes closed because I don't want to see her and I already know what she wants and a part of me wants it, too. Not because I want *her* but because I want to feel *something* that isn't *nothing*. Her hand takes mine and settles it on her leg and I don't take it back. I don't remove it. Then she whispers my name and my eyes snap open and she's undoing the buttons of my shirt she's wearing. And *dammit,* I miss this—not *her*—but I miss this touch, this intimacy, this *need.* Both my are hands on her legs now, drifting higher until I feel the fabric of her panties. I focus on her fingers as they undo the last button and she spreads the shirt open. My gaze moves from the top of her panties, to her stomach, where stretch marks streak down her skin. I trace a single one with my finger, from the bottom of her breasts to the side of her belly button. The marks are faded now, marks we'd created together, back when we thought we were in love and that love would get us through anything.

"I know they're gross," she says. "The guys I'm with are always turned off by it."

"What?" I whisper.

"Yeah…" Her fingers trace where mine had just been, clueless to the fury she'd just unleashed inside me.

I push her away from me so quickly she stumbles into the wall behind her. "Get out!" I shout, getting up and pulling her suitcase out of the closet. I fill it with whatever clothes of hers I can scramble, all while she cries, trying to stop me as she buttons *my* shirt to hide *her* fucking shame. She grabs my arm as I carry her shit down the hallway. I shake her off; the rage, the anger, the fire within me uncontainable, and for the first time ever, I don't hold back. I open the front door and throw her crap from the top of the stairs down onto the driveway.

"Josh, stop!"

I turn to her. "Get. Out!"

She cries harder and it just makes me sick. Like, deep in my gut, *sick.* I push past her and pick up anything and everything that belongs to her. All her shoes at the door, her stupid cookbooks, her stupid owls... so many fucking owls.

CHAPTER 35

BECCA

---

rage

> **noun**
> **violent uncontrollable anger.**

At first I thought the screaming and yelling were that of a celebration. But the screaming got louder. Louder than the fireworks, and then the unmistakable sound of Tommy's cry fills my ears. I push off the covers and race downstairs, meeting Grams in the hallway, our shocked faces matching each other's. The second I open the door I know it's bad.

Josh's at the top of his stairs throwing clothes and books down onto the driveway, adding to the pile already there.

Josh yells.

Natalie screams.

Fireworks go off.

Josh yells louder.

Natalie cries harder.

But Tommy—he cries the hardest.

Josh swears as he pushes Natalie off of him, then goes back in the house, I guess finding more shit to throw. Natalie's still crying, begging him to stop, and Tommy... he just stands at the top of the steps covering his ears and crying in the corner—away from his fighting parents. "Daddy, stop!"

"Get that little boy," Grams says. My bare feet race up the stairs. I pick up Tommy and shield him from the destruction going on around him.

"Take him inside," I tell Grams, handing him to her. And I march right back up there. I don't know what I'm doing but I need to do something so I step in front of Josh and block him. His eyes are wide, filled with rage. He freezes, holding an owl figure in the air. "What are you doing, Becca?" he says through gritted teeth. I wrap my arms around his waist and push him into his house. He trips on his feet and lands on his ass. I raise my hand, telling him to stay there.

Then I close the door just as Natalie yells, "He's lost it!"

I turn to her and in my mind, I punched her—twice; one on her perfect nose and one on her perfect pouty lips. But in reality, I raise my chin and stand toe to toe with her. "He's allowed to lose it," I yell over the fireworks, my voice breaking in and out. "And you need to leave. Now! Before I call the cops."

She rolls her eyes. "For what? Domestic violence?"

"Trespassing." I point a finger into her chest. "Fuck. Off."

I wait at the top of the stairs, arms crossed, while she gathers her shit into a pile on top of her car. Josh's front door opens and keys are thrown, I assume hers, but I don't get a chance to ask because he's running down the stairs toward her. I chase after him, trying to get him to stop. He stands in front of her while a single firework goes off for the last time. Now we're surrounded by nothing but still, dead, air. "You're fucking insane," she says to him. He doesn't respond, just storms past her and opens the toolbox in the tray of his truck. He pulls out a board, flips it in his hand and then raises it above his head...

I yell, or at least try, for him to stop and I rush toward him. With my arms around his waist I beg for him not to do what he does next. I beg and I cry until he pushes me off of him and I find myself on my knees, watching the boy I love destroy one of the few things he loves. Over and over, I watch him smash a skateboard into his truck, shattering it to pieces. And when one board can no longer take his assault, he pulls out another. And then another. And all I can do is watch him—watch the destruction caused by years of pain, of anger, and of neglect, and I cry. I cry into my hands, my heart breaking, until I feel a presence next to me.

Grams kneels beside me, holds my hand, and we lower our heads.

And then we pray.

We pray until the sounds of splinting wood and shattered glass and metal finally stop and are replaced with Josh's quiet sobs. I stand up and go to his apartment where I find his phone on his nightstand and I call Robby.

I need help.

He doesn't answer.

So I call the only other person I can think to call.

CHAPTER 36

JOSHUA

The only source of light comes from the moon and from the porch but still, I can see the cracks and the splotches of blood as they begin to pool in the lines of my hands, all caused by the layers of wood that splinted and punctured my skin. My breaths are loud—heavy—but unwilling to settle and I feel like that same kid three years ago standing in the alleyway between two buildings, kicking the shit out of brick wall because life fucking hates me. And then a light shone upon us and Chazarae showed up, saving us.

But no one can save me now.

I can't even save myself.

And I sure as hell can't save *him*.

A car pulls in and screeches to a stop. The headlights blind me as I stumble to stand. Doors open and close and the familiar outline of a body walks toward me. My eyes narrow at Becca. "You fucking called him?" I snap. And the rage is back because he's the last fucking person I want to see right now.

"What the fuck is going on?" Hunter says, eying the broken boards and my damaged truck.

"Fuck off, Hunter. Go home," I whisper, walking toward him. I push his chest and he pushes me back. Two years ago he was bigger, stronger. Now I'm sure I can take him. Because he's confused, and I'm angry, and anger always wins.

"What the fuck is wrong with you?" he snaps, hiding his wife behind him. His confusion turns to fear and he should be afraid—he has no fucking idea who I am anymore.

He chose that.

Not me.

"You, Hunter!" I press a finger into his chest and stand toe-to-toe with him. "You're what's fucking wrong with me. You said *we*! You said no matter what happens, always *we*! And the first chance you get, you fuck off with Chloe and you leave me and Tommy behind! There's no fucking *we*, Hunter. It's just me. It's *always* been *just* me!" His eyes are wide as he takes in my words. But I don't fucking care. I don't care about anything.

I turn to Natalie, but I don't look at her, because if I do I'm sure I'd puke. "Did you hear that, Nat? Three fucking years I've done everything alone because you're a selfish coward and you can't ever think about anyone but yourself. Do you remember what you said? You said, *'Promise we'll do it together.'* And I did. I fucking promised you and we had son!" I shout. "We had a fucking a son and it meant nothing to you! How the fuck do you live with yourself? *How?*" I wipe my eyes, my tears unstoppable. "And then you come here," I say through a sob, my voice lowering. "You come here and you act like it doesn't matter. Like your fucked up choices didn't affect me or Tommy or *time*, and while you spent the past three years fucking any guy who wasn't turned off by your stretch marks, the marks made by *MY* son... you know what I've been doing? I've been killing myself trying to raise *OUR* kid. Trying to do everything right so he doesn't ever feel like he needed you in his life. But he did,

Nat. He fucking needed you. So did I. And you just left!" Every single part of me breaks. Inside. Outside. All of it. I turn to Becca, her tears matching mine. "And you…"

Next to her, Chazarae warns, "Don't, Joshua." So I turn to her instead. "Do you know how hard it is to not know… to not understand why you did what you did, but every day I feel like I'm under so much pressure to be perfect—to not fuck up—so I'm worthy of you and your fucking generosity and I'm so scared of fucking up. *So* scared. But here I am! I'm fucking up!"

"Josh!" Becca yells.

I face her, watching as her hand covers her mouth and her shoulders heave with each sob. "I *hate* you, Becca."

Chazarae throws her arms around Becca's shoulders and tries to guide her away, but she holds her spot, wipes her cheeks, and lifts her chin.

She wants to hear it.

I'll fucking say it.

"I hate you the most. I hate that I love you. I hate that Tommy loves you. I hate that you're the fucking greatest thing to ever happen to me. I hate that I thought you saw *me*—that you understood *me.* I hate that you came into my life and turned my entire world upside down. I hate that I think about you every second of every fucking day. I hate that you're the last fucking thing I think about. I hate that I still wake up thinking about you. And I hate that in between all that I fucking dream about you. You and your fucking eyes. I *hate* your eyes." Her tears have stopped and she just stands there, unblinking, unmoving, taking every single blow I deliver. "And I hate that you did all this because you're leaving me. You're leaving *us*! You're just like everyone else!"

"What happened to you, Josh?" she whispers.

"You did!" I shout. "You and Hunter, and Natalie, and my *dad*! You all leave us. Because he's fucking dying, Becca, and I can't do anything about it!"

She releases a sob, her hand reaching out for me but I cower away from her touch.

"All I can do is watch him die because he won't even talk to me. He hates me so much he can't even fucking look at me!"

"Josh…" She reaches for me again but I take a step back.

"No! Just don't, okay? It doesn't change shit. It's done. Just like *us*!"

Her gaze drops and the sound of my thumping heart fills my ears. I wait for the anger to pass, but it doesn't, it just builds more and more as I stand there, watching them all watch me.

Then I see Chloe from the corner of my eye as she comes up beside me. "Get in the car," she says quietly.

"What?" I turn to her just as she pinches my ear and drags me behind her and toward their car. Her breath is warm against my ear, or maybe it's because she's about to rip the fucker right off my head. "I said *get in the fucking car!*"

I keep quiet, my head lowered as Chloe drives—more like speeds—through the residential streets to who the fuck knows where. Probably somewhere to kill me and dump my body.

"How's your ear?" she shouts. I think she's pissed and I highly doubt she gives a shit about my ear.

"It's fine."

"I'm sorry," she says, but she's still yelling, and now I'm sure she's pissed. "It's just that you got me so angry. And I don't know. Something else."

"Something else?"

"Shut up!"

I cringe. "Okay…"

We don't speak another word until she drives onto the half-court and parks right in the middle. "Get out!"

I do as she says because right now I think she might be a little crazy.

She waits for me at the front of the car, the headlights still on. I stand in front of her, my hands in my pockets. I watch her. She watches me. Then she shoves my chest just like I'd done to her husband. "You're a dick!"

I roll me eyes. "I know."

"I'm sorry about your dad," she snaps. "But he's not dead, asshole. He's *dying*. There's a big difference. You still have time with him," she says, her voice softer. "If you want to make it right. Make it right. You're old enough to make that choice, Josh." Her voice cracks and so does my heart because, fuck, it's *Chloe*. The girl who's married to my best friend, the girl who was diagnosed with the same cancer that killed her mom and her aunt, and she stands in front me, her shoulders squared and jaw set in determination. She stands tall, *brave*, in the middle of a world she could've given up on.

Just like I have.

But she hasn't.

With a sigh, I pull on her arm and bring her into me, one hand on her back, the other in her hair that wasn't there a year ago. "I'm sorry, Chloe. You're right. About everything."

Her body relaxes against mine and when she pulls back, she wipes her eyes. "I really am sorry about your dad. Please don't tell me it's cancer because I'll kick the shit out of something if it is."

I smile—which is strange given the situation. "It's not. He's got um…" I swallow nervously, knowing it's the first time the words will leave my mouth. "Chronic kidney disease. It came out of nowhere."

"How'd you find out?"

"My mom. She came to see me when he decided to quit dialysis. He'd rather live a full life than a long one."

Chloe nods once, giving me a sad smile before saying, "You know what we need?"

"What?"

She smirks before going back to the car. I follow. She reaches into the glove box and finds what I think is a carton of tampons. "What the fire truck?"

"Relax," she says through a laugh and pulls out a bag of joints.

I step back. "I don't know, Chloe. You remember the last time we did that?"

She rolls her eyes. "I have a script." She points to herself. "Cancer."

I nod. "Right."

"Just don't tell Blake. He doesn't know I have it anymore. Hence the tampons."

"Got it."

She uses the dash lighter to spark one, smiles as she inhales and then hands it to me. I look at the joint between my fingers. "Fuck it." I take a puff and sit on the hood of the car with her. She lies down and I lie next to her.

"So your mom just came to see you because she wanted you to know?"

I pass her the joint and hold my breath, feeling the weed burn in my throat before releasing it. "No. She wanted me to get tested as a living donor."

Her eyes snap to mine. "And did you?"

"Yeah, I got tested."

"And?"

"No go. Something about tissue incompatibility."

"I'm sorry."

I shrug. "Mom says it's for the best anyway. If he ever found out it came from me he'd probably kill me."

"You mean you would've done it without him knowing?"

"Of course."

"Why would you do that?"

"Because he's my dad," I say simply.

She looks up at the stars and I do the same. And we stay that way, passing the joint between us.

"Did it feel good?" she asks.

"What?"

"Yelling and beating the shit out of things and just letting it all out."

"Yeah. At the time. Not so much now, though."

She rolls to her side and looks at me with a smirk on her face. "I want to try it," she whispers.

"Go ahead."

She starts to stand up on the hood of the car. "It stays between us, okay? Don't tell Blake."

"You're keeping a lot of secrets from your husband."

"It's for the best. Trust me." She hands me the joint and I take a puff as I get off the hood, waving my hand through the air.

"The stage is yours, C-Lo."

She clears her throat and suddenly looks unsure. Then she nods once and rolls her shoulders. "Fuck you, cancer!" she shouts, her voice echoing through the night sky.

"Yeah!" I encourage. "Fuck you, cancer!"

Her head throws back with laughter, and then she stops. Her smile fades and her breaths become heavy. She shakes out her hands and I notice her eyes begin to glaze with tears. She sniffs once, her sob following after it.

I swallow anxiously, waiting for her to continue.

"I was eighteen!" she shouts to no one. "No one should have to deal with that at eighteen! Wasn't it enough? My mom? My aunt? Weren't they enough for you that you had to take me, too?"

I stay still, my heart in my throat and my mind on her and Hunter.

"I'm sick. And I'm tired. I'm so fucking tired of acting like it didn't bother me! Do you know what it's like to sit in a fucking chair for eight hours straight while the person you love sits and holds your hand and you wonder the entire time *why?* Why the fuck am I here? Why is *he* here? And I have to pretend like I'm okay with you. I'm not okay with you, cancer. Not at all! I fucking hate you. I hate everything about you." She's pacing up at down on the hood now, her footsteps heavy against the metal. Her fists are balled at her sides—the anger and frustration and hurt all coming out. "And now everyone around me treats me like I'm going to die at any minute. Blake—he watches me like a fucking hawk. He helps me with every little thing and I love him so much but I hate *that.* If I want to jump up and down, I'll fucking jump up and down!" I cringe as she jumps on the hood, denting the fuck out of it. "And I'll do it and I'll laugh about it and he doesn't need to stop me! He doesn't need to tell me that I'll overexert myself and that I need to calm down. *I don't want to calm down!*" she shouts, crying as she does. She wipes her face across her sleeve and looks up. Then she collapses.

"Holy shit!" I rush to her. "Are you okay?"

She's fucking laughing. "You're just like Blake. I'm not going to die, Josh." She takes the joint from me and inhales a drag, then blows it out slowly.

"You overexerted yourself, didn't you?"

She pouts. "Yes. Don't—"

"Tell Blake. I got it."

I lie back down on the hood with her. "Did it help?"

"At the time," she says, "Not so much now."

"Yeah."

"You know what I hate the most?"

"What?"

"The word remission."

I face her. "Yeah?"

"It should be called intermission. Like they have in plays. Or, like, TV shows when they have the mid-season breaks. It's like the diagnosis and the chemo are the first half of the season. Then the intermission comes and you're just sitting there waiting for the next appointment. And it's like... *oh yay, the show ended well, you're cancer free*. Or, it can be like, *oh a cliffhanger... the cancer's still there. Sorry.* And then you have to wait for the next season and the first half is just a fucking recap of everything from the previous season until another fucking intermission. And then you wait for the outcome and it still might not end—it can still be a cliffhanger. I fucking hate cliffhangers." She rolls her head to the side and looks at me. "And I fucking hate cancer."

"Fire truck cancer," I tell her.

She smiles. "Fire truck it right in the ass." She pounds her fist on the hood. "With this car."

"With a fire truck."

She laughs. "Fire truck it with a fire truck, right in the ass."

"We're so high."

"Maybe." She shrugs. Then moves closer and settles her head on my chest. "Hey Josh?"

"Yeah Chloe?"

And I'll never forget what she says next; "There's a big difference between being happy and being selfish. Choose to be happy. Fire truck the rest."

CHAPTER 37

JOSHUA

I wake up in bed, my head throbbing, and I try to remember, or maybe forget, last night. Something warm rubs against my leg and I flinch and pull away, looking to my side. Hunter's in my bed, his head resting on his outstretched arm. "Morning, Princess."

I jump up and as far away from him as possible. "What the fire truck!"

"You were so good last night," he says, puckering his lips and blowing me a kiss. "Best I've ever had."

"You're weird."

He smiles. "What's the plan for today?"

"Apologizing to everyone until I'm blue in the face."

"Who first?"

I start to respond but sirens blaring interrupt me. I wait for them to pass but they just get louder.

"Josh!" Chloe yells from the living room.

I run out of the bedroom and go to her. She's looking out the window, and I do the same and the first thing I see are two paramedics jumping out of the ambulance. My heart stops. I slip on my shoes and point to Tommy. "Keep him away," I tell Chloe and she nods and carries him to his room.

My stomach in knots, I race down the stairs. "What happened?" I ask the paramedics. "Stay there, sir," one says, and the only thing I can think is that something's happened to Chazarae. I try to move, but my feet are glued to the ground and every single breath is a struggle.

More sirens.

Cops this time.

An officer approaches and stands in front of me while another runs inside. The officer's mouth's moving but I can't hear what he's saying.

"Chazarae! Becca!"

Finally, my feet come back to life and I try to run inside but arms around my waist stop me from going any further. The officer speaks again but I can't hear anything over the blood rushing in my ears.

I see Blake.

I see an officer.

And then I see a paramedic, his hands gripping the end of a stretcher. I see feet on the end of it and breathe out Chaz's name. And then I see her. But she's standing, walking next to the stretcher. Her shoulders shake. Her tears fall fast.

Then I look down.

And I see *her.*

"BECCA!"

CHAPTER 38

JOSHUA

Chazarae doesn't let me ride with them so Blake drives me to the hospital.

"Rebecca Owens," I tell the nurse at the desk.

She types on the computer, her eyes darting from side to side. All while I feel like I'm dying from fear of the unknown. "She's just been admitted, sweetheart," she says, her eyes full of pity as she looks up at me. "Are you family?"

I almost say that I'm her boyfriend, but then I realize I'm not. I'm nothing. I check her nametag, hoping if I'm more personal it might help my cause. "No, Nurse Ruby. I'm not."

She smiles, but it matches the pity in her eyes. "You're welcome to wait."

As if I'd be doing anything else.

"Come on, man." Hunter grabs my arm and leads me to the waiting room chairs. I watch the seconds tick by, my heart never slowing. Every fifteen minutes I get up and ask the same nurse the same question. I want to know what the fuck happened and if she's okay. The nurse's answer is always the same. She can't give me much information but as soon as she can she will. I thank her. Because she could be an asshole and tell me to fuck off, but she doesn't. Then I sit back down, wait fifteen minutes and do it all over again. Hunter stays by my side, never leaving. "You can go," I tell him.

His smile matches the nurses. "Always *we*, Josh" is all he says.

And that's all it takes for me to break.

Three hours I've been sitting in the waiting room, living through the questions racing in my mind. I've stayed quiet, stayed as calm as I can. And now—now I lose it.

He stays silent, his hand on my shoulder as I cry into my hands.

"I'm sorry, Hunter."

"Me, too, Warden. For everything." After a sigh, he asks, "Do you want to talk about it? The stuff with your dad?"

"Not now."

"You should, though, with someone. Anyone. You can't keep that shit bottled inside. I don't think your skateboards can handle it anymore."

I'd forgotten about the boards. "Fuck."

Hunter shakes my shoulder and points to the door. Rob and Kim walk in, their eyes frantic as they search the room.

"Rob," I call out. "What are you doing here?"

His shoulders drop with his heavy exhale. They rush toward me. "What happened?"

"I don't know. How did you—"

"We dropped by the house and Chloe told us you were here and… Jesus fucking Christ, Josh. I'm sorry. Do you know anything?"

"Nothing."

"Have you asked?"

I ignore his question because it's stupid and it doesn't deserve an answer. "I'm sorry about the truck."

"Fuck the truck, Josh, who gives a shit? I'm worried about you."

"I'm fine."

He sits down on the other side of me. "Clearly."

"I don't want to deal with it right now," I say, my voice rising. "I just need to focus on Becca. *Please.* Just let me do that."

Kim disappears for a few minutes and returns with coffees for everyone. "I heard one of the nurses talking. It's one of their busiest days. A lot of idiots partying too hard to celebrate the New Year. A lot of overdoses and alcohol poisoning." She sits down next to Robby.

And we wait.

Seconds turn to minutes. Minutes turn to hours. And my heart never slows.

"Josh?" Nurse Ruby calls.

I jump up from my seat, so do the others. "Is she okay?" I ask once I'm at the desk.

"I'm about to finish my shift but I couldn't leave without finding out *something* to tell you. Rebecca—"

"Becca," I cut in. "She doesn't like Rebecca."

She smiles the same sad smile. "Becca's moved from critical to stable. The doctors have been working with her all day. And that's basically all I can tell you."

With my heart in my throat, I sigh, relieved. "So she's okay?"

Nurse Ruby nods once. "Hopefully she will be. I hope you don't mind but I spoke to her grandmother. I told her you were out here waiting," she says, but the look on her face isn't one that's delivered with good news. "She says that Becca doesn't— I mean *isn't* ready for visitors just yet."

"Wait. You said *doesn't*," I say, a sob filtering out of me. I rub my hand against my chest, trying to somehow soothe the massive ache; the pain of my heart breaking. "She doesn't want to see me?"

"That's not what she said," Rob says, his hand on my back.

Nurse Ruby glances at him quickly before returning to me and I can see it in her eyes; that's exactly what she meant and she knows it's more important for me to know the truth than it is to protect my feelings.

"I've convinced Becca's grandmother to come out and at least speak to you, Josh. I think you deserve that much."

I hold my breath and nod.

"I have to go now." She stands up and walks out of nurse's station and stops right in front of me. "Good luck with everything, okay?"

And then I hug her. I don't really know why but I feel like I need to, and she needs to know that right now, I needed her or at least someone like her on my side. "Thank you so much. For everything."

An entire hour passes. We sit in silence. All four of us. Not a single word spoken. Then Chazarae walks out from the ER doors and we stand, in unison, slow but steady.

She looks like death.

I *feel* like death.

There's no smile on her face—not even a pitiful one. There's nothing. And it's exactly what I deserve. She stops in front of me, her hands at her sides as she eyes each of us individually. When she finally settles on me, she clears her throat. "It's not that she doesn't *want* to see you. It's that she *can't.* So go home, Joshua."

My stomach plummets. "I'm not going anywhere."

She inhales sharply, her eyes narrowed. Then she takes a step forward, lowering her voice to whisper. "When Becca moved in, I asked you for one thing; to leave her alone. Why couldn't you have just left her alone?"

I try to swallow the lump in my throat, but it's too fucking big, so instead I speak through it. "Can you just tell me what happened? Please."

"Go home, Josh."

I refuse to go home.

Not until I see her.

Kim takes over watching Tommy for Chloe. Chloe goes home to her parents' house where they'd spent New Year's Eve. I guess that's how they were able to get to my house so quickly last night. Hunter doesn't leave. Robby doesn't leave. Day turns to night. Robby calls my mom. I have no idea why. She shows up with food. They eat the food. I don't. "Let's go for a walk," Robby says. And I agree. Because it's better than sitting in the waiting room, watching people come and go. Some give up on waiting. Some get to see the people they care about. I don't do either. I'm an outsider—sitting still—watching the world move on around me.

But I can't move on without her.

He takes me outside where the air is cool but it doesn't help me to breathe any easier. We walk just outside the perimeter of the hospital, my phone gripped tightly in my hand in case Hunter calls with any news from Chazarae. I know he won't call. I know she won't come.

We sit down on a bench just outside a different entrance. More sitting. I could've done this inside. He doesn't speak. What is there left to say?

"I fucked up," I tell him.

"We all fuck up sometimes," he says.

"I hate New Year's Day," someone else says, and I look up to see two nurses, both male, standing a few feet away. They're smoking. One's super tall. The other's super short.

The short one says, "Me, too. There are so many fuckers in here that take things too far and think they're invincible."

"Right?" the tall one agrees. "I had one come in this morning. Here we go again, I thought. But it wasn't. The girl tried to kill herself."

My entire body tenses. Next to me, Robby sits forward.

We listen.

"Ugh," the short nurse says. "Those are the worst. It's like... I don't know about you, Danny, but I took this job to save lives of those who actually want to live. Don't waste my time with this shit. You want to kill yourself? Die, already."

"Right?" Danny says again, taking a puff of his smoke and crossing an arm over his chest. "It's fucking sad. Like this girl, she's young, hot as hell. Her eyes are fucking ridiculous. How hard could life be that you'd want to do that, you know?"

I stand up, my blood boiling and my fists balled.

Robby stands up next to me. "Be careful, Josh," he warns.

The short nurse says, "That's fucked. What do you think happened?"

Danny scoffs, blowing smoke out at the same time. "Same old shit. Some fucking guy doesn't love her and she thinks the world's over."

Three steps.

That's all it takes for me to get to them. I push the short one out of the way and within seconds, my fist is on Danny's stomach. Blow after blow until he's on the floor. From the corner of my eye—I see Robby holding back Danny's friend. I open my mouth to speak, but no words could ever convey how I feel, so instead I communicate with my fist, twice more, before I stand.

Danny scuffles, but I'm ready, waiting for his exchange. "Call the cops," he tells the other nurse, his eyes on mine. He won't fight back though. He's a pussy. And a fucking asshole.

I step back and start walking away—the adrenaline, the anger, the understanding, all of it pulsing through my veins.

"You call the cops," Robby says, his voice loud but even. "I'll share with the medical board every single thing I just heard." I stop in my tracks and turn back around because Robby's fighting *my* fight and he doesn't need to. "What do you think would happen to your license if they hear what I've recorded?" He holds up his phone. "Maybe next time you can watch your fucking mouths and keep your fucked up shitty opinions to yourselves."

Danny silently brushes down his clothes and heads back into the hospital.

Robby comes up beside me and we walk together, side by side, step by step. "Did you really record it?"

"Nah." After no response from me, he says, "I'm sorry, Josh."

Neither of us mention what they said and whom it was about. But at least I know why she's here. Only now I wish I didn't.

CHAPTER 39

JOSHUA

Hunter sleeps on the floor of the waiting room. So does Robby. Eventually, so do I.

"Joshua?" I hear, and for a moment I think I'm a kid again and it's my mother's voice trying to wake me for school. For a second I'm annoyed—but then reality hits. Fuck, I wish I was that kid. I'd take all the Monday mornings in the history of the world if it took me away from this reality.

I sit up and thank Nurse Ruby when she hands me the coffee. "I figured you could use it," she says, the same pitiful smile from yesterday.

"Do you know anything more?" I ask, not sharing the fact that *I* do.

She shakes her head, her lips pressed tight. "My shift just started. But I checked in on her first thing before I even knew you were here." She glances at Rob and Hunter still asleep in the corner of the room we've deemed as ours. "She's beautiful, Josh," she says, her gaze dropping.

She checked in on her... saw her file. She probably thinks the same of me as those asshole nurses from last night—she just doesn't have the guts to tell me to my face.

"I know," I whisper, a lump forming in my throat. "She's... my everything."

Nurse Ruby clears her throat. "She's still not ready to see anyone, Josh. Why don't you go—"

"Not you, too," I cut in. "You can't make me leave, right? I mean there's no law that states I can't be here."

"No," she says, looking right in my eyes. "You can stay."

She starts to leave but I grab her arm. "I know she doesn't want to see me. I know she hates me. I know that seeing me will most likely make it worse. I know that you know that, too. But I can't *not* see her. I just... I need to talk to her and I need to touch her and I need to know that she's okay. And I need to tell her that I love her, that she's everything to me and that..." I choke on sob. "That I'm sorry. I'm so fucking sorry."

Nurse Ruby takes me in her arms, holding me, all while I cry unashamed.

"I love her," I mumble. "And I don't want to exist without her."

She pulls back, her tear soaked eyes on mine again. With her hands on my shoulders, she nods once, and then she's gone.

She doesn't speak to me for the rest of the day.

Rob and Hunter barely speak to me.

I wonder if they've worked it out—that I'm the reason she's here. I wonder if they hate me as much as *I* hate me.

At some point, Chazarae walks out. She sees me but she doesn't acknowledge me. An hour later she returns, showered and changed, Bible in her hand. Like the fucking Bible can rewind time and erase the past. It can't do shit. And even with that in mind, I find myself pacing the floors, praying to a God who knows I don't believe in him.

. . .

Kim calls. She says Tommy's been asking for me. He wants to talk to me, so I let him. He talks about anything and everything and I listen to his voice, hear the joy in his words, and I try—I try so damn hard—to hide the sadness in mine.

I go back to breathing without really existing, all while the world moves on around me.

Seconds turn to minutes, minutes turn to hours.

And I wait.

CHAPTER 40

BECCA

"I understand," the nurse says to Grams. Her voice is soft and warm, unlike the male nurse I had yesterday. She's not my nurse, though. I know this because she came in this morning, skimmed over my chart and just looked at me—right into my eyes. She smiled sadly and then left.

She comes in often but never checks my chart.

The other nurses check the chart every single time they come in. I wonder what they're looking for—a note that proclaims I'm no longer crazy and they can go back to taking care of people who need it?

"Just think about it," the nurse says, her hand on Grams' arm.

Grams nods and waits for the nurse to leave before coming to me.

She sets her Bible next to my arm and slowly takes my hand. Her fingers skim the bandages around my thumb and I look away because the heartache in her eyes is too much to handle.

"I've been lost," she says, and I can already tell she's crying. "I don't know what the right thing to do is here and I want to do the right thing, sweetheart. I want to protect you but I don't know if that's the best for you. I've been praying and looking to God for the answers but I'm torn. Matthew 6:7 says: *Blessed are the merciful for they shall receive mercy.*" She sniffs once, and I finally look at her. "It's not me who needs to offer forgiveness. It's you. It is you he has wronged. Not I. And it's wrong for me to make that choice for you."

My eyes narrow.

Her tears fall faster.

Next to me, the heart monitor beeps—the space between each sound shorter than the last.

"Josh is here," she says, and I fight to breathe. "He hasn't left. Not once." She lowers her gaze. "Becca, I told him you couldn't see him."

"Why?" I mouth.

"Because I didn't want him near you. I couldn't forgive him for the way he'd treated you. For bringing you back to this place, back to the darkness of your past." She looks up now. "Do you want to see him, Becca?"

Grams waits until there's only ten minutes left of visiting hours before getting him. I know if I see him any earlier, he'll want to stay.

I'll want him to stay.

And he can't.

I don't move when he walks in, his hands in his pockets and his head lowered. He doesn't look at me either. He simply sits down on the chair next to my bed, the same one Grams has been in since I was moved into this room.

His hands rise and pause an inch over my arm. His eyes lock on the bandages around my thumb and circle around my hand down to my wrist. He doesn't touch me. I don't want him to touch me. Then he pulls back, his hands on his lap. He looks up, first at the wall opposite me, and slowly, at me.

And I feel like I've died.

Like the breaths I'd been taking are no longer possible and everything inside me has stopped.

Just stopped.

But I know it's not true because I can still see him. I can see the lifelessness in his eyes, the darkness that surrounds them— the heaving motion of his chest and quivering of his lips. I see him. But he's not himself.

And neither am I.

He clears his throat, his eyes on mine.

"You look beautiful," he whispers, and my eyes drift shut, releasing the tears. His hands jerk forward, wanting to wipe them away, but I beat him to it.

"I looked into schools in St. Louis," he says, "for Tommy. There are some good elementary schools around Washington University. Robby says he'll write me a really good reference. I can get a job there. I've saved up enough that we can move there. All three of us. We can get a two-bedroom apartment or something. Or, I mean, even if you want to live on campus or whatever, we'll just stay close." He sniffs once and wipes his noise. "We can go now if you want. When you get out or whenever. Whatever you want, baby. I don't..." He breaks off on a sob and I do nothing but watch him, tears flowing fast and free. "I don't want to live in a world that you're not part of. I don't know how to live without you. And I'm sorry, Becca." He reaches out now, his hands on my arm. I don't flinch from his touch. I don't move at all. But I don't love it like I used to. "I'm so fucking sorry. And I love you so much. You have to know that—that I'm so in love with you. Becca, please say something. Please?"

"Get Grams," I mouth.

At first he's confused. Then he stands up and gets Grams from just outside the door.

She walks in, her eyes wide in panic.

I point to my throat, and then to Josh sitting back in the chair.

Josh's eyes move from me to Grams when she says his name. "Becca can't talk anymore," she says, her tone flat—but the anger behind it unmistakable.

"What?" Josh whispers, looking back at me.

Grams answers, "She had to get her stomach pumped. The tube they stuck down her throat damaged her vocal cords even more. She can't speak."

Josh swallows loudly, his eyes on mine, and his jaw tense.

Grams leaves.

Josh doesn't.

He just sits there.

I look at him.

He looks at me.

And I can feel the clock ticking.

Each second bringing us closer to the edge of never.

"I'm going to fix this," he says. "I'm going to make it right."

He can't.

Grams comes back in. "Visiting hours are over," she says.

Josh stands slowly. "I'll be back first thing tomorrow, okay?"

I nod.

He leans down, his eyes closing as he drops his mouth to mine.

I let him.

But I don't kiss him back.

Then he leaves.

And he takes my heart with him.

. . .

After Grams walks in and takes a seat, I reach over and grab a pen and paper from the tray by my bed. I write a note and hand it to her.

Her eyes move from side to side before lifting and locking with mine.

"Okay?" I mouth.

She nods. "Okay."

CHAPTER 41

JOSHUA

"What do you mean it's sold?" I ask the guy at the counter behind the only pawnshop in town.

"It sold real fast."

"Can you tell me who bought it?"

He scoffs. Right in my damn face. "I can't give out that information."

With a sigh, I almost give up. Almost. "Can you at least tell me what exactly she sold you? Model numbers? Something?"

He sighs, too. Not from lack of hope like mine, but from frustration. "Sure man, whatever." He goes to his computer, taps a few buttons, and prints off a list.

I look over it as I walk a couple blocks to the camera store. I don't bother asking questions—I have no time. I hand the guy working on the displays the piece of paper. "Whatever's on this list—I need it."

"These are old, dude, we don't carry—"

"So give me the updated versions. And all the lenses, too. And whatever accessories you think I'll need."

His eyes widen.

I look at my watch. Fifteen minutes before visiting hours start. "Can we make it quick?"

He jumps in his spot. "Sure!"

A six grand dent on my credit card and worth every penny.

I hope it makes her smile.

I need to see her smile.

I walk past Nurse Ruby while carrying multiple bags. She smiles and nods and I pause just outside Becca's room, waiting for my heart to settle. I check for my phone in my pocket so I can show her the apartments I'd been looking at. She may not want to live with us and that's okay. At least we'll be together. That's all I want.

I step into her room and my heart drops to my stomach.

The bed is made.

The room is empty.

All but for a single note sitting on her pillow.

> Josh,
> I am broken.
> I am sick.
> You were my Band-Aid.
> I need a cure.

Chazarae answers the door. She must expect what comes next because she opens her arms and lets me collapse into them— the force of my cries the loudest sound I've heard in days.

"It's okay," she soothes. "It's for the best."

"I don't know what happened." My hands grip the back of her dress, her frail body taking the wrath of my emotions. "I didn't mean any of it."

She pulls back, her hands on my cheeks but I can't see her clearly. I can't see anything through my tears and through the anger and the regret and the fucking pain. *The fucking pain*. It hurts so much.

"Please, ma'am. Just tell me where she is so I can make it right. I can't—"

"Shhhh," she coos, taking me in her arms again and leading me to the steps. She helps me to sit and I try to settle every single part of me. "She's okay. She needs to do this—for herself."

"What happened?"

"It's not your fault, Josh. I need you to understand that. Becca—she's had a rough start to life. She's experienced a lot of things that nobody should have to and it's time for her to put herself first. To take care of her. She has the opportunity to do that now… and you—you have to let her do that."

I inhale deeply, and let it out forcefully. "The nightmares?" I ask, turning to her. "Is that—I mean, I knew there was something going on but—"

She nods, cutting me off. Then she takes one of my hands in hers, the other pointing a finger in the air, asking me to wait. She takes a few breaths, trying to stay calm while tears build in her eyes. Her throat bobs with her swallow and I know that whatever she's about to tell me will change everything.

So I sit.

And I wait.

"When I was sixteen, I fell in love," she says. "Twice. Once with a boy, my boyfriend at the time, and again with our son. A baby I held only once before handing him to the nurses so he could meet his adoptive parents."

"Ma'am…"

She keeps her hand up, telling me she's not done.

"Things didn't work out for the baby's father and me. I guess the pregnancy and the child I'd given up had always plagued my mind. I thought about that little boy, more often than I should, and while my boyfriend was out being a teenager and living his life completely carefree, I struggled to move on. Eventually I did, but I did it alone, without the boy I once loved so much. And that's *why*, Josh. That's why when I saw you at the store doing everything you could to be the best father you could be—I knew, deep in my heart, I had to help you. I had to do something to make up for my choices in life. I need you to know that I don't want or expect anything from you. You've given me a family, and God has given me grace. That's all I've ever wanted."

"I didn't mean what I said, Chazarae. I owe you a thousand apologies, along with everyone else. I just lost it and I can't take it back. I can't take anything back."

"Hush now." She squeezes my hand. "That's not why I'm telling you this. I'm telling you because that boy—my son—he found me a few years ago and he contacted me. I felt like you did, like I needed him to forgive me, but he assured me there was nothing to forgive. You know better than anyone the sacrifices we make for those we love." She pauses a beat, a shuddered breath escaping her. "He didn't know about Becca. Not until it was too late."

"Too late? What does that mean?"

"He told me he met Becca's mother at a bar and they had a one-night stand. He works on an offshore oil rig, so it's normal—this behavior... she tried to contact him so many times, but it wasn't until Becca was born that he got back in contact with her. He says he thought she was crazy—the way she talked to him and the things she'd threaten to do if he didn't marry her and take care of her. And he was positive he used protection so..." she trails off.

"So?"

"So he didn't believe her, I guess, and I don't blame him. After finding out what Becca's mom was like—"

"The car accident?"

She nods. "I wasn't sure if you knew about it," she says, the surprise in her tone unmistakable.

"All I know is she was in one and it damaged her throat."

She nods again, her eyes somewhere far away. "Becca was seventeen at the time and she didn't have any other family. Child Protective Services contacted my son from Becca's birth certificate but he couldn't do much. He was offshore and he still wasn't convinced she was his. Becca—she was at the tail end of her senior year and there was no one there to help her. Luckily, there was Olivia, who was able to work out a sort of temporary agreement with CPS once Becca was finally released from the hospital. Olivia took Becca into her home, but it couldn't be forever. She'd been accepted to college in St. Louis and it was important for everyone who knew her, who was involved in her life, that she attend. But with her mother's death there were financial issues and thank God that Olivia was able to contact the school and defer her attendance for a year. In the meantime, my son Martin corresponded back and forth as much as he could from where he was stationed. The department sent him Becca's file along with her pictures and one day, out of the blue, he calls me crying, telling me all about her... about this beautiful girl—his daughter—whose *eyes* held the truth."

I choke on a breath.

"He didn't ask for a DNA test; he didn't need to. What he needed was help. And he asked for it—he asked that I take her until his contract was done and he could come home. He'd set up a life for them in St. Louis so she could actually start living one. He needed to right his wrongs. And I would help, because I needed to right mine. He warned that it might be difficult, that Becca was... *special*, so he sent me her file and the day after I got it, I picked her up from the bus station."

I blow out a long breath, and with a heavy heart, I ask, "What was in her file?"

CHAPTER 42

BECCA

---

sinister
   adjective
   **giving the impression that something harmful or
evil is happening or will happen.**

The first time my mother called me a cunt, I was in third grade.
She smiled as she said it, her eyelids heavy, right before she
downed what I thought back then was classy water.

The next day, I said it in the school playground. This girl,
Teagan, let me play with the ball. "You're such a little cunt,
Teagan," I said, smiling at her like my mother had done
with me.

Apparently that wasn't proper behavior. Not for a third
grader, and not even for grown-ups.

My mother got called in to the school and we were both
spoken to by the principal.

I still remember crying as I walked into our house, knowing
what my fate was. And I remember even clearer the sounds I

made as I gasped for breath after each consecutive punch to my back.

"You're just like your father," she yelled, grabbing a handful of my hair as she dragged me to the bathroom. She sat me on the edge of the bathtub and rummaged through the drawers. "No more!" she shouted, and then spun to me, the blade of the scissors she held reflecting the light above me. She stepped closer, a sinister smile on her face. My eyes drifted shut as the cold steel lightly ran across my neck and up to my ear. She leaned forward, her mouth cold against my ear. "You have hair just like your father's," she whispered.

She cut off all my hair that night, laughing the entire time.

It took me a while to realize there were two versions of Mom's laughter. The first was the one she saved for me; sinister and evil. And the other was one she kept for the boys. *Boys,* she liked to call them, even though they were all men. At least to me and my ten-year-old eyes. Some of the men I feared more than I did her. The ones who watched me, touched me, even when she was in the same room. I stopped being in the same room after one touched my leg and tried to get me to touch his —only higher. Hiding out in my room wasn't my choice, though. It was hers. *She* didn't like it. Not the fact that they were assholes trying to take advantage of her daughter, but because she didn't like that they paid more attention to me than they did her.

She put a lock on my bedroom door.

She had the only key.

Some days she forgot I existed.

Those days were the best days of my life.

How fucked up is that?

Probably as messed up as the fact that nobody noticed, or maybe nobody bothered to care. See, my mom had mastered the art of faking it. Faking *everything*. She lived two lives; the hardworking, single, loving mother who'd brag to anyone who listened about how proud she was of me. And when the people she spoke to told her that she should be—that I was a sweet child or any other form of compliment—she smiled and agreed to their faces. It wasn't until we got home that I'd see *her*—who she really was: jealous, bitter, hateful and violent. I'd say she was a drunk—but she wasn't. She controlled her drinking to only the times when I set her off. I just set her off a lot... by breathing.

She hated me so much.

Almost as much as she hated my dad.

A man I've never even met.

She rambled sometimes—would tell me that I ruined her life. That she'd been raped and that's how I came to be. But she lied, because sometimes when she got really drunk—when her knee was pressed against my chest and her hands were around my neck while I lay on the floor, gasping for breath, she cried. She'd tell me that she should've been enough for *him*. That he should've stayed for her. That she loved him and why the fuck didn't he love her back—whoever the hell *he* was.

She apologized after each "episode," as she liked to call them. She was always sorry. She'd say she didn't mean it. That she just got angry and it set her off, but she loved me. *She loved me so much*. I meant *everything* to her and she couldn't lose me.

She was my mom.

The only thing I had in my life.

So of course I believed her.

Of course I *loved* her.

She was the reason I was born into this shitty life, right? Without her, I'd be nothing.

And she reminded me of it. Over and over again, she'd tell me this.

Her greatest apology came when I was fourteen, right

273

before high school started. She stroked my hair, wiping tears from my cheeks with one hand, the other covering my mouth to block my screams. She kissed my temple and told me it was okay, that everything would be fine, all while one of her "boys" took my virginity. It wasn't him who took my innocence, though. It was *her*. And when it was all over I lay in my bed, naked from the waist down, blood between my legs, and stared up at the ceiling—my tears mixed with my vomit soaked into my pillowcase. "Best two hundred bucks I've ever spent," said her *boy*. "I'll leave the money on the counter."

My mother nodded and stayed in the room until he was gone, then she stood over me—her smile sad, genuine almost. "It's better this way," she said. "You start high school soon and the boys will want to take it from you. They'll break your heart, Becca. Just like your father did with me. We don't want that, do we? This way, it's done. And you'll have no regrets."

"I hate you," I whispered, because I needed her to know it. I immediately closed my eyes, knowing what would come next.

I attended my first day of high school with a black eye and a broken wrist. Surfing accident, apparently—*so my mother said*.

Up until high school, I spent my days staring at the walls of my room, dreaming of a better life, smiling and dodging questions from the CPS officers who came in to check on me. I never found out who called them. I suspected it was the old lady next door. She'd be the only one who could hear my cries. But the officers would come, they'd ask if I was okay, and I'd smile and nod and they'd leave. Because, really? Who would suspect a mother of beating their daughter? Especially a mother like mine: a hardworking, single, loving mother whose only concern was my clumsiness. Like I said, she was so fucking good at faking it.

But high school changed everything.

Ms. Crawford, who I later came to know as Olivia, was the guidance counselor. She called me into her office two weeks in.

I sat opposite her, my gaze lowered and my heart pounding against my chest. "Rebecca?"

"Becca," I whispered.

"Becca," she repeated. And after a long pause she said, "Look at me."

So I did. I looked at her—right into her eyes.

"I *see* you, Becca."

I didn't know what she meant—not at the time. But over the next few months, I began to understand. She saw *me.* And when she loaned me her camera on the first field trip of the year, I began to see *everything*—not through my tainted eyes, but through a lens. And I fell in love for the very first time in my life.

I fell in love with photography.

I fell in love with art.

And I fell in love with a boy who loved both those things.

His name was Charlie and he was three years older. He liked to touch me, and I liked his touch—for the first time ever, I didn't shy away from someone else's hands on me. His touch didn't hurt. It was *safe*. And in his arms, *I* was safe.

And just like I hid my camera from my mom, I also hid him.

I kept him a secret.

Something I shouldn't do to my mother—keep secrets. Because when she found out I loved him more than I loved her —that I'd spent evenings after school not doing all the school activities I'd said I'd been doing but rather, seeing him—it ended… in a night with me in the hospital unable to breathe because she'd punched me so hard it punctured my lung. Another visit from CPS. Another smile and nod followed by another lie. My mother told them it was a cheerleading acci-dent. I didn't even do cheerleading. Something the CPS officers could have found out had they cared enough to check.

My fear stopped me from telling the truth.

My fear stopped me from doing a lot of things.

She apologized to them for wasting their time, yet again. But to me, she *really* was sorry. She loved me. No one could love me more than she did. Not even Charlie. Besides, what would I do when Charlie went off to college? When he'd start loving college girls more than the pathetic fifteen-year-old high school girl back home whom he'd used for sex.

Like she said, *no one* could love me more than her.

At least she'd always be around.

She was my mother, after all.

I ended it with Charlie.

He went off to college.

I never heard from him again.

She was right.

But I missed him—his touch—the *safety* I felt from his love.

So, I found other boys to love. My next Charlie became Alfie, Alfie became David, David became Kevin and Kevin became a bunch of faceless other boys. All secrets. But I'd wear the consequences of the secrets for an hour of feeling safe.

I used them to take me away from the pain of my life.

They used me for sex.

And I loved them all because of it.

Then one day junior year, Ms. Crawford asked me into her office, an office I'd spent a good two hours every week in, sitting in the chair while she spoke to me about my future. Sometimes, she'd ask about my past. I didn't like those questions. "I see what you're doing, Becca," she said. "These boys won't love you."

"You're not my mother," I snapped, not out of anger but because it was the first thing that came to mind.

Her reaction wasn't what I expected. I expected her to agree and to back down. Instead, she looked at me, dead in the eye, and said, "Is that what your mother tells you? That the boys *won't* love you."

She'd said *won't*.

Not don't.

And it was then that I realized she'd known all along, and she'd kept all my secrets.

"I see you, Becca."

I stopped with the boys during senior year. Instead, I took Ms. Crawford's advice and focused on school. Focused on getting into college, and mostly, focused on getting away from *her*. Ms. Crawford guided me through it all and soon after, I was no longer staring at my walls dreaming of better days. I was formulating the dreams into a reality.

But still, I kept it a secret.

And stupid, *stupid* me should've known better than to keep secrets from the one person who loved me more than anyone else—who would *always* love me.

I was pathetic.

So pathetic.

I actually smiled as I showed her the acceptance letter. At first, her eyes narrowed in confusion. She took the letter from my hand and skimmed the words, her eyes quickly darting from side to side. Then I saw it—the same look I'd seen so many times. The *rage*. "You're trying to get away from me?" she yelled, her fist already raised. I flinched and cowered away but I wasn't thinking and I went to the one place I knew not to go. I went to the corner of the kitchen—corners made it harder to escape.

I *hated* corners.

"Who the fuck do you think you are, you ungrateful bitch!"

The first blow was to my face.

"You think I've spent the past seventeen years taking care of you just so you can fuck off and leave me?"

The second blow was to my stomach—so forceful I fell to the floor.

"You can't fucking leave me, Becca!" she cried. "You're all I fucking have!"

I don't know if it was her foot or her fist that hit my left shoulder, over and over. But when I stayed silent, when I forced the tears back and denied her the pleasure of *my* pain, she got out the heaviest pot she owned and went right back to the same shoulder, dislocating it. Then she did it again, only this time, she missed, and it hit me square in the face, shattering my nose. Blood filled my mouth, from the inside and out. I licked my lips, my sobs heavy now, tasting the blood. *So much blood.* "Please," I whispered, "Please stop."

She didn't.

Through my tear soaked eyes I saw her lift the pot over her head. I closed my eyes and for the first time ever I wanted to survive this "episode."

Just to fuck her.

To prove to her that she was wrong—everything she'd ever said to me—every verbal beat down of my self-worth—she was fucking *wrong*. The pot missed my shoulder again, missed my nose, and went straight to my left eye. Liquid filled it, not tears, but blood—and the only thing I could think was that I was grateful it wasn't my right eye—my shooting eye.

She didn't take away my dreams.

Not yet.

My hands covered my face, my legs kicking out—trying to get her to back away. "Please," I begged. "Enough."

"Enough?" she shouted, dropping the pot. Her shoulders heaved—and if I wasn't smart—if I hadn't lived through this my entire life—I'd have thought she was giving up… that she'd finally calmed down. But I knew—it was the calm right before the storm. "Enough? You don't tell me what to do, Becca! God. Fucking. Dammit! I'm your mother! You disrespectful little whore!" She opened the kitchen drawer and pulled out the biggest knife she owned.

Everything in me went still.

Everything.

Then I screamed.

So fucking loud.

"Help!"

Blood spurted from my mouth, my nose, my eye. All I could see was red. I tried to stand. "Somebody help! PLEASE!"

Nobody came to me.

Only my mother.

She was smiling.

Sinister.

Evil.

"You'll never leave me, Becca," she whispered, knife to my throat as she pulled on my hair, making me stand. She held me against the wall, her voice fierce against my ear. "Never!"

She let me go and I fell to the ground. I cried, relieved.

The "episode" was over.

Or so I thought.

Her fingers curled against my scalp, her hands gripping my hair. I slid against the tiles as she dragged me across the kitchen floor. Through the blood whooshing in my ears, I heard her screaming, shouting the same words over and over. "You'll never leave me!"

With my hands on her wrists, I kicked, I screamed, I begged for mercy. "Please stop! *Mommy*! Please!"

She dragged me through the house and outside, all while I kept my eyes shut. I knew it was wrong. I knew the punishment would be worse but I couldn't help it. I kicked. I begged. I screamed for help.

Nobody came.

She opened the front passenger's door of her car and threw me inside like I weighed nothing, then slammed the door shut and ran to the driver's side. I screamed again. "HELP!"

She got in and closed her door. Then turned on the stereo as loud as possible to drown out my pleas. She turned to me, her face red and eyes filled with rage. *So much rage.* Then she held the knife to my throat again. "I'd rather you be dead than leave me."

The life switched off inside me.

The dreams I created were just that.

Dreams.

And I remember thinking that I hope my dreams were the last thing that run through my mind before I died. I couldn't think of anything worse than being trapped in my reality for the rest of mortality.

"Let me dream," I whispered as my mother reversed out of the driveway. I looked out my window with the one eye that still functioned and I saw her—the old lady next door, phone to her ear, tears in her eyes. "Thank you," I mouthed, my blood-stained hands on the window.

I wish she could've saved me when I could have been saved.

With the music blaring, my mother sped through the streets, ignoring everything around her. I put on my seatbelt right after she ran a red light—the last set of lights in town before there was nothing but empty roads surrounded by trees. She turned off the stereo when she knew there would be no one around to hear my screams.

For minutes we drove in silence.

At least on the outside.

Inside, every single part of me was screaming.

And then the strangest thing happened.

She started to laugh.

Not out of humor.

But pure *evil*.

She faced me but I could barely keep my eyes open. I knew I was fading, and fading fast—dropping in and out of consciousness.

She smiled. Not out of happiness.

But pure *menace*.

She picked up speed, swerving from side to side on the empty road.

I grabbed onto the dash. "Mom!"

She laughed harder.

Drove faster.

Swerved farther.

I moved my hands from the dash and gripped my seatbelt.

She hit the brakes. I lurched forward but was contained by the belt as the tires screeched to a halt. I couldn't breathe through my nose. My mouth was filled with blood, but still, I fought for air, and that intake and outpour of breath was the only thing I could hear. Darkness surrounded us. The only thing I could see were her headlights and the trees half a mile in front of us. She unclipped her seatbelt and moved toward me. It seemed slow, the movement, though I'm sure it wasn't. She leaned in close, her dark, tear-filled eyes on mine—her pale skin illuminated by the moonlight. I felt her hand, soft at first, around my neck—right before she squeezed. Her face an inch from mine, she smiled again. "I'm sorry, baby," she said. "I never wanted it to be like this."

Her elbow moved from side to side but I couldn't make out why.

"I just love you so much, Becca. You know that, right? I never meant to hurt you. It's just that you're all I have. *You and me.* That's the way it has to be. *Forever.* You can't leave me. You wouldn't leave your mommy, would you, baby?"

Her smile dropped.

She pulled away—just as I heard my seatbelt wind up.

I looked down—already knowing my fate.

She'd cut the fucking belt.

My gaze snapped from the belt to the trees as she hit the brakes and the accelerator at the same; the wheels spun, but the car was stationary.

"You'll never leave me," was the last thing I heard her say, right before the sound of tires screeching, of screams—not mine, but hers filled my ears.

Metal crushed.

Glass shattered.

And then darkness.

Sweet, peaceful, darkness.

It felt safe—that darkness. Then I remembered my dreams —the dreams that I'd created on my own. The dreams that started this *nightmare.*

I fought to breathe.

Inhale.

Exhale.

But something pressed against my neck, crushing it. I couldn't move. I couldn't feel a thing. I felt the darkness trying to suck me in—trying to take me away from my reality.

I *needed* to see her.

One last time.

I opened my eyes and glanced sideways.

And I saw her.

She was facing me, her head pinned between the steering wheel and her seat. And as I watched the blood trickle from her mouth and her eyes lose the fight for life, all I could think was that she could've been beautiful. If you take away her evil and her anger and her need to hurt me—she could've been beautiful. In a way, she still was. To me, anyway. In her death—she was still beautiful.

"I hate you, Becca."

CHAPTER 43

JOSHUA

"Maybe now you can understand why it's so important for her to go to college… for her to do something for herself," Chazarae says. "It's going to be hard for her. She has a lot of emotional hurdles she needs to overcome. I spoke to Olivia the first time she started showing signs of depression again—"

"Depression?"

Chazarae nods. "Becca's very sick, Josh. She was diagnosed with depression when her mother passed. I'm sure it's something that was there long before the diagnosis. How could it not be? When she got here she was at a very low point in her life—then you and Tommy came along and you changed all of that. She has a tendency to become attached to those who show her love—for people who can make her feel safe. Especially—and please don't take this the wrong way—but especially boys. She feels a level of comfort and safety because their touch is gentle and different to her mother's. I'm sure it's not the same with you, though. In fact, I'm positive it's not. Becca genuinely loved you, Josh," she says, her voice breaking. "I don't want you to think her condition made your time together any less than it was. While you were together, you gave her an extreme level of joy and happiness and when things started to fall apart with you guys, she fell into a deep, dark hole, one I couldn't get her out of." She pauses a beat, as if hesitating to tell me more. After a while, she continues. "After Tommy broke his arm, I caught her in her room at three in the morning, her lights were on and she was rocking back and forth in the corner biting down on her thumb. She wouldn't react to my voice, to my touch, nothing. So I called Olivia and asked her for help. I can't remember the exact words she used, but she likened it to training a dog; when they do something good, you give them a treat and after a while their brains link the two. When Becca thought she did something bad, her mind automatically associated it with pain so she bit on her thumb looking for that link. The other night she bit down on it so hard she broke skin."

"Jesus Christ." I wipe tears off my cheeks. "She took something, right? That's why she had to get her stomach pumped?"

Chazarae nods. "She had pain killers left over from the accident. She took whatever was left in the bottle. I found her unconscious, Josh. We're just lucky the ambulance got there in time."

My hands shake as I stare straight ahead, my mind numb, and my breaths short. "I'll never forgive myself," I tell her.

"You have to, Josh." She places a piece of paper in my hand and stands up. "Becca says you have to."

I wait until she's in her house before looking down at the note—the one in Becca's handwriting.

> Grams,
> Forgiveness is the final form of love.
> Joshua deserves both.
> Continue to love him like I do.
> Like I always will.
> -Becca.

CHAPTER 44

JOSHUA

I look at the framed picture in my hand—the one from her birthday. I stare at her smile, a smile that reached her eyes and I find it so hard to believe that behind those eyes, there was a whole other side of her I didn't know existed.

I should've known, right?

When she'd cried in my arms, I should have asked.

I should've pushed her.

I should've made her talk to me.

I should've done so many things I didn't.

And I shouldn't have done so many things I did.

But like they say, regrets are useless.

They also say that time heals all wounds.

And as I sit here—looking at a still image that makes me question *everything*—I don't see how time, or anything else, can heal me.

Heal us.

A knock on my door has my eyes snapping to the sound—and for a moment, I almost forget that it's not her. It *can't* be.

And when I open the door, it's the complete opposite.

"Natalie."

I look for a sign of compassion in her eyes—something to say that she's sorry for what she did—for being the catalyst that tore me down, wore me out, and finally broke me.

"I want full custody of Thomas," she says, and I blink, tilting my head so my ear's closer to her—because I must've heard wrong. "I'm using my grandmother's trust fund to hire lawyers. And there's a lot of money there, Josh. I'm going to fight for him. And I'll win. I'll spend every spare second of every day, every single cent I have until I get what I want—what Thomas deserves."

With narrowed eyes, I take a step forward. "Who the hell is going to grant you rights to a child you fucking abandoned?"

She doesn't budge. Not an inch. She stands in front of me, toe-to-toe. Eye-to-eye. "A judge who's not going to want a child in danger of your temper. All I have to do is tell them how you acted that night." She holds up her phone. "I have pictures of your truck—the truck you destroyed in a fit of rage all while your son stood in a house ten feet away. He's not safe with you, Josh. He's better off with me."

I slam the door in her face because I'm too afraid of what'll happen if I have to look at her a second longer.

I stand, staring at the door, my fists balled, letting the anger filter through me. And once the anger has passed, I let reality sink in. And for the millionth time since my mom showed up on my doorstep, I break.

Seriously, how many times can a person break before the only things left are shattered fragments too small to piece back together?

I slump down on the couch and look back at the picture again—only this time, my focus isn't on Becca; it's on Tommy.

And I remember one of the first things I ever told Becca: that there are some sacrifices greater than love. And some loves greater than any sacrifice. Tommy is greater than both.

And because of that, I stand up, grab my keys and get in my car.

And I give up the only thing I have left to sacrifice.

My pride.

My mom's eyes widen when she opens the door, then drop to Tommy standing in front of me.

"I need your help."

Without a word, she opens the door wider. She doesn't stop us when I take Tommy's hand to help him climb the stairs to their bedroom. She stays silent as she follows behind and when I walk into the room, my dad's eyes widen, first at me and then at his grandson. He looks behind me, I assume at my mother, his lips part but he doesn't make a sound.

He never does.

Through the lump in my throat, I force out my words. "Tommy this is your…" I look at my mom. "What do you want to be called?"

She sniffs once, covering her mouth with the back of her hand. "Nanni," she whispers.

"Tommy this is your nanni, this is Daddy's mamma."

Tommy's narrowed eyebrows shadow his clear blue eyes. "Daddy's mamma?"

"Yes." I point to my dad. "And this is Daddy's daddy…"

"Pa," my mom says. "Nanni and Pa."

Tommy looks at my dad, lying on his back in his hospital-type-bed, the same way I'd seen him since I found out about his illness. "You is Pa?" he asks quietly.

My mom lets out a single sob.

My dad doesn't move.

Robby and Kim knock on their front door—showing up exactly when I'd wanted them to.

Tommy smiles when he sees them enter my parents' room, even though he just left them.

"This is your grandson: Thomas Joshua Christian. My son. *My world.* And I need your help, because I'm going to lose him."

I ask Kim to take Tommy so I can speak to my parents and Robby and ask them for something I never thought I would.

Help.

I need help.

And I need them.

I sit down on the same chair I've always sat in, only now I pull it to the side of his bed, because I need him to hear me. I need him to see *me.*

"He's a great kid—my *son*. He's kind and respectful and a little crazy but I love him with everything I have," I tell him, the pain of the past few days finally consuming me. "He's smart, Dad. Smarter than I ever was. And he's so funny. He gives me a new reason to smile every single day." I pause when my mom sits on the bed by his legs, taking his hand in hers. She nods, asking me to continue. "He's into dressing up at the moment. Chazarae, the lady who took me in and gave me a home when I had nowhere to go—"

My mother's cry cuts me off, but she nods again. "Go on."

"Chazarae buys him all these little outfits and Becca—my girl—my *ex*, she'd take these pictures of him. She called him a little poser." I reach into my pocket and pull out all the photographs she'd taken of him and hand them to my mom. She lets go of Dad and starts flipping through the pictures, her smile now overshadowing her tears. My dad stays silent, his gaze at the wall in front of him.

"It's been hard—being seventeen and being completely alone to a raise a child. I didn't know anything about being a dad—only what you taught me," I tell him. "And somehow, it was enough to get me here. And Robby and Kim—they've helped me through a lot of it, but there've been times when I needed my parents. And no more so than I need them now. I wouldn't ask…" I choke on a breath, fighting against my pride.

Robby steps up behind me, his hand on my shoulder.

"Natalie—she came back. She wants full custody of him. She has money I don't. She has family I don't. She's his mom and she's going to win. She's going to take my world away from me and I don't know what to do. I can't live without him."

"Fuck," Robby whispers.

I rear back when my dad slowly sits up, his eyes on mine. He tries to speak but nothing comes out. Then he looks at my mother. "Ella, call Jack Newman."

"Our lawyer?"

Dad nods. "Set up a meeting for all of us." He turns to me now, but I can barely see him, not through the tears flooding my vision. "Your son has your smile, Josh."

I get the papers from Natalie's lawyers the next day and the first thing I do is take them to my parent's house. We sit in my dad's room and go through everything we know. The next day, we have an appointment with Jack Newman at their house. My dad sits in the living room with us, dressed in a suit that hangs off his now thin and gaunt frame. He stays quiet while the lawyer explains everything to us. Natalie's lawyers are good. *Really good*. And they're going to take their time finding evidence and character witnesses who are going to be willing to lie on the stand for the girl who was lost at seventeen, found at twenty, and wants the best for her son. In her mind, and in her lawyer's, she has a case. A good one. Especially since she's using my actions and temper from New Year's Eve night for her personal gain. Jack says he'll do his own digging into her past and try to find what she's been up to. I tell him to have at it, but I don't want to know about any of it until I have to.

"How much is this going to cost?" I ask him. "I have money that I was saving to put toward a house but I don't know if it's going to cover it."

Mr. Newman glances at my dad quickly. "It's covered," he says.

I look at my dad, but he's looking down at his lap.

"Your first step is to gather character witnesses, which is what she'll be doing. Anyone you can find who will vouch for you. We need all the help we can get," Mr. Newman says.

"What are my chances here? Be honest. Please."

"We need time, Joshua. We all need to be patient. It could take weeks—months even—before a court date is set."

"And in the meantime, what happens to Tommy?"

"I've called her lawyers already. Nothing changes in the meantime. Natalie doesn't want to do anything to jeopardize her case."

Mom huffs out a breath. "The little bitch," she whispers.

My eyes widen. So do Jack's. My dad doesn't seem surprised at all.

Then Jack chuckles. "Remind me not to put your mom on the stand."

Weeks pass while Jack's law firm gathers the evidence and I gather character witnesses. The only ones I have are the same people who I'd tried to push away the night that started all of this; Chazarae, Hunter, Chloe, Rob and Kim.

I make the most of every day—between work and meeting with the lawyers, I spend every waking second loving the absolute crap out of my kid. Then, one night—out of the blue—I get a text.

From *her.*

Becca: SK8F8 in two days.

I hold my breath and stare down at my phone, my heart thumping a thousand miles a second. Endless scattered thoughts race through my mind while I try to come up with a response.

I'm sorry.

I love you.

I miss you.

I *need* you.

Instead, my fingers skim the screen quickly and come up with the only thing I feel safe enough to send.

Joshua: I'll go if you go.

Seconds, minutes, hours pass while I grip my phone tight, waiting for her to respond. Finally, it comes.

Becca: If I go, you talk. I listen.
Joshua: Anything.
Becca: Okay.

CHAPTER 45

BECCA

---

break
>   verb
>   separate into pieces as a result of a blow, shock, or strain.

Josh freezes mid-step when he sees me waiting by his half-beaten truck the morning of SK8F8. I came home, or at least the closest thing I have to a home, yesterday when he was at work. I didn't tell him I was there. I asked Grams not to tell him either—but I knew she wouldn't. She wasn't happy about me being here, neither were the nurses—besides Nurse Linda —at the psych hospital. Or, as they liked to call themselves, *the home for personal development.*

Josh clears his throat, his eyes on mine, and his lips pulling to a half smile. I look away because it's already started—the stirring of old feelings that I don't want to feel.

293

I get into his truck the second he unlocks it and put on my seat belt, my gaze on the dash in front of me. After getting in, he starts the engine, but he doesn't do anything else. I sit up a little higher, preparing for what he's about to say. "Hey," he says, his voice so low I almost don't hear it.

I don't respond. I wasn't kidding when I told him that I'd go if he talked and I listened. Apart from not actually being physically able to speak, I don't have anything to say to him. At least nothing I want to share.

He exhales loudly and changes gear, then reverses out the driveway.

For the entire two-hour drive to the SK8F8 grounds we sit in silence. It's not until he finds a spot and parks that he turns to me. For seconds, he just looks at me. I keep looking at the dash. Then he shifts, moving closer to me and I flinch, pressing my side against the door. He curses under his breath before reaching into the back seat and placing a black backpack between us.

"It's yours," he tells me.

I settle the thumping of my heart before turning to him, but he's looking down at his hands, his jaw set.

Confused, I unzip the bag and peer inside, and then I close it quickly and shove it back toward him, my heart hammering again.

He turns to me slowly, and if beauty could be found in someone's frown, it would be his.

"I can't," I mouth.

"Please, Becs. I need you to have it. I tried to get yours back because I know it's sentimental but the pawnshop had already sold it and this is everything you had, just updated I guess…" he trails off, his eyes on mine again.

My chest heaves, my breaths silent.

"I charged it all up for you. I got you the lens you wanted, too. The one you said was good for action shots. And I know you probably won't use it after today but…" He shrugs. "I don't know. I don't know what I'm saying. I just need you to have it because…" He sucks in a breath. "Because I know what it's like to sacrifice something you love. And you sacrificed it for me. I can't live with myself knowing that I can at least take away some of that loss for you. Besides, you're going to need one in St. Louis, right?"

I take the camera because I know he won't move on unless I do and I walk beside him as he makes his way to the registration area. "Joshua Warden," he tells the younger guy at the desk, and as soon as his name is said all three guys at the desk, as well as two in the lines beside him, all turn to him.

"The prodigal son returns," the guy practically sings. "We didn't believe it when we saw your name."

Josh simply shrugs and stares down at his feet.

"You his photographer?" the registration guy asks, motioning to the new camera in my hand.

I copy Josh's shrug.

We get handed an envelope each. One for Josh (competitor) and one for me (press).

We find seats high up in the bleachers and make ourselves comfortable. It doesn't take long for the comp to start and when it does, Josh leans forward, his eyes narrowed and focused, and he seems to get lost in a whole other world. His knee bounces—a sign I've learned means he's nervous. "This guy's good," he mumbles, pulling out his phone. He hits a few buttons and holds the phone in the air. "I can't get any more details on him. My phone's got shoddy reception. Can I use yours?"

I grab my phone, and as I hand it to him I hear his name being called. I don't think Josh hears it, though, because he's too busy looking down at my phone. I hear it again only this time I can see the source. Chris, the guy from the skate park is climbing the steps, his eyes wide as he approaches.

He smiles at me.

I don't return it.

"Warden," he says, clapping Josh's shoulder.

Josh's gaze lifts, just for a second, before going back to the phone. "What's up, man?"

"Rumors said you were competing. It's good to see you back in the circuit," Chris says.

"Do you know who's on right now?" Josh asks him.

Chris's response is instant. "Curtis Chutlick."

A half hour later, all three of us are watching the fourth person after whoever the hell Curtis Chutlick is, and Chris and Josh are deep in conversation about the competition. Chris— he's kind of like a walking Wikipedia page on all the competitors and the skate circuit as a whole.

"How do you know all this shit?" Josh asks him.

"Planning for my future" is all Chris says, and it seems to be enough of an answer. "What are you working with?"

Josh clears his throat and lazily points to the humongous bag at his feet. "I trashed all my good boards. I got gear that was shit four years ago."

Chris's eyebrows pinch as he looks down at the bag. Slowly, he reaches down and starts to unzip it. He only gets half way before his face contorts with a look of disgust. "Jesus Christ, Warden," he mumbles. He looks at his watch. "I'll be back," he tells us, and leaves.

Ten minutes later he's back carrying a bag just as big as Josh's. "I keep my stuff in the car. It's not the best but it's better than what you got," he says to Josh. "I spoke to one of the volunteers. There's a training ramp in the corner of the lot. Let's go," he orders, pointing his thumb over his shoulder.

Josh looks from me to Chris, and back again. "You coming?"

I nod.

What else am I going to do?

Josh flies through the first round, and then the second. By lunchtime, word's gotten around that *the* Joshua Warden is present. Chris follows Josh between his rounds and gives him insight into the competition and what their strengths and weaknesses are. I keep quiet, obviously. At one point Chris leaves to get us all drinks and that's when Josh faces me—and without a single emotion on his face, he says, "Thank you, Becca." And that's all he says to me for the rest of the competition.

The day goes by in blur. Everything's rushed and we're constantly on the move. Chris is always by Josh's side, talking to him—training him, almost—and I trail behind. Josh—he's focused. *So* focused. Sometimes he turns around when he feels me lagging behind and he stops and silently waits, and when I catch up, he moves on. He barely speaks a word throughout the entire thing and then he gets on the pipe and I have to force myself to lift the camera and take the shots because, God, he's such a beautiful sight. I feel so many things just *watching* him, but then I'd look at him and *nothing.*

It's as if he feels *nothing.*

Even when he gets on the podium, the crowd cheering his name while he accepts the second place trophy—he shows *nothing.*

And when the sun starts to set and the crowd starts to leave, he thanks Chris for his help and offers him a cut of his *eight thousand dollar* prize—to which Chris declines because, apparently, he doesn't need money.

We walk to Josh's truck in silence, and I wonder when it is he's actually going to start talking to me. He opens the door for me and once I'm settled, he shuts it and then throws his gear along with his trophy in the back seat. Then he starts to drive home, and I start to believe the nurses from the hospital who warned me it wasn't such a good idea to do this, because while I wait for him to talk, I keep looking over at him—at the lines between his eyebrows and the frown on his face and the heaving of his chest and the muscles, tense, in his arms. "My dad—he has chronic kidney disease," he says, and I hold my breath, waiting for him to continue. "He was diagnosed a few months before my mom came to see me that night. He was on dialysis but it didn't seem to help and he made the choice to quit taking treatment and just..." His gaze drops before returning to the road in front of him. "...And just wait to die."

I release my breath, my fingers itching to touch him.

"When my mom came over, she asked me to get tested to be a donor. It didn't work out, so now there aren't any other options, and I guess we just wait. I don't really know why I kept it a secret from you," he says, his voice hoarse. "I think I just didn't want to seem weak, that I could so easily forgive a man who turned his back on us. It was like my pride kept me from sharing my weakness with you and I don't know why because I know now that you—" He chokes on a breath and slowly pulls over to the side of the road, wiping his eyes as he does.

He turns to me once the car has stopped.

But he doesn't look *at* me.

I, however, can't look away.

I see you, Josh.

"You stood by me through all of my bullshit baggage and insecurities, and I should've told you because I know you would've been there for me, but I couldn't. I couldn't express how I felt because I don't think I let myself feel any of it. I pushed back everything I felt because I didn't want to admit it —that watching a man I love, a man I looked up to my entire life, give up hope and just..." He sniffs once, his eyes wide as he tries to push back the tears. "He just gave up, Becca. And that's where I was all those times I told you I had to be somewhere. I was in his room staring at the walls trying to figure out something to say to him to make him stay. To beg him to try. And I thought my presence was enough. That if he saw me in there he'd somehow want to make it—for *me.* Because I was his son and he was my dad. And it should've been enough. But I'd go in there and it just—it wasn't enough.

"And then Natalie came and, God, Becca—I didn't know she was back in town when she was at the hospital. She'd just come back that day, and you have to believe me when I tell you that nothing ever, *ever,* happened with us. And I know it means nothing to you now, but I don't want you to think that I'd ever do anything to hurt you—not intentionally. It's just the shit with my dad made me think of Tommy and the future, and if anything happened to me… *Fuck!*"

He punches the steering wheel.

And then he breaks.

The boy I love breaks.

And there's nothing sadder, nothing harder in the world than watching the person you love fall apart right before your eyes—and you can't *say* or do anything to change it.

"I just want Tommy to have everything and I thought I was doing the right thing, even if I hated doing it. Even if I hated having her there. Even if I hated *her*. I just wanted to do the right thing. And I got so selfish—so caught up in the bullshit of my life that I didn't think about you. I should've thought about you because you're the only thing that makes sense. Having you here, with me, is the only thing that makes sense, and I can't have it. I can't have you. And I don't deserve you. I never did. And I'm so fucking sorry, Becca."

My cries match his.

Not because he's sorry.

Or because I forgive him.

But because I *see* him.

"And I feel so pathetic right now because I know about you, Becca. I know about your life and everything you've been through and, *fuck,* my issues are so fucking insignificant in comparison. And I just—I know it means nothing. Not anymore. I've come to terms with the fact that it's over between us and I *have* to let you go because you're my drug, and I'm your poison."

I open my mouth. Nothing comes.

He shakes his head. "I just need you to know that I loved you. I loved you the first moment I saw you with my son. And I'm *still* in love with you now. There are so many things in my future that absolutely terrify me, but loving you for the rest of it isn't one of them."

I face the front of the car, my eyes wide, and my heart bleeding *for* him.

Without another word, he pulls back on the road and continues the drive home.

I grab my journal from my bag, the book Nurse Linda gave me, and I do what she told me to do. I write down what I want to say—but can't, and when he pulls into the driveway, the same one we've spent so many days falling in love in, I tear out the page and hand it to him.

He starts to open it, but I cover his hand. "Later," I mouth.

Then I open the door, but he grasps my wrist gently, making me face him. He's looking down at the note, flipping it between his fingers. "It was good, right?" he whispers. "For a while… you and me… coasting?"

I nod, my eyes filling with tears again.

He sighs. Then stares straight ahead, his jaw set and his lips pressed tight. "I hate him, you know that right?"

He turns to me to gauge my reaction. "Who?" I mouth.

"The guy who's going to win you over. The one you meet at some Starbucks on campus. The one who'll take a picture of his stupid coffee and upload it to his stupid Twitter and hashtag

'Frappuccino' like it's some fucking cure for world hunger. He'll walk to the exit with his phone in his hand and that's when he'll see you sitting at the table with your laptop in front of you and he'll see you for the first time the way I've often seen you… with your brow bunched and your bottom lip between your teeth. And he'll know right away that it's not because you're confused. It's because you're focused. And he'll know because he can see it in your eyes—the passion and the heart in what you do. But not just that, he'll see your eyes. He'll see your emerald eyes, Becca, and he'll want to ask you a thousand questions, and then a thousand more, just so he can be around you. So he can spend a second longer getting lost in your eyes and you'll love that about him. You'll love that he pays attention to you and makes you feel like you're the only girl in the world. Because to him, you are. And two weeks later, he'll take a photo of you taking a photo of him and he'll post it on Twitter and hashtag 'mybeautifulgirlfriend' and you'll fall even deeper in love with him."

I wipe my tears, my hand pressed against my heart trying to ease the pain.

"And you'll come home and he'll meet your grams and your grams will love him as much as you do. And even though you'll try to avoid me, I show up anyway. So you have no choice but to introduce us. I'll smile. I'll shake his hand. I'll make small talk and I'll store the little secret you'll keep buried and hidden from him and from all your college friends because I'll still love you. But I'll hate him. I'll hate him because he'll give you everything I can't. And I'll hate him because he'll have you and I won't." He looks away. "You deserve all of that, Becca. You deserve the coffee shop and the campus and the college education and all the experiences that come with it. You deserve for someone to look at you the way I have and love you the way I do. You deserve all of it. Even the stupid fucking hash tags."

CHAPTER 46

JOSHUA

"I entered a skate comp today," I say, bringing the chair closer to Dad's bed.

His eyes move to mine, then just as fast, go back to staring at the wall.

He doesn't mind when I come over for the lawyer appointments, because he makes an effort to look normal. Healthy, even. And even though he hasn't spoken to me since the day I brought Tommy here, he at least acknowledges me now. He'll speak to my mom and to my lawyer when I'm in the room. Just not to me. He hates my impromptu visits—the ones where he has no choice but to lie in his bed while I sit with him, watching him die, because he's too unprepared to fake it.

I clear my throat and ignore the knot in the pit of my stomach. "It's the first one I've entered since I found out Natalie was pregnant." I wait for a reaction and when nothing comes, I continue, no longer afraid of what I want to tell him. "It was kind of a last minute thing. Something I completely forgot about until a couple days ago. I was unprepared but luckily there was this guy there—Chris—he kind of knew me from the skate park…

"So this Chris guy—he knows anything and everything about the skate circuit and, between rounds he'd prep me about the opponents and he'd critique my form and he made sure I stopped skating so I could be at the right place at the right time. He carried my gear, and made sure I was hydrated. He kind of did everything for me today. Just like you used to, Dad." I focus on my hands so I can avoid focusing on him. "You remember when you'd take me to the comps and we'd wake up early and mom would pack our lunch but we never ate it because we always liked the food there better? You'd always make sure to know what she'd packed so when we got home and she asked how it was we could always lie about it. And you'd carry my gear and set timers because you knew that no matter where I was I wouldn't stop skating unless I really had to. Then you'd stand at the sidelines with me, waiting for my name to be called, and you'd always just say, 'skate your heart out.'

"So Chris—he did everything you used to do, well, almost everything. He didn't encourage me and he didn't remind me that it didn't matter if I placed or not, as long as I enjoyed it.

"I guess the reason I'm telling you this is because I haven't been in a good place lately, Dad. It's been dark, and hard, and lonely." I sniff once, pushing back my tears. "Hunter called the other day and we joked that I might have postpartum depression. Which is kind of crazy, but not really. I don't know…" I shrug. "I think maybe I just needed someone to encourage me —someone to tell me that it was okay to not be perfect. I think I just needed my dad." I take a few calming breaths, still refusing to look at him. Then I reach down, grab the trophy, and set it on his nightstand. "I came second, Dad. I didn't win, but I didn't care. I didn't even care that I placed. I skated my heart out just like you always told me to do. And I wanted you to know that I get it, and that I *forgive* you. Because I know now—I know that it's really, really hard to be perfect all the time. And you were, Dad. Up until that point, you were pretty damn perfect."

I sit with him for a while, the preverbal weight lifted off my shoulders.

When his eyes begin to drift shut and his breaths become steady, I reach into my pocket and pull out Becca's note—my heart already racing as I unfold it.

I see you, Josh.

CHAPTER 47

JOSHUA

"You look nice," Maggie, the lady in charge at Tommy's daycare says, brushing down my suit jacket. "We're all sorry this is happening to you. You're the last person in the world who deserves this and I just want to commend you for not letting it affect Tommy. The amount of kids we see whose behavior changes because of this kind of stuff... well, you can imagine. My family's been praying for the right outcome. Good luck today, Josh."

"Thank you. I really appreciate it."

She smiles a pitiful smile that changes the moment she looks down at Tommy. Then she takes his little hand in hers while he waves at me. "Bye, Daddy."

I start to wave back, but my emotions flood me and I drop to my knees and hold him tight for as long as I can, knowing it might be the last time. "I love you," I whisper.

"You so silly, Daddy! I see you soon," he says, but he hugs me back anyway because he knows I need it. He just doesn't know why.

Maggie places her hands on his shoulders. "We got some

new toys in the sandpit," she tells him. "They're calling your name."

"Toys don't talk, silly," he tells her, and even through all the nerves and anxiety of what's about to happen, I manage to smile.

I drive to the courthouse, my mind on Tommy sitting in the sandpit in his daycare, and I remember the day that started all this—the day with Becca and the stupid sandpit. I remember their matching pouts as they looked up at me because we forgot the sand, and in that moment, I knew that I'd pretty much do anything to make them happy. Both of them.

She had her first nightmare that night, and the next day she tried to push me away. But I wanted her; even then I knew how badly I *needed* her. So I asked her to coast with me. And she did. For a while, we all did. All three of us coasted through life until, figuratively, Monday came along and we had to deal with real life.

And real life—it was a fucking asshole.

Rob and Kim meet me just outside the courthouse. "You look so handsome," Kim says, kissing my cheek.

"Yeah? I feel like shit."

"Your mom and dad are inside," says Robby.

"Dad's here?"

"Yeah, but he's pissed at your mom for making him roll around in a wheelchair."

"Is he okay?"

Robby shrugs. "He's fine. Your mom's being dramatic."

. . .

Mom, Chazarae and Mr. Newman stand up as soon as they see me and I can tell by the expressions on their faces that whatever they've been discussing isn't good.

"Everything okay?" My gaze shifts from them to my dad, suited up and sitting in his wheelchair looking down at his lap.

"There've been some developments," Mr. Newman says and my eyes snap to his.

"What do you mean *developments?*"

He picks up his briefcase and motions for me to walk with him. I eye them all, one by one, but the only one who seems to know what's happening is Mom. My dad might, but I can't tell because he won't look at me.

I step up beside Mr. Newman as he leads us down a hallway. "Natalie doesn't want to go to court—she wants mediation."

"Can she even do that? We're supposed to be in there in ten minutes."

He stops in his tracks and turns to me. "To be honest, Josh, I don't really know what's happening but her lawyers contacted me this morning and they don't sound too happy about Natalie's decision so I guess this might be a good thing for you. Mediation doesn't mean we *have* to agree with anything that she's asking for. It just means we discuss it. And if we're not happy—we continue with the original plan."

"Okay," I say, because my mind's too busy trying to work out a scenario where I come out on top if this is something *she* wants.

Heated whispers sound from behind me and I turn to see the others walking after us—my mom and Robby deep in conversation. I look back at Dad, being wheeled by my mom, and this time, he sees me, too.

He nods once, his lips pressed together.

And that's all he does.

I turn back and keep walking, one foot in front of the other, until I see Natalie's parents sitting on the chairs just outside a door. Gloria stands up when I approach. Her husband doesn't. "Hi Josh," she says, and I stand still in front of her, my hands in my pockets. I can tell she wants to say more but Mr. Newman says, "Let's go," as he opens the door for me.

Voices stop when I walk into the room and I lift my gaze. The first thing I see is the back of Natalie; she's standing in front of the full-length windows and my fists ball at the sight of her. I want to yell at her to look at me, to see what she's done to me. To see how she's *ruined* me. But I know she won't.

She couldn't face me three years ago, she sure as hell won't face me now.

Our lawyers shake hands and make their introductions.

Mr. Newman sits down.

I don't.

I keep my eyes on Natalie.

And I wait.

"Miss Christian," her lawyer says, "It's time."

Moments pass and the air turns so thick I struggle to breathe. Just like I struggle with the scattered thoughts in my head and the silence surrounding me. I hate the silence the most—the sound so loud it's deafening.

Finally, Natalie turns around, looking exactly the same as the first time I saw her when she came back—tears mixed with mascara streaking down her cheeks. Only this time I'm not shocked to see her. I'm not even shocked that she's been crying. Because after all the shit she's pulled—nothing she can do will ever surprise me.

"I'm dropping the case, Josh. I want you to have full custody."

"What?" I ask, because there's absolutely no way I heard her right.

She takes the steps to get to me, her hands bunching the fabric of her skirt. "There are so many things that I want to say right now and I don't know where to start. *I'm sorry*, I guess is a good place," she says, her voice lowering. "I'm sorry that I walked out on you and our son all those years ago. I'm sorry that I never once—"

"I don't care," I tell her, and then shake my head. "Not that I don't care about your apology, I do. I just… are you serious right now? I mean, *that's it*? I can keep Tommy?"

She nods. "You're the best thing for him and I know that. I've always known that. That's why I left in the first place, because I knew that you'd take care of him better than I could have. It's not what I wanted—to be a mom—and I thought I could do it, but I couldn't. And to be honest I still don't know if I'm completely ready. I just know that I'm not ready to walk away again. But I want to try. I want to do better. *For him*. I still want to be part of his life, Josh. As long as it's okay with you."

I nod quickly.

She adds, "My lawyers have drafted up papers, and I was hoping we could discuss it today—come up with some kind of agreement."

"What kind of agreement?"

Natalie clears her throat and steps closer again. "Two hours a week, two times a week. It can be supervised if that's what you want. And once a month overnight just like you used to do with my parents. I'll make sure that they're home when we set dates."

"That's it?"

She wipes her cheeks with the back of her hand, smearing more mascara all over her face. "There's one more thing."

"Okay?"

"I want you to go to therapy," she rushes out, as if I'm going to disagree. "It's just…" Her gaze flicks to her lawyers quickly before returning. "I know that you're under a lot of stress and you've had a lot going on lately and that's why you lost it the way you did—"

"Nat—"

"No, Josh," she says, cutting me off and raising her hand. "You're completely entitled to feel like that. I don't know if I would've handled it any different. It's just that I know Becca's gone and your dad's not well and I just want to make sure that it all doesn't get on top of you again, because I don't want Tommy to have to witness what I did. He loves you so much, and he looks up to you, and he should never have reason to fear you and I'm just worried—"

"Okay," I interrupt. "I'll do the therapy. I'll do anything as long as I get to keep him."

Mr. Newman clears his throat and I face him, but he's looking down at the papers on the table in front of him. "You just took a job offer, Miss Christian?" he asks her.

"Yes sir," she says, taking a seat next to her lawyers.

My legs carry me, as if on their own, and I slump down on the nearest chair.

"I start in a month," Natalie continues. "For the past couple of years I've been working on a cruise liner, so I'm going back to work. It's all written there, it's three months on and one month off and so I'd like the opportunity to set up Skype calls with Tommy at times that suit Joshua."

"Is that okay with you?" Mr. Newman asks.

Air.

That's all I can feel, filling my lungs, free and easy for the first time since my mother knocked on my door. "That's fine," I say, but I'm still in a daze. "Natalie, is this some kind of joke? Because I feel like—"

"No, Josh," she says. "I love Tommy, and I want what's best for him and that's you. He's such a beautiful, bright, and happy kid and that's because of you." She looks over at my lawyer and points down to the papers. "It also states that I'm willing to change his last name to Warden."

"Why?" I ask, ignoring the numbing ache in my chest. "Why are you giving up like this?"

"I'm not giving up, Josh, I'm giving *in,* because it's the right thing to do. And your dad and Becca—they showed me that."

My heart stops, my eyes lock on hers. "What do you mean? How did they—"

"They came to see me. Last week. Both of them at the same time."

"How did—"

"They didn't want me to tell you," she interrupts. "Even though they may not show you directly, you have the right to know. The two of them—they love you something fierce, Josh."

CHAPTER 48

BECCA

Fight
    verb
    engage in a war or battle.

Both Nurse Linda and I jump when my phone buzzes on the nightstand of my six by eight foot room. Which, ironically, is the same size as prison cells.

"So?" Linda asks.

I hold up one hand, the other reaching for the phone.

Henry Warden: Win.

I smile, which feels strange. Like my mind knows the emotion but my body forgot the sensation.

"So it worked?" she asks, her eyes wide and her smile matching mine.

I shrug, because I really don't know if it was our doing or not. When Josh had dropped me off at Grams' house after

SK8F8, Grams came downstairs, tightening her nightgown as she greeted me. "How was it?" she asked. I held up two fingers and she smiled instantly. "So he's good?"

I nodded.

"Where is he now?"

I shrugged.

"Maybe he's gone to see his dad," she mumbled, and my eyes narrowed. "They've gotten closer since the whole custody thing."

"What?" I would've yelled if I could've, but she knew what I meant anyway.

"I didn't tell you?"

I shook my head frantically.

She proceeded to tell me everything that'd been going on with Josh and Natalie, and I spent the night at her house, tossing and turning until the early hours of the morning. And when the anger had passed and was replaced with worry, I got out of bed, dressed, marched down the hall, and pushed opened Grams' bedroom door so forcefully it hit the dresser behind it. She sat up quickly, her hand to her heart.

"Jesus, Joseph and Mary," she said. "You could've given—"

I didn't hear much else because I was too busy typing out the message on the text to speech app on my phone.

"Do you know where his parents live?" The mechanical voice sounded.

I call her Cordy.

Grams rolled her eyes. She hates the voice on the app. So do I. But Cordy was the closest thing I had to a friend.

"Becca, what are you—"

I hit the green button on the app. *"Do you know where his parents live?"* Cordy said again, and this time I raised my eyebrows and put a hand on my hip. I had to double my efforts with physical responses and mannerisms now that I had no other way of getting my point across.

She sat on the edge of the bed, rubbing her eyes and nodding at the same time.

"Get dressed," Cordy said, *"You're taking me to them."*

I gathered all the pictures from Tommy's birthday, as well as all the ones of him and Josh, and put them in a box, then waited anxiously for Grams at the front door. She seemed to take forever, and when she finally appeared, she looked as nervous as I felt. But my anger had out-won my nerves and I'm sure she could see that. Especially considering the way my feet stomped across the driveway as I marched to her car, clutching the box to my chest.

She'd barely come to a stop when I got out of the car, and marched to his parent's front door. Josh's mother answered. "Becca?" she asked, and my breath caught in surprise. She added, "Joshua's told me a lot about you."

I hoped he didn't tell her everything, and going by the lack of pity in her eyes, I highly doubt he did. I tapped my throat, then started typing a message.

"Is Mr. Warden home?" Cordy asked for me.

She nodded.

"Do you know where that fire trucking Natalie lives?"

She nodded again.

"Go get your husband. I'll be in the car."

"But—"

I tapped the green button. *"Go get your husband. I'll be in the car."*

"Becca—"

"Go get your husband. I'll be in the car."

"Why?"

I sighed, frustrated, my fingers skimming across the screen. *"Because it's time for you both to do what you should've done three years ago."*

It took two people—one practically on his deathbed—less time to get ready than it did my grandmother.

Josh's mom sat in the front seat while his dad sat in the back. Mrs. Warden gave my grandmother directions as they chatted between themselves.

"I don't know if this is such a good idea," Josh's mom said. "The case is soon and this could ruin Josh's chances."

I rolled my eyes, though no one could see me.

"I'm sorry," Grams said. "I don't really know what Becca's plans are."

"She's thinking with her heart," said his mom. "We need to think with our heads."

I typed out another message. *"I'm mute. Not deaf. I can hear you,"* Cordy translated for me.

Next to me, Josh's dad snorted. "Ella, we're all sitting on our asses while this young lady is taking action and doing something about it. Let's just see how it goes."

As soon as Natalie answered the door, the first thing I wanted to do was the exact same thing as the *last* thing I wanted to do. Punch her. Twice. One on her perfect nose and one on her perfect pouty lips. I didn't, of course, but I was pretty forceful when it came to pushing her aside and sitting down on her living room couch, my arms crossed, ready for war.

Everyone else was slow to follow behind, probably because they were busy calming down Natalie's screech of *"What the hell is she doing here?"*

I kept my arms crossed, and waited for them all to take a seat. Surprisingly, Henry—Josh's dad—took the seat next to me. Natalie sat opposite us—her stance matching mine, and for the first time ever, I loved *fear*.

Because it didn't live in *me*.

It lived in *her*.

I opened the lid of the box and emptied its content all over the glass top of the coffee table between us. Hundreds of pictures scattered all over the place, some falling on the floor.

I pointed at her, then at the pictures. "Look," I mouthed, and she slowly picked up one, and then another, and another. Her eyes scanned through the memories of Josh and Tommy's life together—every single moment I was able to capture. Every smile, every laugh, every bit of joy I was blessed to be a part of. Her hand froze mid-movement, her gaze fixed on a picture of Josh and Tommy sitting side by side on my grandmother's porch, a single skateboard across both their laps. Their heads were thrown back, their smiles identical.

The air turned thick.

The silence deafening.

"You see your son?" Cordy said.

"You see his smile?"

"You see how happy he is?"

She didn't respond.

"Do you, Natalie?"

She looked up, right into my eyes.

"Do you, Natalie?" Cordy repeated.

Slowly, she nodded.

"The smile on Tommy's face—the happiness in his life—they don't belong to you."

"You don't deserve them."

"They belong to Josh."

"Because he earned them."

"You haven't."

Natalie swallowed loudly, her fingers shaking as she set the photograph down with all the other ones.

Henry cleared his throat. "It's strange…" he started, and I turned to him. His elbows rested on his knees, his hands clasped together, his head bent and his voice low. "Out of all the people in my son's life, the only one who has the courage to stand up for him is someone who's only been in his life a few months." He sniffed once, his shoulders lifting with the strength of it, but he didn't look up. "It's taken almost four years for the people that should've been there from the moment you got pregnant to be in the same room together—and this is why… because of a little boy you gave birth to—my *grandson*—and we don't even know him. You got scared and you left. I got scared and I turned him away. I was so afraid *for* him—afraid that he'd made a mistake, and that his life was over, and I thought it was my fault—that I didn't raise him right and I was ashamed. What the hell kind of father does that make me?" He finally looked up, his eyes on Natalie. "He's the only one who was man enough to do the right thing. His girl-friend had walked out, and all the parents in his life turned their backs on him… and the one man he looked up to wasn't man enough to deal with it. So we abandoned him. All of us. I lost my son, and for what? So that I can lie in a bed wanting to die because it's easier than living with my regrets?"

I reached out and, without a moment's hesitation, took his hand.

My grandmother gasped and I knew she wouldn't under-stand; me touching a stranger. But he wasn't. Not to me, and not in that moment. Right then, he was just like Josh: a man with regrets living in a world full of unforgiving circumstances.

Henry added, "Do the same thing that Josh did three years ago. Do the *right* thing, Natalie. Please."

We drove Josh's parents' home in silence. It wasn't until we pulled into their house that any of us even moved.

"Josh can't know about any of this," Cordy relayed for me.

"It stays between us," Josh's mom agreed.

I looked at his dad, but his gaze was on his lap again.

I tapped his hand, and when he looked up, I pointed to the

box of pictures I'd taken with me. I lifted it between us and offered it to him.

Then he did something that seemed so out of place on him; he smiled—a smile just like his son's.

He took the box from my hands.

Followed by my phone.

He tapped it a few times and then handed it back. "Thank you," he said.

And that was it.

Two days later I got a message.

> **Unknown:** Don't give up on him yet. But don't wait four years like I did.

CHAPTER 49

JOSHUA

"So how's things with Natalie?" Dad asks, sitting up in his bed, sniffing whatever the hell Mom had just brought in for him. I chuckle as he places it on his nightstand next to my SK8F8 trophy.

"Things are good. She Skyped with Tommy last night, says she misses the crap out of him. She's only been gone a month."

He shrugs. "Tommy's an easy kid to miss. I missed him yesterday."

"Well, I have to share him around now. I've got Chazarae and Rob and Kim—who's not too happy about the new Tommy schedule, by the way—and now you and Mom, plus I still want him to go to daycare so he's around other kids, you know?"

"Makes sense."

"Besides, he told me you gave him a chocolate bar before lunch."

"That little—" Dad averts his gaze. "I told him it was our secret."

"Yeah? I guess he's only good at keeping the secrets he wants to keep," I tell him, thinking about him and Becca's secret language. He still won't tell me what holding up one, two or three fingers means. I've asked, numerous times, and every time I do he asks about her. *Where Becs? What Becs doing?* I wish I could tell him, but I have no idea. So I tell him she's out on adventures with her camera, because that's what I hope she's doing. Out there somewhere in the world, creating adventures, living dreams, capturing moments that make her question *life*.

"He's not the only one good at keeping secrets," Dad murmurs, and I wonder for a moment if he's thinking about Becca, too—about their little secret. A secret I'll take to the grave.

I shrug, not knowing how else to respond.

"And therapy?" he asks.

"Same old. There's really not a lot we discuss. I asked Natalie to think about dropping the clause. It's just a waste of my time and money."

He sighs, but he doesn't press on. Instead, he asks, "What are you doing here, anyway?"

"Tommy and I were going to skate for a bit… thought I'd drop by to see if you were up to coming with, but looks like you're not doing too well."

He throws the sheets off of him and sits on the edge of the bed. "Let's go."

"Mom said—"

"Son, I love your mother. For many reasons. Giving me you is the main one. But, Jesus Christ, that woman doesn't quit *nagging*. I go downstairs, and it's twenty questions about every-thing. The other day she tried to sneak in getting my tempera-ture while I was sleeping on the couch."

He waits for me to stop laughing before adding, "Sometimes I'm just happier in here staring at the wall and sitting in silence."

"So what? We have to sneak you out of here now?"

"Leave it to me."

I wait for him downstairs while he gets changed and when he comes down the first thing he says is, "I'm going out, Ella, and I don't want to hear it."

She pauses halfway through pulling a Lego out of Tommy's pants. "What do you mean you're going out? What's the weather like? Did you eat? Have you gone to the bathroom? What are you wearing? Who are you going with? What are you doing?"

My dad looks at me, his hands on his hips and his eyebrows raised. "Told you," he mouths.

I stand up, laughing under my breath. "Ma, we're just going to skate. I'll take care of him. Promise."

She walks to the entryway and opens the closet, then pulls out his wheelchair and coat. "He has to be in the chair," she says. "He gets too tired too quickly, and it's not good for his immune system if he catches a cold and—"

"I'll sit in the damn chair," Dad shouts, sitting in the damn chair.

"Damn chair!" Tommy yells.

I cringe.

"I'll make you boys some lunch," Mom says, fussing with his coat.

"Ella! We're grown ass men," Dad grumbles.

"Yeah!" Tommy shouts. "We grown ass men."

"You can't say stuff like that in front of Tommy," I tell Dad.

He drops his head. "Ah, *shit.*"

"Dad!"

Tommy laughs. "Ah, shit!"

"Dammit!" Dad mumbles.

"Dammit!" Tommy yells.

~

"Hey, Warden! What's up?" Chris, the guy from the SK8F8, says from behind the counter at Deck and Check, the only dedicated skate store in town.

I slowly release Tommy from my back as I walk over to him. "You work here?"

Chris shrugs. "Something like that."

"Like a summer job?" I ask. "Aren't you still in high school?"

"Just graduated and nope." He leans back a little and nods a greeting at Dad rolling in behind me. "I own the store."

"What?" I ask, surprised. "What happened to Aiden?"

"He wanted out so I bought it."

"So no college?"

"Nah. Not my thing."

"And your parents are okay with that?"

"My dad's a TV producer, Warden. All the trashy, reality bullshit you see on TV? That's his doing. He didn't go to college. He worked hard on the AV side, and slowly worked his way up in the business until he was able to meet and talk to the right people. My dad doesn't care for college. He thinks it's a waste of time, and for what I want to do, I agree with him."

I nod slowly. "So that's why you used to follow me around with a camcorder? Your dad's influence?"

"I knew you remembered me!" he says through a laugh. "What can I help you guys with today? This your old man?" he asks, dropping his gaze to my dad.

"Yeah, that's him." I introduce them quickly then say, "I just need to get me and my kid some new boards."

He eyes me for a long moment, but he doesn't speak.

"So, I'll just take a look around I guess."

He nods, then moves around the counter and leads Tommy and me to the back wall where dozens of boards are on display.

"So the online skate world kind of blew up after SK8F8. You were the number one topic. That must've been cool?" he says, shoving his hands in his pockets.

"I don't know. I didn't really check or anything." I pick up a junior board for Tommy and show it to him. He says it's poop.

Dad laughs from behind me.

I put the board back.

"Listen…" Chris leans his shoulder against the wall. "I actually wanted to call you after the comp, but I didn't really have things worked out yet…"

I stand taller. "Call me about what?"

"Just hear me out, okay?"

"You're kind of freaking me out a little, dude."

He laughs once, pushes off the wall, and bends down to Tommy's level. "What's your favorite color, Tommy?" he asks.

I say, "How do you know his name?"

"Research."

"You mean stalking?"

Chris laughs again. "Just a little." He focuses back on Tommy. "So, little man. Favorite color?"

"Poop," Tommy tells him, and my dad chuckles again.

"So brown?"

Tommy nods.

Chris searches the board stock on the floor and when he finds the one he's after, he opens it and shows it to Tommy. A shit-brown Torpedo board. "You like it?" Chris asks him.

Tommy pulls out the board and inspects it, then drops it to the floor and settles one foot on the deck, rocking it back and forth. Then he looks up at Chris. "Yep."

"Good," Chris says, patting Tommy's shoulder. "It's yours."

"Whoa. You can't give—"

He ignores me and speaks to Tommy again. "Whatever you want in the store, Tommy, it's yours. Take it."

I step in front of him. "What the fire truck are you doing?"

"You, too, Warden, anything you want in the store, it's yours."

I throw my hands in the air. "Okay, seriously, what the hell is going on?"

He sighs dramatically and crosses his arms. "This store—it's just a stepping stone for me. It's small and that's cool for now but I want to open another one, and another one. Then the biggest one in the state. And then the country."

"Why not just use your dad's money and open another one? Also, if you want to make money then you have a lot to learn. Giving shit away is probably the first thing you're doing wrong. They probably teach that in Business 101 in *college.* Maybe it's not too late for you."

"Joshua," Dad chides. "Language."

"Sorry," I mumble, even though he said the same thing in front of Tommy no less than fifteen minutes ago. Apparently being schooled by my dad still has the same effect, even at twenty-one.

Chris rolls his eyes. "I don't want my dad's money. I want to earn it. I want to be able to look back and say that *I* did it. That I became successful and it was because I worked hard for it. And that's not even the point. The point is the store is just something to keep me busy while I work on the major stuff."

"What major stuff?"

"You, Warden."

"Me?"

He nods. "Like I said, you can have anything in the store… you *and* your son. All you have to do is wear the Deck and Check gear at skate comps. You promote me and my brand, and I promote you."

Amusement sets in. And then confusion. "Who says I'm doing more comps?"

"Who says you aren't?" Dad chimes in.

Chris and I face him. "What?" I ask.

"So?" Chris says, raising his hand between us. "Deal?"

"What? No."

"You'll also be my client."

"What client?"

"I'll be your agent, your PR rep, your assistant. Your everything, basically. And you know I'll be good at it because I know the skate scene better than anyone. Not just the amateur or the underground, but the pro circuit, too. And that's where I plan on taking you."

Dad speaks again. "Josh, is he the kid from the skate comp you told me about?"

I nod, my gaze switching between them.

"Sounds like a good deal," Dad says. "Your mother should be your manager."

"Okay," Chris agrees.

"What?" I ask everyone.

Dad says, "Who else would look after your best interest better than your mother? Plus, she needs something to do when I kick the bucket."

"Dad!"

He shrugs.

"Mom doesn't know anything about skating," I tell him.

"I'll teach her about the skate side. That's not a problem," Dad says.

"So?" Chris asks.

And I don't really know what happens next or what the hell makes me say: "I'll pay you."

Chris smiles. "I take a cut of anything you earn from the competitions, and any sponsorship deals I might make from it. So will your momager."

"Momager?"

"Mom/Manager."

Tommy laughs from the corner of the store, a dozen hats on his head. "I'm a fat-hat-man!"

I turn back to Chris. "I don't think any sponsors would be interested—"

"They already are, Warden."

My mouth opens, but nothing came out. Maybe it's the shock… or maybe it's something else completely. "I don't want anything that's going to take me away from my son."

Chris shrugs, and looks at Dad. "That's cool. We can put it in the clause, right? You'll speak to your wife about it? Actually, I'll get her number and we can set up a meeting."

"What clause? What meeting?"

"We'll work on it. I'll have my lawyer draft up the contract." He jerks his head to his hand still raised between us. "Deal?"

I swallow loudly. "I um…"

"Just shake his hand, son," Dad says.

So I do, because he's my dad, and I always do what he says.

"Good." Chris grins from ear to ear, and pats my arm twice. "This is going to be good, Warden. I can feel it."

"Me, too," Dad says, shaking Chris's hand.

"Me poop!" Tommy yells.

Chris makes his way behind the counter again. "And I wasn't kidding when I said you could take whatever you wanted. Just tell me what it is so I can remove it from inventory." He busies himself with paperwork behind the computer. "I'll get some shirts printed for you and your son." He points to my dad. "And you and your wife, too?"

He nods.

"Just give me a list of sizes for whoever else will be in your camp at the comp next weekend."

"Next weekend?" I shout.

"Yep. We got a lot of work to do," he mumbles, still not looking up.

"I work full time, man, I can't just drop it to train."

"Did you train for SK8F8?"

"Well, no, but... I mean, I *should* train, and I can't get enough time in at the skate park while I'm watching Tommy and working and—"

"Robby?" Dad interrupts, his phone to his ear. "Can Josh take the next week off?"

CHAPTER 50

JOSHUA

Chris takes care of everything, from my clothes to my decks, registrations, schedules, etc. Luckily, this comp's local—only an hour away. He says he and my mom will look at the full tour schedule and go through "logistics" later.

Whatever that means.

Chris's good at what he sets out to achieve. I don't have to worry about anything but skating, and that's pretty damn perfect for me.

Of course everyone shows up to the event, even my dad, forced—again—into a wheelchair by my mom. They wear their matching Deck and Check shirts and hats, the same ones I wear.

They sit and watch me skate and move on to the next round, round after round, and each round they sit together and show their support.

My mom claps.

Robby whistles.

Tommy squeals.

But my dad—he just smiles the same proud smile I've seen at every comp he's ever taken me to.

And when it's over, I drive us back to my parent's house; set the first place trophy right next to the other trophy on Dad's nightstand, and I face him. "I skated my heart out today."

～

After that comp things get a little more major. Chris starts getting calls, and turning down sponsorships and interviews, etc. He tells me not to worry too much about all of it, and that if anything worthy comes up he'll definitely tell me.

I trust him. I have to. Because really? I have no fucking clue what I'm doing.

He does, however, say that I need to work on my brand. He sets up a website and all the other social media bullshit, and when I tell him it's too early for any of this kind of stuff, he just looks at me with a twinkle in his eyes and says, "Just you wait."

The first post I get on my Facebook wall is from Hunter:

You're still the best I've ever had.

I didn't tell Hunter about the event, but it doesn't surprise me at all that he knew.

So, I spend most of the summer working and skating.

One comp turns to two and plans for many more. I seem to coast through everything.

Well, almost everything.

I think about her a lot.

More than I like to admit.

And I miss her.

God, did I miss her.

Then, one day, my mother calls with news that puts a shadow on everything.

My dad's in the hospital.

He'd suffered a stroke.

The doctors stand in front of my mom and I while they throw out terms I've only read about while researching the disease. Apparently the stroke and his failing kidneys go hand in hand, resulting in his entire body shutting down. We knew it was coming, but still, hearing the words and seeing it take action is a whole other experience. Mom asks him to go back on dialysis, but at this stage, it'll be useless, and under the doctor's recommendations and my father's request, the best thing to do would be to "make him as comfortable as possible."

In other words: continue to watch him die.

For weeks I put off skating.

I work as little as possible.

I spend every spare moment in his hospital room making sure he's "as comfortable as possible."

Slowly, I watch the life, the light, the hope leave his eyes. And in my heart, I know he's already gone, but the constant beeping of his monitors remind me that he's still holding on.

Still fighting.

Still *waiting*.

Then one Sunday, Chazarae knocks on the hospital room door. "Let's pray," she says.

So we do.

She takes me to her church and we pray. Not just us, but every single person in the room. They pray for a man they've never met before.

They pray for a husband.

For a father.

And for a grandfather.

And when I get back to the hospital and my mom's eyes lift as I enter the room, her cheeks still wet from the tears she's shed, I feel the darkness surround me.

And for a moment, I let the blackness of my life consume me.

"It's time, Joshua," she whispers, getting up from the seat. She grasps onto my hand as she walks by. "Time to say goodbye."

I release a breath as my eyes drift shut and my feet carry me toward his bed.

And there's one distinct moment that flashes in my mind.

One sound that accompanies it.

It's the moment I realized Becca had left.

The feeling of my heart being crushed as my lungs fought for air.

And the sound?

It's the sound of my breaths as I struggle to push on.

Just one more inhale.

One more exhale.

I'm trapped in that pain…

…In that sound.

Inhale.

Exhale.

Only now, I share that pain with the man in front of me.

A man waiting for death.

Welcoming it.

Seeing his battle for air should make my struggle easier.

Only it doesn't.

Because I want the same thing he does.

We all do.

We want him to die.

So that the pain of his breaths will no longer trap him.

Inhale.

Exhale.

"I love you," he whispers.

And I forfeit my breaths and give them to him.

Because he needs them more than I do.

And because he has a lot more to say.

"You remember the talk we had when you were twelve, and I was trying to convince you to start competing but you said you were too scared of failing?"

I nod once.

"Do you remember what I said?"

"You said that life's just like skating; I just need to *kick* forward and take a chance, *push* off the ground and follow through. And when everything works out, I'll *coast.*"

He smiles. "Kick. Push. Coast," he murmurs, his eyes drifting shut. "Time to *coast*, son."

CHAPTER 51

JOSHUA

It's easy to fall into the darkness, to drown in the pain and heartbreak and submerge myself in black, day after day, nothing but black. And just like that I feel like I'm falling and falling and there doesn't seem to be an end, and when the ground hits—so does reality—and it hits me hard. I claw against the walls, fighting against the desperation seeping into me. I bargain my life. I promise to give up my last breath so that he has one more and I do this over and over and over and over. Until the pain becomes too much and I can no longer fake the smiles as I shake hands with everyone that passes through the house I grew up in—plates of food made for mourning held tightly in their hands. So I turn to my mother, who seems to be coping a hell of a lot better than I am, and I tell her that I'm sorry—that I have to leave, and because she's my mother—a woman who raised me and raised me right, she nods and says, "I understand."

I ask Rob and Kim to take Tommy for the night, and of course they agree because they, too, understand.

I say goodbye to Chazarae, who's doing everything she can in the kitchen, sorting out plate after plate of mourning food, as if any of us can actually eat after losing someone who meant so much.

Then I get in my truck and I drive home so I can sit alone in my darkness and bargain some more even though I know it won't do shit.

A figure stands as soon as my headlights hit my apartment stairs and I know who it is even before she comes into view.

And I feel like that kid again—the same one kicking the shit out of a brick wall, when suddenly, a light shone upon me. I get out of my truck, my head lowered because I don't want her to see my tears… because the cause of my tears are nowhere near equivalent to the ones she's shed. I stand in front of her at the bottom of the steps, but shame prevents me from looking at her.

Then her hand comes into my vision, her palm up, ready for me to take it.

She wants to touch me.

And I *need* to touch her.

So I look up, my heart stopping the second my eyes make contact with hers—tear filled, just like mine.

She taps a finger to her nose, and then to her heart. *I love you.*

And I release the first sob that's fallen on anyone else's ears since my dad died.

I reach out, take her hand, and pull her into my apartment, closing the door behind her.

Because I don't just need her touch.

I need *her.*

And she knows that.

Somehow, she sensed it.

Because she knows *me.*

She *sees* me.

Time stands still.

And so does she.

"I love you, Becca," I tell her.

Because I know *her*.

I *see* her.

And I know it.

I can *feel* it.

It's our last goodbye.

"I love you, too," she mouths.

Then she kisses me.

And I kiss her back.

We kiss away the tears coated on our lips while she holds me in her arms until my sobs fade to level breaths. She pulls back, her emerald eyes on mine. And then she nods once, telling me it's okay. It's okay to hurt. To cry. To let the immense pain consume me.

For one night.

It's okay to let physical pleasure help heal me.

So we ignore the desperation in our kiss, the ache in our touch.

We ignore the voices in our heads, the ones that tell us it's wrong, that it's over, and that God, it'll hurt.

We ignore time as we slowly take each other in; our clothes coming off just as slow as our eyes and our hands and our mouths explore each other for the last time.

We ignore the taste of our tears as we hold each other, kissing, touching, moving as one.

And as I hold her in my arms, naked and grateful for a moment's reprieve from the pain of it all, I stroke her hair and wonder how I'm supposed to move on. How I'm supposed to wake up every day and breathe new air and fake it through the numbness that will no doubt live inside me. Then she looks up, and she smiles.

She *smiles*.

I think about my future. I wonder how I'll look back on this time in my life... a time that changed me. When the fucked up circumstances of her life brought us together, and the messed up circumstances in mine tore us apart. But as I look down at her, her eyes boring into mine and her smile still in place, I make a choice. I'll remember her as the girl who *saw me*. The girl who *loved* me. I'll stop questioning the why's and the how's because in her heart and in her mind, she felt like I was worthy of it. And I owe her that much—to remember her as the girl who loved me... more than any spoken word could convey.

I'll love her for that.

I'll love her forever.

I ignore the shattering of my heart as I watch her dress for the last time... as she stands up without looking back... as she walks to the bedroom door and I just lie there, knowing it's over.

It's all over.

"I'll always love you," I tell her. "You'll always belong to me, Becca."

CHAPTER 52

JOSHUA

My body awoke to the sound of knocking on my door and I already know she's gone.

I know because she's taken half my heart with her.

The other half now standing in front of me. "Hi Daddy. I missed you."

"I missed you, too, buddy."

Kim asks, "How you doing today?"

I shrug. "As good as can be."

She smiles sadly, and lifts an envelope in her hands. I take it from her and look at my name scribbled in Becca's handwriting.

> To Josh,
> Your emerald eyes have never been so sad.

"Becca was home?" Kim asks as Tommy pushes past me and into the house.

I flip the envelope in my hands. "Was. She's gone now."

"I'm sorry, Josh. I know she meant a lot to you."

I shrug again. "Thanks so much for taking him. I needed the night to myself."

Kim smiles. "Of course. You know I love having him. Tommy drew something last night. I think you should take look at it. I put in his backpack."

"Okay. Thanks."

I close the door, anxious to see what Becca had left me. The second I hear Kim's footsteps stomp down the stairs, I carefully rip open the envelope. It's a black and white picture—a picture of an old man with his hand out, palm up. His head's tilted back, his eyes rolled high, looking at the skies. There's a single drop of rain on his forehead, and I instantly remember the moment Becca told me about taking this picture—the moment she fell in love.

I flip the photograph over and there, on the back, is a single sentence.

Six simple words:

Now you own all of me.

My smile's slow, starting at one corner then the other, and the next moment it's taken over, not just my face but my entire body. I look over at my son—the little boy who holds half my heart in his little hands. "I love you, buddy."

He looks up from his train set and he smiles.

I realize it then; what everyone always tells me. His eyes may be like his mother's, but his smile's mine.

His happiness belongs to me.

"Your aunt said you drew something?"

"Wanna see?"

"I'd love to see it." I place the photograph on top of the fridge, and grab his backpack before sitting down on the couch. He takes a seat next to me and waits while I pull out his drawing from his bag.

I unfold it slowly as he climbs onto my lap.

It's a stick figure drawing of a bunch of people—the smallest in the middle. "That's me," he says, pointing to the figure. Then he points to the ones next to him, "That's you and Momma." He goes on and tells me who the rest are; Natalie's parents, Robby and Kim, Hunter and Chloe, *his Nan and Pa*, and then he points to Chazarae and Becca.

My eyes fix on his image of Becca—of her darker skin and her flowing dark hair and her eyes—her bright-green crayon eyes. "Daddy?" he asks, grabbing my chin between his hands and getting me to face him. His gaze flicks between my eyes, and then he says, "It's my *family*. You like it?"

"Your family?"

He nods enthusiastically. "Do you like it?"

"I love it, Tommy. It's one of greatest pictures I'll ever own."

He laughs at that, and follows me to the kitchen so I can stick it on the fridge along with all his other ones.

"I might sell it online," I tell him. "I think I might be able to get a trillion moneys and then you can take care of Daddy for once. How does that sound?"

He cackles with laughter. One that spreads my heart completely open for him. I pick a magnet on the fridge and that's when I see it; something that wasn't there yesterday.

Two magnets.

Both white.

Red ink.

Choose to be happy. Fire truck the rest. -C-Lo.

I look down at Tommy quickly—still laughing, still happy.

Then I gaze back up at the picture of Tommy stuck on the fridge—the first one of him that Becca ever showed me. His face is covered in dirt mixed with sweat, and his smile prominent.

Then I see the magnet used to keep it in place.
One word:

COAST.

Yeah…

It's extremely easy to fall into the darkness.

But then I see my son.

And I hear his laugh, because I've sheltered him from the pain of it all.

Just like my dad had sheltered me.

Then the storm passes and the blackness turns to light.

And I wake up.

Breathe new air.

And fall even deeper in love with a kid a created.

I search for the light.

And my light is his words.

His last words.

"Time to coast, son."

CHAPTER 53

JOSHUA

So, for the next year I do as he says.

I coast.

I think about him every second I'm out there.

I train when I can, travel only when I have to, and work in between. I place more times than not, and even win a few comps. Each trophy sits on the mantel at my parent's house right beneath a picture of three generations of Warden men. *The Warden Warriors*, my mom calls us.

The sponsors start coming through—ones that are actually worthy of my attention. Chris and my mother take care of everything. The number one clause in all the contracts is that it doesn't take away from my time with Tommy. Along with the exposure, comes interviews and social media awareness— things I don't really enjoy but know I have to do in order to get myself out there. It all happens so quickly that I'm not really prepared for any of it—especially the phone call from Chris when he tells me that *Globe Shoes* wants to be my major sponsor. They offer a six-figure deal that'll entail me wearing their gear, promoting their brand, and they'll take care of everything else. "You'd be an idiot not to take it," Chris says. "I've gone over every single detail of the contract, and they don't want anything from you, Josh. They just want *you*."

I take the deal. I'd be stupid not to.

Chris says the online skate world blew up when it was announced. I start getting messages from everyone and their dog congratulating me. I even make front page of the local newspaper. The day after the newspaper comes out I show up to the job site just like I've done many other days, and as soon as Robby and all the other guys see me, they drop their tools and cross their arms.

"What's going on?" I ask Robby.

"They refuse to work with a celebrity," he says, patting my shoulder.

"Don't be assholes," I shout, strapping on my tool belt.

They don't move.

"Get out of here, Josh," Robby says. "You can't be wasting your time on a job like this when you have so much else going for you."

"Shut up," I say incredulously. Then repeat it, softer this time.

"I'm serious. And so are the boys. We're all proud of you, man. You've worked hard and you've earned it. You deserve everything coming your way. And as much as we love/hate seeing your handsome face every day, we don't want to see it anymore." He smirks. "So, you either walk off my job site or I fire you. Your choice."

"You're kidding, right? I need this job. I need a fall back in case anything happens. I could get injured tomorrow and—"

"The job will always be here, Josh, and you know that. But right now, you're living the dream. Take some time. Soak it in. Enjoy life." He quirks an eyebrow. "*Coast*"

I look around at all the guys I'd been working with for the

past three years. Their smiles match Robby's. "Okay, I guess. Um... I quit?"

The room erupts with shouts and cheers so loud it echoes off the walls, and the next thing I know I'm being tackled by the waist and dropped to the ground; a dozen men laughing, ruffling my hair as they all celebrate for me. "What the fire truck are you doing?"

"Tools down!" Robby shouts, and we spend the afternoon drinking beers and eating pizza.

I guess it's a farewell to me, and to a life I used to know.

The rest happens in a blur.

I dedicate every win, every loss, every spin of the wheels to the man who created me. And as I watch the sun dip below the horizon from whatever half-pipe I find myself on, I close my eyes and I feel him with me, watching me. And when the sun disappears and the night takes over, I laugh and smash the shit out of my skateboard—not out of anger, but to remind myself that our raw imperfections make us real and make us human but they don't *make* us.

And when the comps are over, and the media and the hype of the event dies down, and I find myself lying alone in a dark hotel room, I give in to the forever numbness of my half missing heart and I think about *her.* I close my eyes and I see her in my vision—feel her hair between my fingertips and her warm skin against my lips as I kiss her neck, holding her, keeping her with me forever. Then she pulls back, her bottom lip between her teeth, and she smiles. She smiles and opens her eyes, and even though deep down, I know it's a dream—a memory—and that when I come back to reality, my heart will break and she'll be gone, it's worth it. For those few imaginary seconds, it's worth every single ounce of pain and heartbreak. I smile back at her, call her Emerald Eyes, and I tell her that I love her.

That she was the *only* girl I've ever loved.

And that love is the only one worth sacrificing.

EPILOGUE

BECCA

JOURNAL

*I woke up in a pool of sweat, my mind racing and my heart
hammering in my chest. My heart—my poor, sad, broken heart.
I dreamt about him—the version of him that had me thrashing
against the sheets and my fingers gripping tightly to the covers
surrounding me, suffocating me in my own thoughts. My own fears.
I hated it.
I loved it.
Which pretty much describes everything I feel for him.
My heart loves him.
My head hates him.
Even now, over a year later.
The first thing I did when my eyes snapped open was clutch a hand to
my chest wondering how my heart was still beating after the painful
onslaught the visions my dream had created. Only they weren't just
visions, they were memories.
True, life, memories.
He stood over me, his eyes glazed from tears mixed with rage. "I hate
you the most, Becca," he'd said, and I'd stood still, afraid of him.*

Him.

The boy with the dark eyes and shaggy dark hair whose smile had once lit up my entire world.

*And in that moment, I **feared** him.*

It's an overwhelming feeling, one I can't put down onto paper like Linda had suggested I do, yet here I am, trying to justify it.

*If there was a single word to describe it, it would be **torn**.*

My head.

My heart.

The two parts of myself ripping my being in two.

I should be used to it by now, right? How many times have I woken up in fear, my nightmares grounding me to my spot?

Fear.

Love.

Hate.

Caused by two entirely different people and circumstances.

One is dead.

One is Joshua Warden.

ALSO BY JAY MCLEAN

Sign up to Jay McLean's Newsletter

Visit Jay McLean's Website

See all Jay McLean books on Amazon & Kindle Unlimited

See Jay McLean on Goodreads

Jay McLean books on BookBub

ABOUT THE AUTHOR

 Jay McLean is an international best-selling author and full-time reader, writer of New Adult and Young Adult romance, and skilled procrastinator. When she's not doing any of those things, she can be found running after her three boys, investing way too much time on True Crime Documentaries and binge-watching reality TV.

She writes what she loves to read, which are books that can make her laugh, make her hurt and make her feel.

Jay lives in the suburbs of Melbourne, Australia, in her dream home where music is loud and laughter is louder.

Connect With Jay
www.jaymcleanauthor.com
jay@jaymcleanauthor.com